THE BOOKS OF
eLsewHeRe

volume five

STILL LIFE

THE BOOKS OF
ELSEWHERE
volume five
STILL LIFE

by Jacqueline West

illustrated by Poly Bernatene

DIAL BOOKS FOR YOUNG READERS
an imprint of Penguin Group (USA) LLC

DIAL BOOKS FOR YOUNG READERS
Published by the Penguin Group
Penguin Group (USA) LLC
375 Hudson Street
New York, New York 10014

USA/Canada/UK/Ireland/Australia/New Zealand/India/South Africa/China
PENGUIN.COM
A Penguin Random House Company

Library of Congress Cataloging-in-Publication Data
West, Jacqueline, date.
Still life / by Jacqueline West ; illustrated by Poly Bernatene.
pages cm. — (The books of Elsewhere ; v. 5)
Summary: "An old magic resurfaces in twelve-year-old Olive's house, and in order to save
herself, those she loves, and all of Elsewhere, she must uncover the complex history of this
eerie, painted world, its magical origins, and its creator"— Provided by publisher.
ISBN 978-0-8037-3691-7 (hardback)
[1. Space and time—Fiction. 2. Dwellings—Fiction. 3. Magic—Fiction.]
I. Bernatene, Poly, ill. II. Title.
PZ7.W51776Sti 2014   [Fic]—dc23   2013041383

Printed in the United States of America

3 5 7 9 10 8 6 4 2

Designed by Jennifer Kelly
Text set in Requiem

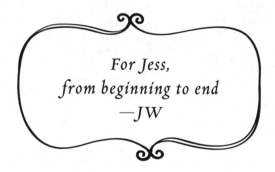

For Jess,
from beginning to end
—JW

WINTER IS A dangerous time.

There is ice to slip on. There is snow to skid through. There are whiteouts and wind chill, frostbite and head colds. And there are all kinds of winter sports—like sledding and skating and downhill skiing—that will help you hurt yourself very efficiently.

Simply stepping outdoors in the wintertime can be dangerous. If you're the kind of person who tries to avoid danger and discomfort, you might step outdoors as rarely as possible. If you're a gangly, distractible twelve-year old girl who is prone to falling down even without snow and ice to help you do it, you might avoid the outdoors whenever you can.

And if you are a gangly, distractible twelve-year-old girl with a huge stone house to nestle inside, and if you have far more chilling reasons than frostbite to avoid the outside world, you might hardly leave your house at all.

You'll burrow down inside those thick-walled rooms with a book to read and something warm to drink, perhaps with a costumed cat for company, and you'll feel almost safe.

Almost.

Because no matter how many blankets you hide under, or how many lights you turn on, you'll remember what is waiting for you outside. You'll hear shards of blown ice tapping at the windows. You'll hear the moan of cold wind battering the walls. You'll know that the ice and the darkness are waiting for their chance—any tiny gap, any unlocked door—to get in.

And out there, in that cold and darkness and ice, something else is waiting for you. It's as cold as the snow that blows around it, as slick as the icicles that drip from the eaves, as dark as the longest nights of the year. It watches you through the glowing windows as you huddle inside its house.

Deep down, under all your blankets and bravery, you'll know that even with the windows sealed, and the doors locked, and the sturdy rooftops and solid walls all around you, that dark, cold thing *will* get inside.

It's only a matter of time.

MR. HAMBERT, REALTOR, puffed his way along the creaking downstairs hall. He didn't like this tall gray house. He didn't like the way his footsteps echoed disconcertingly from every side at once. He didn't like the way the stiff white furnishings seemed to be waiting for someone to come back. He didn't like the way this house *felt*: chilly and muffled and half-petrified, like something stuffed into the back of a freezer.

This made him think about frozen steak.

Which made him think about dinner.

Which made him all the more eager to finish this tour and get out of here.

He put on his shiniest smile.

"It's an unusual situation, of course," he told the client trailing quietly behind him. "Selling the house complete with its contents, that is. Though it's not unheard of on this street." Mr. Hambert cast a glance through the parlor windows at the towering stone house next door. Then he made his smile even shinier. "Besides, you are a rather unusual client!"

The young man behind him gave a start.

"You must be the *youngest* homebuyer I've worked with," Mr. Hambert explained.

"Oh," said the young man—the very tall, very thin young man, in a voice so deep that it seemed to be coming from somewhere beneath his feet. "Mmm."

Mr. Hambert beamed. "They just don't build grand old places like this anymore, do they?" he asked, moving onward down the hall. "So much space. So much charm." He opened the next door and groped for a light switch. A gust of air, thick with spice and smoke, drifted out into the hall. "So much history."

The light switch clicked. A dusty chandelier flared to life, illuminating what had once been a formal dining room.

It was clearly not a dining room anymore.

The long table was littered with bits of strange plants: purple leaves, fuzzy blue berries, flowers on black stems that twisted like corkscrews. The sideboard was arrayed with trays of unfriendly looking brass tools. A huge stuffed raven perched on the curtain rod. In one corner, a human skull, which might or might not have been made of plastic, grinned from atop an ink-spattered desk.

"Oh," said Mr. Hambert, in a wobbly voice. "Well. As I was saying." He closed the door with a decisive bang. "So much history." He gave the client another smile. "Shall we continue?"

Puffing a bit more loudly now, Mr. Hambert trundled to the end of the hall. He had just reached the foot of the stairs when a soft thump came from the floor above.

"Did you hear that?" Mr. Hambert asked.

The young man shook his head.

Mr. Hambert stood still for a moment, listening. The tall gray house kept quiet.

"Never mind," the Realtor said loudly. "Must have been the house settling. These old places, you know. These grand, historic old places!" The stairs groaned under his tasseled loafers. "The house has three good-sized bedrooms, along with—"

He stopped. Another sound—the soft, rapid rhythm of running feet—seemed to echo from the head of the stairs before dwindling quickly away again, leaving the house as still as it had been before.

Mr. Hambert pulled a tissue from his pocket and blotted his forehead. "What was I saying? Oh yes: Three bedrooms, two and one-half baths . . ."

They stepped into the upper hall. Just ahead of

them, a wisp of pale fabric vanished through an open doorway.

Mr. Hambert swallowed audibly. "Bedroom number one," he announced, sounding a bit like someone who's just been punched in the stomach. He reached out and gave the door a nervous inward push.

The door pushed back.

It closed with a slam right in Mr. Hambert's shiny face.

The sound Mr. Hambert made was something between a gasp and a honk. He wheeled around, loafers squealing, and bounded back down the staircase three steps at a time.

"I'll buy it!" the young man called from behind him.

"Excellent!" shouted Mr. Hambert, streaking toward the front door. "I'm sure you'll be very happy here!" He wrenched the door open with both sweaty hands. "Congratulations!"

"Congratulations!" echoed two voices from the other side of the door.

Mr. Hambert gave another gasp-honk.

An oldish woman and a youngish boy stood on the porch of the tall gray house. The woman's body was made up of large, round shapes, which balanced on her little booted feet like several scoops of ice cream on a tiny cone. The boy had messy brown hair and smudged glasses. A T-shirt with a picture of a dragon on it peeped through the lapels of his flapping winter coat.

"I'm Lydia Dewey, and this is my grandson, Rutherford," said the round, smiling woman. "We're here to welcome our new neighbor to Linden Street." She wafted a plate of cookies under Mr. Hambert's nose. "My Dutch-cocoa-sour-cream swirls," she said. "Maybe you'd like to try one? Or two? Or three?"

In the towering stone house next door, a girl and a splotchily colored cat sat on the sofa in the front parlor, their noses mashed against the frosty windowpane.

"Now he's eating his fourth Dutch-cocoa swirl," the girl murmured. "He's probably already forgotten what he's doing here."

"I believe your postulation is correct, Inspector Olive," the cat replied in a lofty British accent.

Through the glass, they watched Mr. Hambert totter down the sidewalk to his car and drive off in the wrong direction.

"Now Walter is officially our neighbor," said Olive.

"Indeed," said the cat. "He will make a valuable addition to the Yard."

"But it isn't really his house." Olive skimmed a fingernail through the frost in a long, looping swirl. "If Morton ever finds his parents, it will be *their* house again."

"Another logical conclusion."

"Inspector Harvey, do you think . . ." Olive hesitated. "Do you think *this* house is still waiting for someone else to come back?"

The cat narrowed one bright green eye. "No, Inspector Olive. I do not. But is someone else waiting to return to this house? *That* is another question entirely."

Olive turned back toward the window. The Deweys had disappeared into their own cozy white house. Mr. Hambert's car coasted past again, now heading in the opposite direction.

She took a deep breath. "I should go next door," she said, sliding reluctantly off of the slippery silk couch. "Maybe Morton has finally found something that will help."

"I shall join you," Harvey answered. "Officers Leopold and Horatio can oversee Scotland Yard while we are away."

"I've always wondered, why do they call it 'Scotland Yard' if it's in England?"

"An excellent question," said Harvey, with a knowledgeable lift of his chin. "You see, Inspector Olive, the force maintains a strict dress code. Men in kilts are required to remain outside police headquarters, in the yard. Thus: Scotland Yard."

"Oh. Like 'No shirt, no pants, no service'?"

"Precisely."

Olive turned toward the door. "I'm getting my sweater. I'll be right back."

Leaving Inspector Harvey to monitor the street, she dashed out of the parlor, skidded across the hall, and started up the creaking staircase. On the walls around her, gilt-framed canvases glimmered softly. Whorls of paint caught the sheen of electric lights.

Aldous McMartin, the original owner of the old stone house, had been a very talented—and very unusual—artist. Though Aldous himself had been dead for nearly a hundred years, he had left all of his paintings behind, firmly stuck to the house's stone walls. And inside of those paintings, a host of McMartin family secrets lived on. Aldous had used his paintings to hide treasures, trap enemies, and create deathless versions of himself and his beloved granddaughter, Annabelle. And now, as Olive knew all too well, Aldous's final self-portrait was free of its painting, wandering the real world beyond the old stone house.

Waiting to get back inside.

Olive scanned the paintings carefully, looking for any suspicious changes. She was halfway up the staircase when something jerked her to a stop.

To her left, just above the stairs, there hung a painting of a small, silvery lake. Olive had seen this painting a thousand times. She passed it every day on her way to breakfast, on her way back to her room to find the homework or book or pants she'd forgotten, and on her way to bed each night. But when she looked at the painting now, she felt vaguely certain that the sky above the lake had changed color.

It was twilight inside the painting. Feathery silhouettes of pine trees stood in the distance, and a handful of stars poked through the violet sky. At least, Olive *thought* the sky had been violet. Now its color was closer to plum. And perhaps she had miscounted them (Olive was prone to miscounting everything, including her own fingers), but there appeared to be fewer stars than usual.

A cold, unpleasant gust, like winter air blowing through an unlatched door, swept through Olive's body. With a glance over both shoulders to make sure she was alone, Olive picked up the antique spectacles that hung from a ribbon around her neck and placed them on her nose.

Around her, Aldous McMartin's artworks rippled to life.

In the painting of the moonlit forest that hung at the head of the stairs, bare branches shivered above a twisting path. Heather fluttered in the painting of the Scottish hillside. The still life between the bedroom doors didn't move, but the strange fruits in their silver bowl seemed to shimmer a bit more juicily.

Olive turned back to the painting of the silvery lake. Wrapping her hands around the frame, she leaned forward until she felt her nose touch the surface of the canvas. Then, as if she were smooshing her face into a bowl of warm Jell-O, she pushed her head into the painting.

A lake-scented breeze fluttered her hair. Waves whispered to the sand. Distant pine trees swayed like sleepy dancers. Olive stared up at the sky. She waited, the nape of her neck prickling, to see that familiar darkness rush through the air, eating the light and swallowing the stars. It was the darkness that would mean Aldous McMartin was near.

Olive had seen it within that very painting, when the living portrait of Annabelle had tried to drown her. She had seen it in the painting of the moonlit forest, when darkness had swirled through the night sky and out of the frame, filling the house with Aldous's presence.

But she didn't see it now.

The sky's deep purple hue didn't change. The stars shone against its darkness, their light soft and steady.

Slowly, Olive pulled her head back through the picture frame.

In the upper hall, she checked the other canvases. The moonlit forest didn't seem any darker than usual, but it was already so dim, it might have been hard to tell the difference. The painting of Linden Street that hung outside her bedroom door hadn't changed either.

Or had it?

Olive squinted into the canvas. Far away, in the center of the usually deserted street, something pale and soft gave a twitch.

With an awkward somersault, Olive toppled through the frame and landed in the misty grass on the other side. The Linden Street of a century ago wound up the hill before her. The residents of a century ago—the ones who had learned too much about the McMartin family, anyway—waited there as well, inside their silent houses, trapped in Aldous's painted world until they had become paintings themselves.

Olive rushed up the hillside. Dewy grass straightened itself in her footprints. Painted mist swirled and settled back into place. She ran past houses with candlelit curtains, past empty front yards and quiet porches, toward the hulk of one tall gray house.

An old man with a long bristly beard was standing on its front lawn. His striped pajamas seemed to glow against the darkness.

"Oh, Mr. Fitzroy—it's *you*," Olive panted, jogging to a stop beside him.

"Evening, Miss Olive. I just walked over to check on the place." Mr. Fitzroy nodded at the tall gray house. Its windows stared down at them, dark and unanswering. "Of course, nothing ever changes here, but with Morton gone . . ." He gave Olive a little smile. "Well, I suppose some things *do* change."

Olive, not knowing what to say but wanting to say it anyway, made an agreeable little "hmm" sound.

"We miss him in here," said Mr. Fitzroy.

Olive's heart squeezed. She'd liked knowing that Morton was safe and sound inside this painting, right beside her bedroom door. Now that he was outside, in the real world, a low, constant worry for him vibrated inside of her, like the bottom string of a piano. "I miss him in here too," she said, but she was talking more to her shoes than to Mr. Fitzroy.

The old man bent down and plucked a weed out of the dewy lawn. So quickly that Olive couldn't see it happen, the weed had vanished from his fingers and popped up again in its original spot. "Old habits . . ." Mr. Fitzroy sighed. "Any sign of Mary and Harold Nivens yet?"

"No. But we're still looking." Olive looked up at his bushy profile. "Mr. Fitzroy, you said once—you said there was something special about Morton's mother, didn't you?"

"Mary Nivens," Mr. Fitzroy said softly. "Nobody could keep a secret around her. And there were people on this street who wanted to, believe me."

"I believe you," said Olive. "Do you think that got

her into trouble somehow? Like someone told her something big and dangerous, or—"

Mr. Fitzroy's paint-flecked eyes sharpened. "You're pretty good at digging up secrets yourself, aren't you?" He examined Olive over the crinkles of his beard. "You might want to be more careful. Some secrets are safest where they are."

Before Olive could think of a reply, the old man turned and strode up the street. Olive stood still, staring after him, until his striped pajamas had vanished into the mist.

Back outside the picture frame, Olive tugged off the spectacles and looked anxiously around the hallway. The gaping doorways of unoccupied bedrooms watched her like hollow gray eyes. She checked the painting of Linden Street again. For a moment, she thought that its surface looked dimmer than before— but then she remembered how dim the hall itself was, with the darkness of a winter afternoon already pressing at its windows.

With a little shiver, Olive dove through her own bedroom door. She flicked on the lights before leaping toward the bed, kicking her feet safely out of reach of the shadows beneath, and landing with a noisy *cre-THUNK*.

On the vanity, a massive orange cat glanced up from its own reflection.

"Hello, Olive," the cat said dryly. "You are moving through the house with your usual calmness and grace, I see."

"Horatio, you haven't noticed any of the paintings changing, have you?" Olive gave Hershel, her worn brown bear, a squeeze. "Maybe growing darker, or changing color?"

"I have not," said Horatio. In the mirror, his vivid green eyes focused on her. "And I have been keeping a very close watch."

Olive squeezed Hershel tighter. "Because Aldous *will* try to come back, won't he?"

"Whether he will return is not the question," said the cat. "The question is *when.*"

"And *why,*" Olive added. "I mean, Annabelle is gone, the shades are gone. What else does he want? Elsewhere? Me? You?"

Horatio gave a soft snort. "There are many things in this house that Aldous will not give up. Not willingly. Not as long as he exists." The cat's green eyes flicked sideways. Olive followed them to her collection of old pop bottles—and to one bottle in particular.

Wrapped around its dusty green neck was a gold locket. Olive crossed to the vanity and picked it up. The filigreed pendant was cool and heavy in her palm. Reluctantly, like someone lifting up a bandage to look at the blood beneath, Olive pried open the locket's halves.

The face of Aldous McMartin stared up at her.

It was a powerful face, ridged and craggy, with long, hard features and a stern mouth. Its sunken black ink eyes seemed to gaze straight into hers.

Olive snapped the locket shut again. Then she yanked its chain off the bottleneck and tossed the locket into the back of her top vanity drawer.

"I'm going to see Morton," she said, slamming the drawer shut. "Do you know where my purple sweater went?"

"As I'm not in the habit of borrowing your clothes, my answer would be an emphatic *no*." Horatio turned back to his fluffy reflection. "Be careful out there," he added. "Don't stay out after dark."

"I will," Olive promised. "Or—I won't. Or both."

With a little wave at Horatio, she tore out the door and raced back down the steps.

At the bottom of the staircase, the library's carved wooden doors stood open. Inside the huge room, rows of bookshelves towered toward the ceiling, and ancient velvet couches leaked wisps of stuffing onto the rugs. Olive's father, Alec Dunwoody, sat at his desk in the center of the room, holding a neatly sharpened pencil. His head was raised. His gaze was distant. The cheery glow of the fireplace formed two smaller cheery glows in the lenses of his glasses.

"I'm going next door," Olive called from the doorway.

Mr. Dunwoody went on staring straight ahead. The pencil in his hand made invisible scribbles in the air.

"Dad?"

Mr. Dunwoody turned the pencil around and erased one of the invisible scribbles.

"*Dad?*"

"Ah! Olive!" Mr. Dunwoody's face broke into a smile. "Did you just get home from school?"

"It's one in the afternoon," said Olive. "And it's Sunday. And I just sat next to you at lunch, remember?"

Mr. Dunwoody's eyes unfocused. "I remember a lentil salad . . ."

"You said the lentils were softer than usual, and Mom said she'd made .25 cups of lentils—"

"—to .4 cups water, and I suggested a ratio of ¼ cup lentils to 1/3 cup water instead, or .25 to .33 repeating. Of course!" Mr. Dunwoody beamed at Olive, his eyes focusing again. "So, how was school?"

"It was fine," said Olive. "I'm going next door for a little while. Is that all right?"

"Certainly," said Mr. Dunwoody. "It's good to get out of the house and enjoy the—the *inverse!* That's it!" The pencil began to scribble on the air again.

"Hey, Dad?"

Mr. Dunwoody glanced up. "Oh, hello, Olive!" he said brightly. "Back home already?"

Olive decided to skip this question "Have you seen my purple sweater?"

Mr. Dunwoody looked down at his own blue dress shirt. "I don't believe I have," he said. "Not today, that is. I *have* seen it in the past, approximately once a week, for a period of—"

"Thanks anyway," said Olive.

She hurried around the staircase and down the hall-way to the kitchen.

Alice Dunwoody stood at the kitchen counter. Her brown hair was pinned into a bun, and she was stirring something in a large blue bowl.

"Are you *baking?*" Olive asked dubiously.

Her mother smiled down at her. "I prefer to think of it as combining a series of precisely measured ingredients which then undergo various chemical processes. But I suppose 'baking' is a simpler way to put it."

Olive peeked over the rim of the bowl. "What is it?"

"Two teaspoons of vanilla, 6.8 ounces of sugar, a quarter pound of butter . . ."

"I mean, what will it make?"

"Oh." Mrs. Dunwoody consulted her cookbook. "Snickerdoodles, apparently."

"Mom, do you know where my purple sweater went?"

"I washed it yesterday," said Mrs. Dunwoody, starting to stir the batter again. "It's probably in the dryer."

Olive let out a sigh. *The dryer* meant *the basement.* And *the basement* meant lots of unpleasant, basement-y things. Leaving the warm, vanilla-scented kitchen behind, Olive headed across the hall to the basement door.

The basement of the old stone house was chilly in the height of summer. In mid-December, it was *frigid.* Olive wavered at the top of the staircase, her toes inching reluctantly toward the next step. Then, with a deep breath, she plunged down the creaking wooden planks into the darkness below.

She groped for the chain of the hanging bulb. The light clicked on, its glow pressing through the shadows like a flashlight dropped in an icy lake. Olive glanced around. Dusty cobwebs dangled from the rafters. Empty boxes cluttered the floor. In the uneven stone walls, fragments of gravestones—the markers of McMartin ancestors, brought across the ocean by Aldous to build a new family home—revealed their carved and timeworn names. Olive paused for a moment, recalling the smoky, twisting, whispering darkness that had poured from the graves and chased her and flaky Delora and pompous Dr. Widdecombe up the stairs just a few weeks ago. She shook the memory away.

The washer and dryer stood in one corner, looking as cheerfully out of place as two tourists from the future in a medieval dungeon. Dancing from one foot to the other to keep either one from freezing, Olive hurried across the floor and yanked open the dryer. The door's metallic creak echoed through the basement.

"Hello, miss," said a gruff voice.

Olive spun around. A pool of shadows with bright green eyes watched her from the darkest corner.

"Hello, Leopold," she whispered back. "Aren't you freezing down here?"

"Not at all, miss." One very large cat-shaped shadow split from the pool and moved closer. "It is my duty to stand guard at all times, in all seasons." The cat puffed out a chest covered in sleek black fur. "Fortunately, I am well equipped for service."

"Well, I'm not," said Olive, rooting through the dryer. "That's why I need a sweater."

"If you will permit my saying so, miss, it might have been wiser on your part to be born with fur."

"Hmm," said Olive, finding the fuzzy purple sweater at last. "It's a little too late for that."

"I suppose you are correct, miss." Leopold watched Olive wedge her head awkwardly through the neck of the sweater. "But never mind. We all have our deficiencies."

"I'm going to see Morton," said Olive, patting at her staticky hair. "Keep watch over the house while I'm gone, okay?"

The big black cat sat up even straighter. "You can rely on me, miss."

Olive gave Leopold a scratch between the ears. "I know I can."

She found Harvey waiting for her beside the front door, wearing a tiny bowler hat that appeared to have been made from a hollowed-out pincushion.

"Inspector," he said, with a businesslike nod.

"Inspector." Olive nodded back. Then she tugged her coat over her sweater, and together, they stepped onto the porch.

Olive paused at the railing to gaze down the slope of Linden Street. Drifts of snow swamped the houses in a sugary white sea. Frost coated their glowing windows.

Nothing moved but the branches of the surrounding trees, shoved back and forth by the cold wind.

"All clear," whispered Harvey from his spot near her feet. "Shall we proceed, Inspector?"

"Yes, Inspector," Olive whispered back. "We shall."

Side by side, they raced across the snowy lawn, through the clattering lilac hedge, and into the shadow of the tall gray house beyond.

W**ALTER THREW OPEN** the door before they could
knock.

"Come in!" he exclaimed, his bass voice making the
floorboards vibrate. "Now that we live here—mmm—
officially, you can walk right up to the door any time
you'd like!"

Olive and Harvey stepped inside, and Walter closed
the door behind them.

"We don't have to hide anymore!" Walter rumbled
happily on, leading them into the chilly white living
room. "I can turn on the lights whenever I want to.
I can study in the parlor. I can even build a fire!" He
beamed at the lifeless fireplace. "Of course, I haven't
done that, because—mmm—because of Morton—but
I could!"

Olive looked around the parlor. The fireplace wasn't the only thing that was lifeless. All of the furnishings remained exactly where Lucinda Nivens had left them, looking fragile and feminine and faintly unfriendly. A few china figurines posed daintily on the mantel. The room was coated with dust, as though each surface had been draped in mouse-colored velvet. No one had touched this place in months, Olive realized—not since Lucinda herself had fizzled up in a ball of fire.

But beneath the couch, Olive spotted something strange. A wad of blankets and pillows had been stuffed between the couch's wooden legs. Next to the bedding was a lumpy sack of clothes, one sock protruding from its mouth like a limp brown tongue.

"Walter," Olive asked, "are you sleeping down here?"

Walter's smile faded. He rubbed his shaggy hair with one hand.

"An astute question, Inspector," said Harvey, wedging his head under the couch. "Aha!" He whirled back to the room, shoving a pair of fluffy gray objects before him. "*Bunny slippers!*"

"Mmm . . ." said Walter uncomfortably.

"Why are you sleeping on the couch when there are three bedrooms upstairs?" Olive gave the figurines on the mantel a distrustful look. "You don't have to leave everything exactly the way it was, you know."

"But—I *do*." Walter's Adam's apple bobbed like a yo-yo on a very short string. "Morton doesn't want to change anything, unless we're changing it *back*. He says—mmm—he says everything has to be exactly like it was when his parents come home."

Olive let out a little sigh. "Where *is* Morton?"

"Upstairs, I think." Walter pushed his sweater sleeves up his spindly arms. "He's—mmm—he's reorganizing."

"Reorganizing?"

"I'm not allowed to help." Walter's sleeves slipped back down again. "He says I don't know where things belong, and—mmm—there are things I'm not supposed to see."

Harvey nudged Olive's ankle. "The game is afoot, Inspector Olive!" he whispered.

"And that game is hide-and-seek, Inspector Harvey," Olive whispered back. She turned to Walter, who was watching the two of them with wide, worried eyes. "We'll talk to him," she promised.

As Walter returned to the dining room, Olive and Harvey crept up the stairs to the second floor.

Three quiet bedrooms lined the hallway. In the first room, the walls were painted pale blue. Yellowing pictures of baseball players and old-fashioned cars dangled limply from the plaster. A small iron bed stood in one corner. On the floor, a wooden bat, a drum, and a half-deflated ball sat in the box of a rusty wagon, like passengers waiting for a trip that would never begin. Olive knew that this had been Morton's bedroom, many years ago. But he wasn't inside it now.

The next room was as delicately dead as a white-winged moth in a specimen jar. This room had belonged to Morton's older sister, Lucinda, and her frilly coverlet and china rosebuds waited stiffly in their places. Lucinda Nivens had worshipped the McMartins, and had even changed herself into paint to be like them. But Annabelle had turned on her in the end. Someone had cleaned up the dead leaves that had blown into the corners, and the broken window had finally been replaced, but the scorched spot where Annabelle had incinerated Lucinda still marked the floorboards, as black and deep as an empty hole.

"No trace of him here," Harvey murmured. "Carry on, Inspector."

Olive had never entered the last room in the hallway. But if the first room had been Morton's, and the second had been Lucinda's, she knew the third must have belonged to Mary and Harold Nivens.

The heavy wooden door was shut. From the hallway outside, Olive could hear the soft shush and thump of drawers opening and closing, followed by the patter of bare feet. She grasped the brass doorknob. It didn't budge.

"It's locked," she whispered to Harvey, who sat watchfully beside her.

But then, with Olive's fingers still wrapped around it, the knob began to turn. Olive took a step backward.

Groaning softly, the door inched open, and a small figure in white slipped out. Its round head was covered in pale, wispy tufts. Its long cotton nightshirt billowed past its bare toes, all the way to the floor. In the dimness, she might have mistaken it for a ghost— if it weren't for the very unghostly squeal it let out when it spotted Olive.

"Hi, Morton," said Olive cheerfully.

"You *startled* me," said Morton, not cheerfully at all.

"What were you doing in there?"

"Nothing," said Morton. "Just—sorting things. Organizing things."

"Have you found anything that might be a clue? About your parents, I mean?"

Morton pulled the door shut before Olive could crane inside. "Not yet."

"Can we help you look?"

"No!" Morton flung his arms across the closed door. "There are things you're not—you can't—" He scowled up at her. "Don't be such an *intruder!*"

"I believe you mean *inspector,* Master Nivens," said Harvey. "Inspectors Olive Dunwoody and Harvey Cattisham, Scotland Yard." He nodded his pincushion bowler. "No case too confounding. No clue too concealed. No suspect too surreptitious. No—"

"Fine, Morton," said Olive. She took another look at the door, Morton plastered across it like a stubborn starfish. "You can keep *reorganizing* all by yourself."

Morton's frown unpuckered slightly. His arms dropped to his sides. "You can help me fix the pictures in my room," he said at last. "If you want."

Olive and Harvey followed Morton back down the hall to the blue bedroom. As Morton rummaged for some pins, Olive looked at the bookshelf, where a familiar black-and-white photograph sat in a tarnished frame. It was the photograph she and Morton had discovered Elsewhere; the photograph Morton had brought back to his house on the painted Linden Street. Now he had brought it here. Olive looked down at the soft gray picture. In it, a small, round-faced boy, and a tall, sharp-featured girl posed for a portrait with their parents. The father had a mustache and warm, crinkled eyes. The mother had long skirts and a sweet, welcoming smile.

Harvey dove into the shadows under the bed. "No spot too dark," Olive heard him mutter. "No space too confined. No bunny too dusty."

Morton and Olive got to work reaffixing the newspaper clippings to the walls. The papers were yellowed and brittle, their edges as fragile as dried maple leaves.

"I could bring you some new magazines," Olive offered, pinning a picture of a Model T into place. "You could put up fresh pictures. Ones that are in color."

Morton shook his head. "Everything has to be the *same*," he said. "It has to be just the way it was when Mama and Papa come back."

Olive tacked a torn sketch of a long-dead baseball player back into its spot. "Morton . . ." she began, making her voice as gentle as she could. "Is that why you're making Walter sleep on the couch? Because you want everything to be just the way it was?"

"I'm not *making* him sleep on the couch," said Morton, avoiding Olive's eyes. "I just said he couldn't have any of the bedrooms."

"But you don't need them. You don't even *sleep*."

"He promised!" said Morton. "His aunt and uncle already changed the whole dining room without asking. Everything has to be the same, so Mama and Papa can come back!"

Olive looked down at Morton's round, pale face. The bedroom's curtains were drawn, but just enough wintery daylight seeped through that she could make out the shiny streaks and whorls of his painted skin. She had the sudden urge to wrap him up in his bedspread and squeeze him as hard as she could, to keep him safe.

Or to suffocate him.

Or both.

"Couldn't he have just one room?" she asked, when the squeezing urge had passed. "Maybe your parents' old room? You could always change it back."

Morton's eyes went wide. "No!" he shouted. Then he looked quickly down at the floor, twisting one toe into a knothole. "I suppose . . . I suppose he could have Lucy's room," he mumbled. "But just to sleep in. Not to *keep*."

"Morton, you know that everything won't be exactly the same if—I mean *when*—your parents come back, right?" said Olive. "I mean, you've changed, and Lucinda is gone, and the street outside is—"

But before Olive could finish, Morton whirled away. He hopped up onto the bed, bouncing on both bare feet. "Watch how high I can jump," he demanded. "Watch!"

Morton bounced until his tufty hair nearly brushed the ceiling. The heavy iron bed began to shake. One pillow slipped from its spot and toppled to the floor.

Harvey shot out from under the mattress. "An earthquake!" he shouted. "In *London!* It's an unheard-of disaster! Alert the citizenry!"

Just as suddenly as he had started jumping, Morton stopped. He bounced off the mattress. His bare feet hit the floor with a smack. He whirled back toward the rumpled bed, his eyes wide. "Oh no," he breathed.

"What?" asked Olive.

"It doesn't go back." Morton tugged desperately at the blanket, pulling it farther out of place. "It has to go back the way it was."

"It's okay, Morton," said Olive. "It's just a messy blanket."

But Morton didn't seem to hear. He ran to the other side of the bed, yanking at the quilt, shoving the tumbled pillows. "Everything changes out here." His voice was choked. "It keeps changing. And nothing changes *back*."

Olive grabbed the side of the blanket, tugging it evenly across the bed. She smoothed its wrinkles away with her palm. "There," she said, plumping a fallen pillow. "Now it's just like it was before."

Morton took a breath. He looked down at the bedspread, still frowning, his chin tucked defensively to his chest. "You put that pillow crooked," he said.

"I think Morton is keeping something from us," Olive whispered to Harvey as they raced back through the yard half an hour later.

"Indeed, Inspector Olive," Harvey whispered back.

Their footsteps crunched in the thick crust of snow.

"He didn't want to let us help him," Olive added.

"And he *really* didn't want us to see inside his parents' bedroom. What do you think he found in there?"

Harvey raised one whiskery eyebrow. "Perhaps it is something that he did not want to find *himself*."

Olive pushed apart the twigs of the lilac hedge. "Like what?"

"Perhaps his mother was a jewel thief," Harvey proposed. "Perhaps she stole the cursed diamonds of Koala Lumpy and hid them in her closet, fearing the harm they would bring upon her family."

"Koala Lumpy?" Olive echoed.

"*Or,*" said Harvey, his eyes widening, "perhaps Morton discovered that his father was a trainer of the world's most lethal snake, the deadly Mambo Italiano! Perhaps he used the snake to murder his rivals for a grand inheritance, in a perfect, untraceable crime!"

"Hmm," said Olive. "Perhaps *you* should take a break from Victorian detective stories."

Harvey sniffed.

They hurried up the steps to the old stone house. Olive paused on the porch, taking another anxious look down the slope of Linden Street. It was only midafternoon, but already the sky had dimmed to a faint gray-pink, its clouds mirroring the snowy world below. Fresh drifts had gathered on the rooftops of the staid old houses, where windows glowed and wisps of smoke drifted up from sooty chimneys.

Shivering, Olive gazed along the row of houses and thought of all the secrets that could be shut inside— some little and harmless and vaguely embarrassing, like Mr. Fergus's legendary doll collection, and some deep and old and dangerous, like the paintings that filled the house behind her. She wondered what kind of secrets Morton's might be.

"What say you, Inspector?" Harvey interrupted her thoughts. "In the Case of the Bewildering Bedroom, shall we attempt to extract the truth on our own?"

"No," said Olive slowly. "Morton will tell us when he's ready. I hope."

Turning away from the street, she pushed open the heavy front door. Harvey trotted through it. Olive lingered on the threshold for another moment, taking a last long look at the tall gray house next door. Then she stepped in and closed the door behind her, shutting her own house's secrets safely inside.

"... And *that was* how I met the museum director while standing in a Dumpster!" Ms. Teedlebaum concluded.

The art teacher beamed around the classroom. Today, a blue silk scarf was wrapped around her head, making her frizzy red hair shoot up like strawberry pop exploding from a bottle. A clump of keys and pens and notebooks dangled from cords around her neck. She raised both hands, letting her stacks of plastic bangles swing. "In fact, these bracelets are all made from sliced yogurt containers!" she crowed. "One hundred percent Dumpster treasure! I can't *begin* to count the number of art materials I've fished out of the garbage!"

Her students glanced worriedly around the classroom.

"Now . . ." Ms. Teedlebaum's eyes focused. "Where were we?"

Near the front of the room, a knot of girls put their heads together and snickered.

A boy in a baggy sweater spoke up. "You were talking about how you got asked to join the board of the art museum."

"The *museum!* Yes!" Ms. Teedlebaum clapped her hands. The keys and pens jingled cooperatively. "We're all ready for our field trip to the museum this Friday." She pulled one hanging notebook from the clump and flipped through its pages. "I just need permission slips from control-top nylons, non-drowsy cough syrup, and Miracle-Gro." Ms. Teedlebaum blinked down at the notebook. "This may be the wrong list."

The knot of girls giggled harder.

"Well, you know who you are," said Ms. Teedlebaum, dropping the notebook and swiveling toward the chalkboard. "Back to our painting terms." She gestured to a series of loopy scribbles. "You'll be looking for an example of each of these inside the museum. We've covered chiaroscuro, pentimento, impasto, and still life. I also want you to look for a self-portrait . . ."

At the very back of the art room, Olive Dunwoody twitched. She'd been watching Ms. Teedlebaum's hair sweep from side to side and daydreaming about strawberry pop, but the words *self-portrait* zinged her back to the present.

She glanced nervously around the classroom. There was no one here who shouldn't be. The art room was on the third floor of the school, and its windows revealed nothing but a square of white sky and a few bare black branches. Still, as Olive stared through the glass, her mind began to fill it with a horrible image: a face made of shadows and brushstrokes, a face with sunken, burning eyes and—

"Olive?" said a voice.

Olive jumped. Her table rattled, sending three colored pencils clicking to the floor.

Several students turned around.

"I asked why an artist might create this kind of picture." Ms. Teedlebaum smiled encouragingly.

Olive swallowed. "Because he might want to . . . um . . . scare somebody?"

The girls at the front of the room snorted. One of them swiveled in her seat to smirk at Olive, and Olive caught a glimpse of thick black eyeliner.

"Well . . . I suppose a landscape painting *could* scare someone who is afraid of the outdoors," said Ms. Teedlebaum. She turned to the chalkboard and scribbled the word *Agoraphobia*. "All right," she said, "why else might an artist paint a landscape?"

It's difficult to slump on a high metal stool, but

Olive managed it. She let her spine flop like a piece of cooked pasta, placed her elbows on the table, and buried her face in her hands. She could hear her own heartbeat rumbling in her ears.

Watch out, it seemed to say. *Watch out.*

Rutherford Dewey was waiting for her in their usual seat on the school bus. Olive hadn't even stepped out of the aisle when he glanced up, fixed her with his dark brown eyes, and demanded, "What's your opinion of intentional anachronism?"

Olive plunked down on the green vinyl seat. "Tension and what?"

"Do you believe that an author should include historically inaccurate elements when writing about well-understood time periods?" Rutherford asked in his rapid, slightly nasal voice.

Olive found that she tended to lean toward Rutherford when he spoke, as if this might help her ears to catch up with his words. All it did was help his words reach her faster.

Rutherford tapped the copy of *The Once and Future King* lying in his lap. "Personally, I find it implausible that Eton College, which wasn't established until 1440, could have existed in any similar form during the sixth century, and thus I find the reference highly distracting."

"*That's* what you're thinking about today?"

"That's what I'm thinking about *right now*," Rutherford corrected her. "I'll be thinking about something else in a few seconds, I'm sure. And I'm equally sure that you're thinking the same pointless thoughts you think every day during our ride home." Rutherford lowered his voice slightly. "Aldous McMartin will not have gotten into your house while you were at school, Olive."

"But what if—"

"It isn't possible," said Rutherford. "My grandmother is keeping watch, and Walter is right next door, and the cats are standing guard."

"Two of them are, anyway," said Olive. "This morning, Harvey put on his Sir Lancelot outfit and jousted with the coat tree."

"Who was the victor?" Rutherford asked.

"My dad's hat, I think."

The bus hit a snowdrift, bouncing them in their seat.

Rutherford straightened his glasses. "When Aldous does attempt to return, he'll most likely do something completely new. Something we won't expect."

Olive kicked a clump of slush along the bus floor. "I wish you could read *his* mind."

"Paintings, strangers, and various non-living entities are beyond my abilities, unfortunately."

"Well, what would you *guess* he's going to do?" Olive

whispered, sinking deeper into the seat. "Annabelle said he was *hard at work*. We know he has some of the paints. He used them to put the fake version of me on the deck of the ship, and Leopold says some jars are missing from the room below the basement. What do you think he's painting?"

"A fascinating question," Rutherford whispered back. "How do you think like an enemy, when that enemy is trying to think like *you*?"

"What do you mean?"

"If Aldous is seeking revenge, then it's likely that he will attempt to paint whatever would scare *you* the most."

Something cold and slippery tunneled to the pit of Olive's stomach. "Oh."

"And he could paint anything, real or unreal, extinct or alive," Rutherford went on, sounding more excited with each word. "A fire-breathing dragon. A gigantic spider. A herd of tyrannosaurs—although in actuality the tyrannosaurus is believed to have been a solitary hunter. A razor-toothed—"

"He *can't* paint the thing that would frighten me most," said Olive, cutting off Rutherford's unpleasant list. "He can't paint Annabelle."

"An excellent point," said Rutherford. "Both the living subject and the last living image are gone for good."

"No matter what he paints, he can't set it free from the canvas anyway," Olive continued, trying to make her voice sound braver than she felt. "Not without the cats or the spectacles. And those are safe with me." She patted the lump beneath her collar.

"Another excellent point," said Rutherford.

A fine, dry snow had begun to fall. Flakes coasted over the bus windows like white pollen. Olive stared through the glass, seeing menacing patterns in the swirling whiteness.

"However," Rutherford added, after a moment of thoughtful silence, "Aldous might find a new way to access Elsewhere. He *did* create the paintings and the spectacles in the first place."

Olive shot him a look that said YOU'RE NOT HELPING in fiery red capitals. Rutherford didn't really need the look, but it did finally make him stop talking.

The bus stopped at the foot of Linden Street. Olive and Rutherford hurried up the sidewalk between the rows of quiet houses. Their yards lay buried in smooth sheets of white, like the frosting on an uncut cake. High above the street, leafless branches wove a black net against the sky.

Olive blinked through the snowy air, checking every house, every tree. There was nothing to see—but the fact that she *didn't* see it made her all the more certain that it was there, hiding. Watching her.

"Run," said Rutherford.

Olive gave a start.

"It would make you feel better, wouldn't it?" he asked. "So let's run."

Together, they tore up the sidewalk, kicking up clumps of snow behind them.

On that wintery afternoon, Mrs. Dewey's cozy house looked cozier than ever. Butterscotch-colored light glowed in its windows. Pine boughs and waxy red berries twined through its porch rails. Rutherford ran up the steps and threw open the door, releasing a burst of warm, spicy air into the cold.

"We're here!" he called.

"In the kitchen!" a woman's voice called back.

Stomping the snow off of their boots, Rutherford and Olive followed the scents and sounds around the corner, into the coziest room in the whole cozy house.

Walter and Mrs. Dewey were bent over the kitchen table. Bowls of dried leaves and sparkling seeds cluttered its surface. Canisters of cocoa and sugar and cinnamon and other, more unusual, ingredients waited on the kitchen shelves. A copper teakettle puffed softly on the stove. Pots of bright red blossoms pressed against the steamy windows.

"Now, Walter," Mrs. Dewey was saying, "you only need the peel of the stormfruit, but it's very thin. Remove it gently." Her round, smiling face turned toward the door. "Hello, you two! How was school?"

"Very informative," said Rutherford. "We started a new unit in science on the anatomy of invertebrates. It should provide interesting connections to my already existing knowledge of prehistoric life forms."

"Why don't you warm up with a cup of cocoa?" Mrs. Dewey suggested. "And then, Rutherford, we'll continue your lesson on memory spells. Olive, you could watch Walter, if you'd like."

This was the way things went in Mrs. Dewey's kitchen. Rutherford and Walter learned increasingly difficult recipes using increasingly strange ingredients, while Olive—who had as much natural talent for magic as she had for mathematics—handed them spoons. This was all right with Olive. Her own attempts to use magic had resulted in one awful fight with the cats and one truly disastrous painting. It seemed safer to leave the actual spellcasting in Mrs. Dewey's dimply hands.

While Rutherford fetched the cocoa mugs, Olive ventured closer to the table. Walter stood beside it, squinting down from the top of his very tall body at the very small fruit below. He bowed down, bringing his face close to the tabletop, and tried to get a pair of tweezers around the pea-sized ball.

"Hi, Walter," said Olive.

"Hello—mmm—Olive," said Walter, trapping the teeny fruit.

"Where's Morton?"

"He stayed home. I asked him to come, but—mmm—he wouldn't. He said he had too much to do." The fruit popped out of the tweezers and flew upward, beaning Walter on the forehead. "He's safe. The house is surrounded by spells. I wouldn't have left him alone if—"

"I know you wouldn't." Olive watched Walter sprawl on the floor, hunting for the escaped stormfruit. "I think I'll go over and talk to him by myself."

"Good idea," said Walter. "Mmm—there are locking charms on the doors, but the house should recognize you." He made a sudden dive under the table. "Got it!" he exclaimed, just before a rumble of thunder burst through the kitchen, making the canisters rattle. Rutherford spilled a slosh of cocoa across the stovetop. Olive clamped both hands over her ears.

Mrs. Dewey sighed. "That's why you have to be gentle with stormfruit."

Leaving Mrs. Dewey's kitchen for the outdoors felt like climbing out of a warm bath onto a freezing tile floor. Olive dashed across the lawn, around a clump of birch trees, and through the back door of the tall gray house. Only once it was closed behind her did she realize she'd been holding her breath.

The house was silent. Olive ventured across the empty kitchen and into the hall, listening hard. There was no sound but the creak of her boots against the floorboards.

"Morton?" she called.

No answer.

Olive clomped softly up the staircase. Morton's bedroom was empty. Lucinda's bedroom was as stiff and still as ever, though Olive noticed Walter's bag of clothes had moved from its spot under the couch to a new spot under Lucinda's ruffly bed.

The last door in the hallway was closed.

Olive crept nearer. This time, there was no sound from within. She waited for several seconds, listening for the thump of Morton's feet or the slam of closing drawers and hearing only the muted drumming of her own heart. Slowly, she reached up and touched the brass doorknob.

It turned in her hand.

The room inside was dim. "Morton?" Olive whispered. She already knew that he wouldn't answer, but pretending that she was still looking for him made her feel a bit less guilty. Olive pulled the door shut behind her and hurried to the nearest window, tugging the dusty curtains apart. Blue-white daylight rushed in. Olive spun around, scanning the room.

A high bed stood against one wall, piled with pillows and worn patchwork quilts. A layer of dust had spread across the covers, like one more delicate blanket. The rest of the room was soft and cozy and faded, with patterned wallpaper, and a round, hand-braided rug, and wooden furniture draped with fine white strands of spiderweb.

Except for the cobwebs and the dust, this seemed like the perfect room for crinkly-eyed Harold and softly smiling Mary.

The only thing that didn't seem quite right was that the walls were bare. There were no wreaths, no photographs, no decorations at all—except for one large, framed portrait above the dresser.

Olive squinted up at it. It wasn't one of Aldous's paintings, she was certain. The brushstrokes were bumpy and inelegant, and there was no spark of life inside of it, even when Olive put on the spectacles.

It was a portrait of a girl a little bit older than Olive—a girl with a narrow face and sharp, sallow features that made her look like she'd been carved from a stick of butter. The girl was gazing into the distance, and her mouth wore an awkward little smile, as though she hadn't practiced it enough. Olive recognized her immediately: She was Morton's older sister, Lucinda. Olive sprawled across the dresser top for a better look. In the bottom corner of the canvas, in the shade of gold used for Lucinda's hair, were two little initials: *MN*.

Mary Nivens?

The back of Olive's neck began to tingle.

Without her brain telling them to, Olive's hands yanked open the top dresser drawer. Instead of being filled with clothes or accessories or anything else a person might actually get *dressed* in, the drawer was stuffed with stacks of papers.

Olive pulled out a handful.

The yellowing pages were covered with sketches. There were drawings of a girl with perfect hair bows and a stiff little smile, and of a man with big hands and a thick mustache, and of a boy with a round face and soft, pale hair. In the bottom corner of each sketch, there were the same initials: *MN*. And, at the top of some of them, there was another, changing note. *Lesson with AM, March 13. Lesson with AM, February 28. Lesson with AM, April 9.*

Olive groped through the drawer, pulling out another sheaf of papers. Here was a sketch of Morton on a swing. Morton with a striped ball. Morton running down a hillside. A sketch of Harold leaning against a tree. A drawing of a slender, long-haired woman staring sadly up at the sky.

She was so absorbed in the papers that she didn't hear the door creak open.

"Olive!"

Olive jumped.

A flapping white figure shot across the room,

wrenching the curtains closed. The papers flew out of Olive's grasp. The dresser drawer banged shut.

"I was just looking," said Olive lamely.

"You're not supposed to be in here!" shouted Morton, shoving Olive toward the door. "You're not supposed to snoop in Mama's things!"

"Your mother was an artist?" Olive asked as Morton hustled her into the hall.

"No!" Morton exploded. He slammed the door behind them. "She was my *mother!* She—she just liked to draw!"

"That's all I meant," said Olive. "She liked to draw."

Morton folded his arms. He glared across the hall, not meeting Olive's eyes.

Olive studied his face. He must have seen the same things: *Lesson with AM.* He must have known exactly what this meant. Olive had a guess of her own, but Morton's scowl told her that now was not the time to ask.

"I'm sorry," she said at last. "I just want to know the truth."

"Hmph," said Morton.

"I'm probably a little too curious."

"Not *probably,*" said Morton.

"I'm sorry," said Olive again. "Really. I shouldn't have looked, when you told me not to. I was just trying to help."

Morton didn't answer.

For a few seconds, they both kept quiet. Olive gazed through a gap in the hallway curtains, at the softly snowy world beyond.

"Hey, Morton," she began. "Do you want to have a snowball fight?"

Morton's eyes met hers. ". . . What about the Old Man?"

"It's still daylight," said Olive, trying to sound confident. "Besides, Walter and Mrs. Dewey and Rutherford are right next door. They would know if anything happened."

"Don't you think the snow might"—Morton wiggled his painted hands—"*wipe* me?"

"We'll bundle you up. We'll find boots and a coat and scarves and mittens and a hat, and you'll be completely covered. What do you think?"

Five minutes later, Olive and something that looked like a woolly fire hydrant burst through the front door of the tall gray house.

Olive bent down to gather a handful of snow. Before she could even close her mitten around it, a ball of cold, wet ice smashed against the side of her neck.

"Ow, Morton!" she shouted. "That hurt!"

There was a self-satisfied snicker from the woolly fire hydrant.

Olive straightened up, packing the snow between

her mittens. Another clump of slush struck her on the back of the head.

"Morton! You throw too hard!"

"You throw too *slow*," Morton countered.

Olive hurled her snowball. It landed with a harmless *piff* at Morton's feet.

Morton's snicker turned into a giggle.

Olive dodged his next snowball and even managed to hit Morton's shin with her own. Morton let out a happy shriek before whipping a missile that smacked Olive directly in the chest. She giggled too, feeling the startling explosion of snow on her cheeks and chin.

She ducked to pack another snowball, and Morton dove behind a tree.

"Wait!" he called from the other side. "Don't throw any more."

"Don't try to trick me." Olive inched closer, patting her snowball into shape. "Is this an ambush?"

"*No,*" said Morton. His scarf-wrapped face peered around the trunk. Even from a distance, Olive could see that his eyes were worried. "There's something wrong."

"What happened?" Olive dropped the snowball and ran nearer. "Did you get wet?"

"No. I just . . ." Morton flexed his hands inside their fuzzy mittens. "It feels—like—*thickening*."

"What do you mean?"

Slowly, Morton wriggled his shoulders. "It doesn't *bend* right. It's like . . . like taffy. When it cools."

There was a honk from the street. Olive glanced out from behind the tree trunk to see her parents coasting past in the station wagon, Mrs. Dunwoody at the wheel, Mr. Dunwoody smiling from the passenger seat. They gave Olive and Morton cheery waves.

"You should go inside," said Olive, brushing the clumps of snow from her jeans. "Maybe this wasn't a good idea."

Morton stared after the station wagon. He nodded absently, still flexing his fingers inside of his mittens.

"I should go too," said Olive. "It's getting dark."

Morton nodded again.

"Tell Walter how you're feeling," Olive commanded.

With one last little nod, Morton stumbled toward his house.

"Good night, Morton," Olive called after him.

Morton didn't reply, but as Olive ran toward the lilac hedge, she felt the thud of a snowball between her shoulder blades. She turned around. The front door of the tall gray house slammed, shutting Morton safely inside.

By the time Olive reached her own front yard, her parents had gone indoors. She knew they would be switching on lights, opening cabinets, starting dinner.

And Morton would be trudging through the quiet, dim house where no parents were waiting for him.

Most of Olive felt sorry for Morton. But there was a small, frustrated part of her that wanted to grab him with both hands and squeeze the answers out of him like the last squiggle of toothpaste from a stubborn little tube.

Had Mary Nivens studied with Aldous McMartin? What had she wanted to learn from him—the skills of a painter . . . or something more?

Who had Mary Nivens *been*?

Olive stepped through the front door of the old stone house.

"It's the snow maiden!" shouted Mr. Dunwoody from the kitchen. "Come and tell us about your day!"

"Coming!" Olive called back.

She tossed her coat over the coat tree and hurried along the hall. Around her, old picture frames glimmered softly. Lights glowed in their antique sconces. The whole house felt so warm and bright, Olive didn't notice that within each painting she passed—the Parisian street scene, the silvery lake above the stairs, the stonemasons and their dog in the kitchen corner—a thick, eclipsing darkness was just beginning to fade, as if something that cast a huge shadow was slowly backing away.

THE ART MUSEUM had once been a small college. It still had a slightly college-y shape, with high brick walls and latticed windows, but inside, all the classrooms had been removed, and everything that was left had been painted white. Its ceilings were very high. Its parquet floors were dizzyingly shiny. Footsteps echoed through its rooms, as if other, invisible people followed its visitors everywhere they went.

It was the kind of place that would compel anyone to whisper.

Anyone, that is, except Ms. Teedlebaum.

"It's just like a *garden,* isn't it?" the art teacher exclaimed. She paused in the center of the first gallery, swaying happily from side to side—possibly because she was wearing two different shoes. "Creativity is blossoming everywhere!"

The collected sixth graders gazed around. Olive and Rutherford, who were standing to the teacher's right, ducked just in time to avoid a swinging clump of keys.

"This would be the rose garden," Ms. Teedlebaum went on, gesturing to a row of bright paintings. She whirled to the left, and the keys around her neck swung again. "Those weavings would be the vegetable patch. Does anyone know what those clay pots would be?"

The students blinked at her.

"Pumpkins!" said Ms. Teedlebaum. "All right, everyone. Remember the things we're looking for: examples of impasto, chiaroscuro, self-portraits, landscapes . . ."

There was a soft giggle from the other side of the crowd. Olive glanced up to see the group of girls from her art class smirking at her. The one with black eyeliner went on staring until Olive looked away.

"Most of all, drink it in!" Ms. Teedlebaum cried, swaying from her green pump to her black moon boot. "Be inspired! Enjoy!"

The students scattered, winter coats and thumping boots charging off in every direction. In the jostle, Olive felt a hand touch her arm.

"Tell us if you see any really *scary* landscapes, okay?" said the girl with the eyeliner. She gave Olive a smile that was too bright to be real before gliding away with her giggling friends.

"Why are you thinking about spending the rest of this field trip hiding in the restroom?" asked Rutherford's loud, nasal voice from over her shoulder.

"I'm *not,*" said Olive. She pulled her collar up over her burning cheeks. "Come on. Let's get started."

They headed quickly into the corridor, leaving most of the other sixth graders behind.

The hallway was long and quiet. Chambers branched off from it in surprising places, one room leading into another like gigantic cars on an empty, motionless train.

"I know it's rather unlikely in a local museum, but I hope the collection includes at least a few pieces dating from the Renaissance, if not the Middle Ages," said Rutherford as they swerved around a corner into one of the unoccupied rooms.

The gallery was lined with paintings of all shapes and sizes. There were tiny pictures of flowers in little round frames, and huge pictures of people in velvet coats with too many buttons. Rutherford headed straight toward a canvas depicting a castle. Olive trailed toward a portrait of a woman in a filmy white gown. The woman's face was rosy and cheerful and nothing at all like Annabelle McMartin's, but something about her old-fashioned dress and paint-flecked brown eyes made Olive's stomach twist. She backed quickly away again.

"Shall we move on?" Rutherford asked.

They wound past a dark-suited security guard and turned into a chamber that looked exactly like the one they had just left, except for the changing paintings. Olive stopped beside a picture of a clothesline dangling with strange objects. A bullhorn, a tutu, a striped ball, a top hat, and a baby elephant were all pinned to the clothesline, floating on an imaginary breeze. Olive glanced at the tag beside the picture.

"Rutherford!" she shouted. "Look! It says this one is by Florence Teedlebaum!"

Rutherford skidded across the floor to Olive's side. He leaned close to the canvas, blinking at it through his smudgy glasses. "Interesting," he said. "What do you think it means?"

"I don't know. The tag says it's called *The Inescapability of Laundry.*"

"That is completely unhelpful."

Olive giggled.

"I think I see another Teedlebaum over here," said Rutherford, darting to the right.

Olive followed him, passing a still life with two dead birds, a misty purple landscape, and a portrait of a small boy in a straw hat. The boy was turning away from the frame, as though he was looking at something in the distance. But even at that angle, and even with his tufty white hair hidden under the hat, Olive knew who the boy was.

She rushed toward the frame.

The face was flatter and more lifeless than the ones in Aldous's portraits, and there was something strange and sloppy within the brushstrokes, making them bend in thick, crooked swipes, but Olive would have known that pale, round face anywhere. In the canvas's bottom corner were the two painted initials, just where Olive knew they would be. *MN.* And on the label that hung beside the painting were the words *Portrait—Mary Nivens.*

"Rutherford . . . ?" she breathed.

"This one is titled *The Sweet Security of Breakfast,*" said Rutherford, gazing up at a painting of a house made of pancakes. "I'm not sure I understand this concept, either."

"*Rutherford!*" said Olive again.

This time Rutherford turned around. Seeing the look on Olive's face—or the thoughts in her head— brought him hustling across the parquet.

"*Look,*" Olive whispered. They were the only people in the gallery, but other students were thumping through the corridor outside. Someone could pop in and overhear them at any moment. "It's Morton," she went on, keeping her voice low. "And his mother painted it."

Rutherford squinted critically at the canvas. "I didn't know she was a painter."

"I didn't either," said Olive. "I just found out."

Together, they gazed up at the picture. And, as they gazed, something inside of the painting—something so faint and small that Olive's brain almost didn't catch it—*twitched.*

Olive grabbed Rutherford's sleeve. "Did you see that?"

"See what?"

Olive leaned closer to the bumpy brushstrokes, her heart moving from a steady drumbeat to a roll. "It *moved.*"

Rutherford frowned. "I didn't see anything. And Morton appears to have remained in the very same position."

"It wasn't Morton. I think . . . it was something *behind* him." Her hand flew to her collar, tugging out the spectacles. "Is anyone watching?"

"No," said Rutherford. "We're alone."

Olive set the spectacles on her nose.

The painting kept still.

There were no flickers in Morton's eyes, no fluttering strands of hair, no shimmering light on suddenly three-dimensional surfaces. There was nothing at all.

Rutherford watched her closely. "It's not working, is it?"

Olive shook her head.

The longer she stared, and the longer the painting *didn't* move, the more Olive began to wonder if she had imagined that tiny twitch. Maybe what she'd seen was just an accidental blot of color, or a glint on a thick smudge of paint. And the paint *was* awfully thick and smudgy. Some of the brushstrokes in it didn't seem to be part of the portrait at all. They bumped up under Morton's image like scars under a thin bandage.

Olive glanced over her shoulder. A uniformed security guard stood in the doorway, too far off for Olive to see his face, or to know if his eyes were following her. A group of students tromped past the door. The security guard turned to watch them, and Olive whirled back toward the portrait.

She raised one hand, fingers outstretched, and pressed them carefully against the painting.

It didn't feel like one of Aldous's artworks—like a window with a sheet of warm, invisible Jell-O where the pane of glass should have been. It felt tighter, and thicker, more like a piece of well-chewed bubble gum. Morton's image kept still as Olive pushed harder, making the canvas bend. She had just felt something begin to break, sending a gust of cool damp air over her fingertips, when a voice behind her said—

"I saw that."

Both Olive and Rutherford spun around.

The girl with the eyeliner stood in the doorway. Her hands were on her hips, and her dark eyes were fixed on Olive.

An invisible snowball struck Olive's chest.

"You touched that painting," the girl said.

"No I didn't," said Olive pointlessly.

"Yes, you did." The girl turned back toward the hall. "Ms. Teedlebaum!" she called. "You should come in here!"

Olive froze. From the corner of her eye, she could see Rutherford staring at the girl, his dark eyes focused and sharp.

With a jingle of keys, Ms. Teedlebaum swept into the gallery. Her eyes went straight to Olive, who was standing like a startled snowman in front of Morton's portrait. A huge smile spread across the art teacher's face. "Wonderful!" she cried.

"Olive was—" began the girl with the eyeliner.

"Oh, I know just what Olive found," Ms. Teedlebaum cut her off. She beamed across the room. "I had hoped somebody would notice it—and I'm not surprised that *somebody* turned out to be Olive!"

Olive's throat clenched. A last gulp of air flew through it, like a bubble sucked into a straw. Her nose made a frightened wheezing sound.

Ms. Teedlebaum shouted back into the hallway.
"Come here, everybody! Quickly!"

More footsteps clomped along the hall as the other
sixth graders hurried in.

"Come along!" Ms. Teedlebaum called. "Everyone
get nice and close to the portrait where Olive and
Remington are standing!"

Soon a semicircle of students was clustered tightly
around the picture, with Olive and Rutherford trapped
in its center. Olive threw Rutherford a panicked look.
He gave her a tiny nod.

"Now," said the art teacher, sidling into the crowd,
"does anyone else see what Olive noticed?"

Olive wished with all her might that some gigantic distraction would choose that instant to smash its
way through the museum. A blizzard would have been
nice. So would a marauding band of art thieves. Or a
herd of rhinoceroses. She held perfectly still, hoping
to catch the sound of approaching rhinoceros feet. Or
did rhinos have hooves?

"The rhinoceros is actually a three-toed ungulate,"
whispered Rutherford.

But there were no blizzards or trampling toes—
just the murmurs of the other sixth graders, and Ms.
Teedlebaum's jingling keys. Olive started to think that
her lungs might actually explode.

Ms. Teedlebaum placed one hand on Olive's frozen

shoulder. Then, as though she were announcing the next contestant on a game show, she belted out, "*Pentimento!*"

The security guard stepped back into the doorway.

"We discussed that term in class, remember?" Ms. Teedlebaum went on just as loudly. "It's the underlying image in a painting when an old picture has been painted over with a new one. Sometimes artists reuse their own canvases; sometimes they paint over another artist's work. Look at the brushstrokes in the sky, right here . . ."

Olive squished herself to one side as three dozen faces craned closer. *Don't move,* she thought. *Please don't move.*

"I'm not," Rutherford muttered.

Not YOU, thought Olive.

But the other sixth graders weren't jerking away from the canvas with startled or mystified expressions. The painting kept still.

Thank you, Olive thought. *Thank you, thank you, thank you.*

"You're welcome," whispered Rutherford.

"If there was anything on our list of terms that I thought might go unfound today, it was this," Ms. Teedlebaum was bubbling on. "Even some experts wouldn't notice it!" Her paint-splattered hand landed on Olive's shoulder again. "I think you've got an artistic destiny ahead of you, Olive!"

Olive swallowed. Her cheeks felt like toasted marshmallows. Out of the corner of one eye, she could see the girl with the eyeliner staring past the painting, straight at her.

"You know, I think it must be fate that you spotted this picture." Ms. Teedlebaum's hand gave a squeeze. "This very painting was given to the museum by the former owner of your own house! Remember when I told you that Annabelle McMartin had made a sizable donation to the museum? Well, *this* was part of that donation!"

Hearing the name *Annabelle McMartin* made Olive's skin crawl with invisible wasps.

"Olive's house used to be owned by a well-known painter," Ms. Teedlebaum added. "Maybe someday Olive will give him a run for his money!" With a last smile at Olive, Ms. Teedlebaum sashayed away on her mismatched shoes. "Now, who's found a good example of impasto? Anyone?"

The other students backed off, two or three at a time, scattering toward other canvases. But the girl with the eyeliner stayed, watching Olive with narrowed eyes, until Olive and Rutherford both turned and wandered reluctantly away.

"It moved," Olive whispered as she and Rutherford trudged up the snowy slope of Linden Street. "I'm positive."

"It moved when you *weren't* wearing the spectacles?" Rutherford asked.

"Yes. Something inside the painting moved, just a tiny bit. And then it stopped."

"Interesting." Rutherford frowned. "But I didn't see it. Ms. Teedlebaum and the other students didn't appear to see it, and they were all looking very attentively. When you touched it, did it *feel* like the other pieces of Elsewhere?"

"No. It didn't." Olive blew away a strand of damp wool that trailed from her scarf to her lip. "At first, I thought I felt something—I don't know—*bend* a little. But now I'm not sure."

"Are you certain that you weren't merely noticing the effects of the pentimento, as Ms. Teedlebaum assumed?"

"I'm certain," said Olive uncertainly. "I think."

"Well, let's extrapolate," said Rutherford. "Assuming that you recall correctly, and the painting *did* move, what would that mean?"

"It would mean that Morton's mother knew how to use magic in her paintings." Olive gazed up the hill, at the old stone house looming through its leafless trees. "And *that* would mean either she was like Mrs. Dewey, and used magic in good ways, or that she was like . . . *them.*" Olive looked warily around the street once more. "And since I saw it move without the spectacles, it would mean that there was something inside that portrait that came from the real world. Something Mary wanted to hide."

"*Or,*" said Rutherford, "maybe it means that the combination of layered paintings reacted in a way that caught your eye and created illusory motion. That's when visual artists use certain techniques to trick the viewer's eye into believing that something is moving, when in fact it's perfectly stationary."

Olive stared into Rutherford's smudgy glasses. "How do you know this stuff?"

"There was an article in *Scientific American.*"

"Scientific American?"

"It's a magazine. It's generally the only reading material in my parents' bathroom."

"Oh," said Olive.

They paused at the walkway to Mrs. Dewey's house. Warm yellow light poured from the front windows, making the snow outside glitter like powdered gold.

"Maybe I imagined it. About the painting," said Olive, after a quiet moment. "But when I saw that picture, and that it was painted by Mary Nivens, I thought there had to be something special about it."

"Pareidolia," said Rutherford knowledgably. "When vague or arbitrary stimuli are perceived as something significant. Like seeing Satan in the scorch marks on a piece of toast."

Olive blinked at him.

"Scientific American," said Rutherford again.

"Oh." Olive backed toward the street. "Maybe you're right. But if I find anything else, I'll let you know."

"Good." Rutherford nodded. "I'm planning to use the winter break to complete my diorama of the Battle of Crécy—although, of course, dioramas themselves postdate the Hundred Years' War by several centuries. How will you be spending your vacation?"

"Inside," said Olive. "If I didn't have to go to school, I'd barely leave the house. And now I *won't.*"

"Perhaps that is the safest course," said Rutherford.

He swept her a chivalrous bow. "Until we meet again, enjoy your hermitical vacation!"

Olive watched him stride up the walkway and disappear through the door of the cozy white house. Then she turned and ran.

Safe inside the old stone house, Olive turned on the hallway lights. She flicked on the porch lamps and the parlor lights for good measure.

"Horatio?" she called, tossing her coat onto the rack. "Horatio!"

"In here," said a voice from the library.

She found the huge orange cat crouched on the rug. His green eyes were honed on the ceiling. The tip of his tail twitched like a furry whip.

Olive flopped down beside him on the woven curlicues. "Hi, Horatio. Is the house safe?"

Horatio's eyes didn't leave the ceiling. "As safe as it can be when it's besieged by a dimwitted pirate."

"*Dimwitted?*" snarled a voice from above. A splotchily colored cat dove from one high bookshelf to another. "I've keelhauled men for less! How dare you insult the legendary Captain Blackpaw?"

"Captain Blackpaw forgot to take off his Sir Lancelot costume," said Horatio.

Harvey used the eye that wasn't covered by a miniature eye patch to glance down at his tuna can breastplate. "That's pirate armor," he said quickly.

Horatio read the can's faded lettering. "'Chicken of the Sea'? Is that what they call Captain Blackpaw?"

"*Outrage!*" yowled Harvey, leaping from the bookcase onto the huge brass chandelier. "Prepare for battle, ye scurvy scalawag!"

Olive and Horatio ducked as one of the chandelier's lightbulbs sailed down and landed on the velvet sofa.

"BOOM!" Harvey bellowed.

"But otherwise, the house was safe?" Olive asked, getting to her feet. "You didn't notice any changes?"

The chandelier gave a tinkly creak. Another lightbulb soared down and buried itself in a potted fern.

"BOOM!" shouted Harvey again. "Avast, ye scoundrels!"

"No," said Horatio dryly. "Everything was perfectly normal."

That night, the Dunwoodys' dinner consisted of a large pizza cut into equal fourteenths. There were five-fourteenths for Mr. Dunwoody, five-fourteenths for Mrs. Dunwoody, and four-fourteenths—"Or two-sevenths!" as her father pointed out—for Olive, who didn't care what fractions she got as long as there weren't any mushrooms on them.

After dinner, the three Dunwoodys settled down in the living room with their books and newspapers.

Olive was in the middle of an especially creepy mystery book, which meant that she had to sit very close to the lamp. It also meant that, after twenty silent minutes, she almost jumped off the couch when the grandfather clock began to chime.

She glanced nervously out the living room window. The evening was already dark, turning the glass into a blurry mirror. Olive could see herself and her parents reflected there, settled in their seats around the glowing lamps. On the other side of the window, above the backyard, a quick, dark shape glided through the trees—an owl or another night bird. Its blackness slid through the Dunwoodys' reflection like a shadow beneath a living portrait.

Pentimento, Olive thought.

"Can I go visit my friend Morton?" she asked, shooting to her feet. "You met him on Halloween, remember?"

"I think that would be all right." Mrs. Dunwoody glanced at her wristwatch. "It *is* only seven oh two. The sun sets so early at this time of year—"

"Four thirty-three this afternoon," Mr. Dunwoody chimed in.

"—that it already feels like night," Mrs. Dunwoody finished. "Go ahead. Just don't stay out too late."

Stuffing her arms into her coat sleeves, Olive raced out the front door. A blast of cold air swirled around her. The porch was dark and empty, but as she stepped over the threshold, she heard the soft crinkle of paper beneath her shoe.

She looked down. On the frosty floorboards, just outside the heavy door, there lay an envelope. Olive stooped to pick it up. Its thick ivory paper was as chilly as the air. By the moon-pale glow of the streetlamps, she could read her own name on the front, scrawled in angular black strokes.

Olive Dunwoody.

She recognized the handwriting, she was certain. It wasn't Morton's, or Rutherford's, or Mrs. Dewey's, and yet it seemed foggily familiar, like new words put to an old melody.

Inside the envelope was a single sheet of paper. As Olive tugged it out, something cold and thick and awful cracked open inside of her body, its chill seeping from her shaking fingers to the soles of her feet.

I know what you have found, the note read, in the same angular black writing. *If you are wise, you will leave it there, turn away, and forget that you saw it at all.*

Olive glanced around. Layers of footprints, too many and too messy to trace, trampled the snow that led down the steps toward the silent street. She didn't need to follow them to know the truth, anyway.

Aldous McMartin had been here.

He had climbed the steps and left that note, just

inches from her family's door. He had stood right where Olive stood now while the Dunwoodys were eating dinner and talking and reading, with only that barrier of wood between them. Maybe he had stopped to listen to their voices and their clinking plates. He must have been getting stronger than Walter's and Mrs. Dewey's protective charms. Almost strong enough to step inside.

The two-sevenths of a pizza bubbled queasily in Olive's stomach. With a deep breath, she leaped down the stairs. The twigs of the lilac hedge clattered as she plunged through them, their brittle tips scratching at her face. A light glinted within the tall gray house on the other side, beckoning her onward.

Come on, Olive! the light seemed to say. *Come inside! RUN!*

Olive pounded at the gray house's front door.

"Walter!" she shouted. "Morton! It's me!"

The door stayed shut.

Olive glanced fearfully over her shoulder. The lawn was dark and quiet—too dark to tell if any dark, quiet shape within it was slinking closer.

"Let me in!" she yelled.

No answer.

Telling herself that just this once being *safe* might be more important than being *polite,* Olive grabbed the doorknob, wrenched it to the side, and stumbled gratefully through the unlocked door. She slammed it shut again behind her.

The tall gray house was still. The lights in the entryway and the hall were switched off, but Olive had seen the ruddy glow of light through the windows, she was positive.

"Hello?" she called. "Walter? Morton?"

She stepped forward. The old floorboards creaked beneath her. And then, from somewhere down the hall, there came a high-pitched, frightened scream.

"Morton!" Olive shouted.

There was no reply—only the distant, crackling sound of something being consumed by fire.

7

OLIVE TORE ALONG the hallway.

Her boots thudded on the floor, but she could barely hear them. Her heart was beating twice as loudly. With a surge of panic, she skidded around the corner, following the crackling sound of fire straight through the living room door.

Morton stood alone in the center of the chilly white room. His arms were crossed in front of his face, blocking the glow from the fireplace. In the grate, a fire roared. Heat made the air ripple like melted glass.

"Morton!" Olive grabbed him by one skinny arm, pulling him farther from the light. "What happened?"

Morton didn't answer. He just blinked, wide-eyed, at the fire.

"Are you all right?" Olive demanded. "Can you hear me?"

Morton turned to Olive. "*Of course* I can hear you," he said. "You're shouting *in my ear.*" His eyes flicked back to the fireplace. "I just didn't know they would catch so fast."

Olive squinted across the room. A heap of papers writhed in the grate, each page gusting with white flames. "Morton," she whispered, "what did you burn?"

Morton tugged his paint-slick arm out of Olive's grip. "Well, I wouldn't have burned them if I wanted you to *know.*"

"It was those sketches, wasn't it? The ones your mother made?" Olive's words came faster. "She was studying with *him,* wasn't she? She wanted to learn about the things he could do?"

"Shush!" Morton exploded. "Just *shush!* We're not supposed to talk about it!" He wrapped his scrawny arms around his body. "I *knew* somebody was going to find them, somebody *nosy,* and *wrong,* so it's better if nobody ever sees them at all!" Whirling away, Morton stalked across the room and threw himself down on the stiff white couch.

Olive took a breath. The fire snapped softly behind her, nibbling away at Mary Nivens's secrets. She looked back at Morton, who had curled up into a small, tufty-headed ball.

"Where's Walter?" she asked.

"At Mrs. Dewey's," the ball muttered.

Olive inched across the room. She sat down on the edge of the couch, far from the spot where Morton had wedged himself.

"Morton," she began, "I found out something else about your mother today. Something strange. I think she might have had . . . *talents,* like Aldous McMartin. I think she might have been able to make paintings that weren't just ordinary paintings."

Morton gave a jerk at the sound of Aldous's name. "She just liked to draw," he said, squeezing his nightshirted knees.

"I don't think that's all," said Olive. "I mean, everybody says there was something special about her. That nobody could lie to her. Maybe . . . maybe she had other magical talents too."

"Shh!" Morton grabbed a pillow from the end of the couch and clamped it over his ears.

"I saw a painting by your mother in the art museum," Olive went on stubbornly. "It's a portrait of you. It isn't perfect, but it's kind of like Aldous's artwork. Like Elsewhere. I think—I think it might have something *alive* inside of it."

Morton let go of the pillow. It bounced to the carpeted floor, sending up a puff of dust. "Mama wouldn't do that," he said. "She wouldn't trap anybody."

"Well, she might have wanted to learn to use her talents for *good,* like Mrs. Dewey, and Walter, and Rutherford. Or . . ."

"Not *or,*" said Morton. "She was good."

"Okay," said Olive. She paused, watching Morton tuck his legs back under the nightshirt. "So, *was* she studying with Aldous McMartin?"

"Maybe," Morton mumbled to his kneecaps. "Yes. But it was for *nice* reasons. To learn to paint. And to watch him."

"To watch him?" Olive repeated.

But Morton didn't go on. Olive waited, looking down at the tufts of Morton's hair, which turned from amber to pale gold as the fire burned down. Inside her mind, something else began to change. It turned from something wispy and gray into something strong and solid, something that gave off sparks of its own radiant, promising light.

"You know what I think?" she asked, very slowly. "I think maybe your mother was a threat to the McMartins. Maybe she was learning to use Aldous's magic so that she could undo it. Maybe he had to trap her before she could stop him. Maybe . . . if we find her . . . maybe she could defeat him for good."

Morton glanced up at Olive. "Maybe," he said. His eyes went back to the fireplace. "But I just want her to come home."

Something in Olive's chest—that same warm, solid, strong thing—spread its way through the rest of her body. She stood up and strode across the dimming room, straight to the fireplace. The last of Mary's sketches was crumbling into red-seamed ash. Olive pulled the envelope from her pocket. With a little flick, she dropped it into the grate. The heat in the embers rushed up, breaking through the paper with fresh jets of flame. In seconds, Aldous's message was gone.

OLIVE CALLED RUTHERFORD first thing the next
morning.

"I knew you were going to call," Rutherford said,
before Olive could get any further than *Hello*. "And I
know that you want to go back to the museum as soon
as possible, and you're hoping that I will accompany
you."

Olive sighed. "Do you know how it feels to have
someone know everything you're going to say before
you say it?"

"I can read thoughts, not feelings," said Rutherford.
"So my answer to that question would have to be *no*."

"It's a little annoying."

"I can imagine. You were thinking we'd meet at three
o'clock, as the museum closes at four, weren't you?"

Olive let out another sigh. "Why do we need a phone at all?"

"Because of *feelings,*" said Rutherford. "Your thoughts are not the only things that interest me."

Olive smiled, in spite of herself. But she was glad Rutherford couldn't see her do it. "Just so you know, I feel . . ." She trailed off. She knew Rutherford could read the word *grateful* scrolling through her mind anyway.

"I shall see you at three." Rutherford hung up.

At precisely 2:45, Olive was in the basement of the old stone house, kneeling in front of Leopold with her empty purple backpack held invitingly open.

"I am reluctant to leave my station, miss," said the cat in his gravelly voice. "Particularly when we know that *what* I'm guarding could be an invader's first target."

"But Leopold, I need you," Olive pleaded. "The other two cats can stay here to guard the house while you come with us for backup. You're the perfect choice for this mission. You're brave. You're wise. You're *quiet.*"

Leopold's chest inflated in a gratified way. "Simply doing my duty, miss."

"I know. That's why we need you. This will require stealth and secrecy." Olive gave the trapdoor a significant look. "And you know all about keeping secrets."

The cat inclined his head. "I don't know what you're talking about, miss."

"I'm talking about the secret room with the—"

"Yes," said Leopold quickly. "I *do* actually know what you're talking about."

"So . . ." Olive rustled the backpack. "Will you come with us?"

Leopold eyed the bag's purple pockets dubiously. "It's not especially dignified," he said at last, in his very deepest voice.

"Well—you'd be riding on my back, so it's kind of like a saddle," said Olive. "You'd be like the Duke of Wellington, and I would be the Duke of Wellington's horse."

Leopold's eyes flickered. "Copenhagen?"

"Sure," said Olive. "We can pretend we're going there." She held out the backpack. "Mount your steeds, gentlemen!"

With a deep, decisive breath, Leopold strode into the bag and let himself be zipped inside.

The Dunwoodys weren't surprised that Olive wanted to spend Saturday afternoon at the art museum. They had stopped being surprised by Olive's artistic tendencies when she was five, and they had given her a beautiful wooden abacus, which Olive had taken apart and used to make a beaded headdress for her teddy bear.

"You're *sure* you'd rather go to the art museum than help me grade these math quizzes?" said Mr. Dunwoody, waving a sheaf of papers enticingly.

"I'm sure," said Olive.

Mrs. Dunwoody looked up from the latest issue of AUSOM: *The Absolutely Unrelenting Seriousness of Mathematics.* "Have a good time," she said. "Just don't stay out after dark."

"I won't," Olive promised, wrapping a scarf around her neck. "I'll be home by dinnertime."

"And don't forget your hat. It's freezing out there." Mr. Dunwoody gave Olive's back a pat. Her backpack squirmed.

Olive yanked a knit cap over her hair, shouted "Good-bye!" to her parents, and raced out the front door.

Rutherford was waiting for her at the corner.

"Hello, Copenhagen," he said, with a little bow. "And good afternoon, Your Grace."

"Good afternoon, sir," muttered the backpack.

"The appropriate address is *Your Grace,* not *Your Highness,* you know," said Rutherford as they headed down the slope of Linden Street. "The Duke of Wellington was not a *royal* duke. If, on the other hand, he had been born into the ruling family, as the second son of the king or queen, for example . . ."

Rutherford rambled on about titles and hierarchies

as they hurried up one snowy block after another. Olive, who was shivering in spite of her coat and the warm lump inside her backpack, was grateful for the distraction. She kept her chin tucked into her scarf and her eyes on the streets around them, making certain that they weren't being followed. It was still light enough that Aldous McMartin would probably have avoided the outdoors, but the sun was sinking behind the rows of snowy houses, and the sky above them was the steely shade of a mirror in an empty room.

They wound their way around corners and across quiet streets until the houses gave way to stores and offices, all decked with wreaths and small, colored lights. By the time they reached the museum, the streetlamps had blinked on.

". . . Although until the Hundred Years' War, the royalty of England spoke Anglo-Norman French, which is why they're called *royalty*—from the French *roi*—in the first place," Rutherford concluded as they climbed up the wide stone steps.

Somewhere nearby, church bells clanged a carol.

"It's three thirty," Olive murmured. She put her mouth close to the backpack. "Are you all right in there, Leopold?"

"Perfectly. Thank you, miss," Leopold's voice rumbled back.

Olive hesitated at the doors. "We'll need to find

a place to hide, so we can explore the painting after everyone else leaves," she whispered. "It would probably be safest if no one noticed us at all."

"Agreed," said Rutherford. "We should avoid making contact with anyone."

He pulled open one of the heavy glass doors, and they stepped into the museum's entryway. And there, behind the information desk, with her frizzy red hair curling out from her head like the bristles of an overused toothbrush, sat Ms. Teedlebaum.

"Well, hello, art lovers!" she hooted, hopping to her feet. "What are you two doing here?"

Olive's heart plunged. "Um—"

"We were so inspired by yesterday's visit that we decided to return," Rutherford interrupted.

"Wonderful!" Ms. Teedlebaum beamed. "I'm this weekend's information officer, so if there's anything you'd like to know, just ask!"

"As a matter of fact," said Rutherford, "we would like to learn more about one of the paintings we discussed yesterday."

"I'd be delighted to help, Livingston!" Ms. Teedlebaum stepped out from behind the desk with a tinkle of pens and keys. "Which artist are you interested in?"

"The one with the pentimento," said Rutherford. "The portrait by Mary Nivens."

Olive stifled a gasp.

Ms. Teedlebaum's smile widened. "Of course!" she exclaimed. "Follow me!"

"What are you doing, *Livingston?*" Olive asked between her teeth as she and Rutherford followed the rippling hem of Ms. Teedlebaum's orange kaftan through the hallways.

"As we have already been noticed, it seemed wiser to give a plausible explanation for our visit than to act mysterious and uncomfortable," said Rutherford.

"Hmph," said Olive, even though she knew that Rutherford could read her thoughts, which were all grudgingly agreeing with him.

"Here we are!" Ms. Teedlebaum's voice rang through the quiet room. A few other visitors looked up, startled. "Mary Nivens's portrait!"

Olive stared hard at the double-layered image of Morton, with its strange bumps and swirls. It wasn't moving. The longer she stared at it, the more she began to fear that Rutherford was right. What if it *was* only a trick of the brushstrokes, a shift of light and color? What if she'd been fooled by an illusion, and her hunches meant nothing at all?

"We believe that the artist, Mary Nivens, once lived between our houses on Linden Street," Rutherford was saying.

Olive threw him a dark look, but Ms. Teedlebaum's smile was bright enough to eclipse it entirely.

"Really?" she exclaimed. "How fascinating!" Her refractive green eyes hit Olive. "I wonder if she was acquainted with the famous Aldous McMartin!"

"Mmm . . ." said Olive.

"Are there any other pictures by Mary Nivens in the museum's collection?" Rutherford asked.

"No, Cunningham, unfortunately not," said Ms. Teedlebaum. "This is the only piece by Mary Nivens that's in public ownership, as far as we know."

Olive squinted up at the painting again. It remained perfectly still.

"Has there been any attempt to remove the outer portrait to see what is beneath it?" asked Rutherford.

"That's a tricky process," said Ms. Teedlebaum, "and our art historians have determined from the canvas itself that the underlying painting must be very close in age to the painting on top of it. It's most likely that Mary painted over one of her own artworks. Painters do that a lot, to save money, or to hide embarrassing mistakes!" Ms. Teedlebaum laughed, turning to Olive again. "But it's fun to imagine something more mysterious, isn't it?"

Olive tried to answer, but her tongue was stuck to the roof of her mouth, and all that came out was a little clicking sound.

"It certainly is," Rutherford answered for her.

"It's like buried treasure," said the art teacher, raising

her paint-splotched hands. "Once you dig it up, it isn't buried treasure anymore. It might just be a box of old car parts!"

"I suppose that is possible," said Rutherford agreeably.

Olive finally managed to get her tongue unstuck. "Um, Ms. Teedlebaum? You said that Annabelle McMartin donated this painting to the museum. Did she tell you why she was giving this one away?"

Ms. Teedlebaum nodded. "I asked her about that. She told me that it wasn't one of her grandfather's artworks, which were the only pieces she *had* to keep, and she thought it would be safest at our museum, and that I shouldn't look a gift horse in the mouth. Isn't that a wonderful old expression?" Ms. Teedlebaum clasped her hands delightedly, bracelets jingling. "Do you have any other questions?"

"No, thank you," said Rutherford. "It's been very informative."

"Good." Ms. Teedlebaum smiled down at both of them. "Enjoy the paintings. Just remember that we close in fifteen minutes!"

"Thank you, Ms. Teedlebaum," said Olive and Rutherford.

"Thank you, madam," said a deep voice from Olive's backpack. Fortunately, Ms. Teedlebaum was already sailing away on a ripple of orange kaftan.

"I know what we should do," Olive whispered, glancing around the gallery to make sure no other visitors were close enough to overhear. "There are bathrooms in the entryway, just past the information desk. We'll wait until Ms. Teedlebaum is distracted, call good-bye to her so she thinks we've left, and then hide there until everyone's gone. Okay?"

"The men's bathroom, or the women's bathroom?" Rutherford asked.

"Does it matter?"

"Well, *two* of us are male . . ."

"Fine. The men's room then," said Olive. "Ms. Teedlebaum will be less likely to come inside it, anyway."

"Excellent thinking, miss," said Olive's backpack.

They slunk back along the corridor. The museum was emptying for the night. A few whispering grownups still wandered in the huge, unfurnished rooms, but everyone seemed to be drifting toward the exit.

At the end of the main hall, Olive craned around the corner. Ms. Teedlebaum was back at the information desk. Her frizzy head was bowed over the worn wooden surface. She appeared to be folding tissues into origami shapes before tucking them back into their cardboard box, which wouldn't have made sense if anyone else had been doing it.

Olive gave Rutherford a nod.

"Good-bye, Ms. Teedlebaum," they said loudly, trotting across the entryway.

"Good-bye!" Ms. Teedlebaum called back, glancing up from a Kleenex crane to give them one more smile.

The instant her head was down, Olive and Rutherford dove toward the restroom. Rutherford peeped through the doorway first. "All clear," he whispered.

They tiptoed inside, letting the door swing gently shut behind them.

The bathroom was painted a dingy yellowish color, like a dish of dusty butter. A row of stalls with chipped metal walls faced a row of matching pedestal sinks. Olive slipped into the farthest stall. Rutherford took the one beside her.

"I'm going to stand on the seat, so my feet don't show," Olive whispered through the wall.

"Good idea," Rutherford whispered back.

After arranging several strips of toilet paper and readjusting her backpack for maximum sturdiness (she didn't want to lose hold and drop Leopold into the toilet bowl, for *many* good reasons), Olive climbed up onto the old wooden seat. Her hands were starting to sweat, so she took off her mittens and stuffed them into her coat pockets.

Then she waited.

It took about thirty seconds for her legs to start to ache. Her knees were locked at an uncomfortable angle, but she couldn't change position without losing her balance or making noise. Every tiny sound seemed to thunder through the room, growing louder as it echoed from the yellowish walls. The hair twitching against her ears sounded like claws on a window screen. Her heartbeat was a fist striking a punching bag.

Finally, when she knew she would have to move her legs or lose her mind, there was the creak of an opening door. Olive held her breath, listening to the jingle of keys, followed by the snap of a light switch.

The butter-colored room turned black.

In the distance, there were more soft clicks, and then the thump of a heavy door . . . and then, at last, there was silence.

Olive waited for another minute, counting the seconds in her head.

"You skipped the forties," Rutherford whispered from next door. "But I think we can safely emerge, with or without them."

Olive climbed down from the toilet seat and stumbled out of the creaking metal stall. To her right, she could hear Rutherford doing the same. In the blackness, she crouched down and unzipped her backpack. Leopold emerged, his eyes like two fireflies against the dark.

"Shall we make our exit?" Rutherford's voice whispered.

"Let's hurry!" Olive whispered back.

They slipped out of the restroom. The museum's entrance was silvery and silent. Fading daylight pressed through the glass doors. The big wooden information desk was abandoned, only a box of origami tissues marking the spot where Ms. Teedlebaum had been.

In a cluster, they darted across the entryway and back down the hall, Leopold soundless, Rutherford quiet, and Olive trying to be quiet and failing miserably. Her backpack made annoying rustling sounds, and her boots struck the creakiest floorboards. Even her breath seemed to reverberate through the cavernous rooms.

They turned into the gallery. The hanging lamps above the artworks had been switched off for the night. Light from the windows reflected in the polished floors, turning the air to gray mist. The canvases gleamed dully.

"Here we are," Olive breathed, stopping in front of Morton's portrait. She tugged the spectacles from her collar and set them on her nose.

The painting remained perfectly still.

Even though she had been telling herself not to get her hopes up, Olive felt a wave of disappointment pushing them down again.

"Do you see anything?" Rutherford whispered.

Olive shook her head.

"I do," Leopold whispered, from his spot near Olive's knees.

Olive looked down. The cat's eyes were fixed on the canvas, their gaze so vivid and bright that they seemed to make the painting itself glow. "You were right, miss," he said softly. "There is something alive inside this painting."

"Are you sure?" Olive whispered back.

"Absolutely certain, miss," said the cat. "But Mary Nivens did not put it there."

The back of Olive's neck prickled. With one slightly shaky hand, she reached up to touch the painting. It flexed softly against her palm, like the peel of a huge, ripe fruit. She pushed harder, and again, she felt the painting shift against her fingertips, letting out a sudden gust of cool, damp air.

"We have to climb inside," she breathed. "Rutherford, will you stand guard? If something happens to one of us, the other one can bring you the message."

Rutherford nodded intently. "I'll be your sentry," he said. "For historical accuracy, I should be armed with a halberd or a glaive of some sort, but I didn't think to bring mine along.

"I've just perceived a problem, however," said Rutherford, before Olive could grasp the picture frame. "If something were to happen to both of you, I would be unable to come to your aid."

"Oh. You're right." Olive lifted the spectacles from around her neck. "I suppose you should keep these with you. But be very, *very* careful."

"Your warning is unnecessary, though it will not go unheeded," said Rutherford, taking the spectacles from Olive's hand. "And I'm certain that *you* will be very careful as well."

"Ready, miss?" Leopold offered her his sleek black tail.

Olive grasped it. Together, they climbed into the thick gold frame.

The image of Morton stretched and warped as they pushed forward. Leopold raised his chin, marching determinedly on. Olive wriggled after him, and around her, the painting itself began to soften and tear, letting her head and shoulders push their way inside.

She could smell something earthy and faintly rotten in the air, and the sky went from a soft blue to gray-white, and the pale streak of Morton's face gave way to wild marshy ground, and suddenly Olive was toppling through the frame onto a thick tuft of damp brown grass.

She looked up. The frame hung above her in the foggy air. The portrait of Morton, its profile now facing the opposite direction, mended itself as though it had never been disturbed at all.

Leopold had landed on a tussock a few feet away.

His ears stood up like spear points. He sniffed at the air.

"Scotland," he said, in a soft voice. "The bogs."

"Like . . . *cranberry* bogs?" asked Olive hopefully, who had learned all about cranberry bogs in the report she'd done on Wisconsin for geography class.

"No," said Leopold. "Not like cranberry bogs at all. Be very careful where you step, miss."

Olive got cautiously to her feet. The world inside the painting was stark and harsh and strangely beautiful. In the distance, she could see the crags of painted hills, and a few delicate birch trees clustering against the sky. But between them and the hills, stretching away for hundreds of yards on every side, was a flat expanse of moss and mud.

This didn't look like one of Mary's sketches.

This looked like . . .

"Aldous painted this, didn't he?" she whispered.

Leopold gave one sharp nod.

Olive looked around again. The ground on every side was dark and shaggy and still. What living thing had she noticed inside this deserted place? What had moved in this gray-brown emptiness?

She took one slow step forward.

"Keep to the dry grass, miss," Leopold warned. "People who fall into the bogs aren't found again for a very long time. Sometimes for thousands of years."

Olive paused. Arms out for balance, she stared down at the land in front of her. A few steps away, in a patch of dark earth, there was a tiny, almost invisible quake.

"It moved!" Olive shouted. "Right there! I knew it! I knew I saw something!"

"Where, miss?" Leopold asked, examining the ground with narrowed eyes.

"Right there." She pointed. "Something must be buried there!"

Olive took an eager step forward. The solid layer of moss and mud beneath her crumbled into nothing. She let out a gasp as a gush of freezing liquid rushed over the tops of her boots. All around her, in a wobbling, widening circle, the ground began to shiver.

"It's a quaking bog," she heard Leopold murmur. "One huge, hidden pool, with a little skin of grass on top. Miss, listen to me: Back up very, very carefully."

But Olive had already taken two quick, terrified backward steps. A mass of floating sedge dissolved under her feet, and her body plunged downward, into a pit of icy, liquid mud. She didn't even have time for a last breath before the darkness closed around her.

FREEZING MUD PLUGGED her nose. Bitter grit slipped through her teeth. Olive thrashed upward, sputtering, shaking. Oily water stung her eyes. She couldn't see. Gasping for air, she swiped at her eyelids with one hand, reaching out for solid ground with the other. But there was no solid ground to grasp.

"Listen, miss!" Leopold paced frantically along the edge of the pool. "Don't splash, or it will pull you deeper! Swim slowly toward me, and—"

The cat froze. Olive felt a rush of wind chill the wet strands of her hair. She squinted up through the mud, following Leopold's eyes. The gray sky above them was darkening. Blackness rippled across its painted surface like an invisible fire, leaving only ash behind.

"He's close," Leopold breathed.

Olive knew who Leopold meant. Aldous McMartin was nearby, close enough to control this part of Elsewhere.

But *how?* Had he followed them here, into the museum? How had they not noticed him, when they'd been watching for him the entire time?

Panicking now, Olive thrashed harder, kicking her legs against the mud. It was like trying to swim in a giant bowl of frozen oatmeal. She felt it thickening around her, the sunken dirt stirred into motion, pulling at her feet, filling her boots with liquid cement.

"Don't panic, miss!" Leopold called. "Move *slowly!*"

Olive's brain tried to obey, but her body wouldn't listen. Everything inside her demanded that she fight, that she kick and struggle, that she get out of this pit of foul black water. Overhead, the wind was rising, rattling the tussocks of grass. Bits of flying bracken stung her face. She groped for the edge of the pool, trying to keep her chin above the liquid. Her coat dragged at her arms. Her soaked jeans felt cold and heavy as iron. Leopold reached out with one paw, but Olive was still too far away, and no matter how hard she fought to stay afloat, she could feel her body being sucked back.

"Shall I get Rutherford?" Leopold shouted over the noise of the wind.

"No!" Olive screamed back. "Don't leave me alone in here!"

She squinted at the picture frame hanging in the

distant, darkening air. The wind was pummeling her now, and between the mud in her eyes and the dimming light, she could barely see. The frame became a golden blotch amid the blackness. Rutherford should have caught her terrified thoughts by now. Why wasn't he climbing inside?

"Stay calm, miss!" Leopold shouted. "I'll be right back!"

Olive tried to answer, but the mud washed up and over her mouth, filling it with the taste of painted dirt, and she knew that she was being pulled deeper.

. . . Pulled into that lightless, sloshing, rotten pit by something whose hand had just locked around her ankle.

Olive gave a frantic kick.

The hand didn't let go.

She felt its fingers tightening, pulling harder, as the black water slid up and over her nostrils, over her eyes, over her head.

Olive's body writhed with panic. Her limbs thrashed. Her lungs burned. The cold, slick fingers hung on.

Aldous McMartin.

He was waiting down there, in the darkness, ready to drag her into this cold, black, awful swamp where even her body would be hidden forever from anyone who might try to find her.

Something solid knocked her on the head.

Was she getting attacked from *above* too? Olive lashed out, grasping for the solid object, and felt her hand break the surface of the bog. Something long and bumpy and firm scraped against her fingertips.

Olive grabbed it. Locking both hands together, she dragged herself upward until her nose and mouth just cleared the foaming surface. She took a deep, spluttering breath of the windy air.

"Hang on, miss!" she heard Leopold yell. "Smooth, slow movements! Don't let go!"

Squinting through the mud that clotted her eyelashes, Olive spotted his bright green eyes. The cat was pinning the other end of a large branch to a piece of solid ground.

"Pull, miss!" he shouted. "You can make it!"

Olive kicked both legs, paddling forward. The freezing fingers around her leg held on.

"Something's got my ankle!" she shouted. A burst of wind shrieked across the bog, whipping the surface of the mud into a black froth.

"Just keep moving!" Leopold shouted back. "Hurry!"

Olive gave another kick. She wrenched one numb hand free of the branch and lunged forward, grasping a spot closer to its root. Leopold's teeth closed on her sleeve. Wriggling like an oil-slick seal, Olive squirmed toward the place where the cat stood, feeling the surface beneath her turn from slippery mud to semi-solid earth.

The hand still hadn't let go.

As Olive dragged herself onto the grass, she felt something else beginning to move. The forward momentum of the creature beneath her was pushing her up onto dry ground. She fell on her side, twisting around to stare at the shape emerging from the pit.

It was a man.

A man with old-fashioned clothes, and mud-wet hair, and a thick mustache.

A man who was most definitely *not* Aldous McMartin.

He crawled up onto the grass. "Mary?" he croaked, in a voice like a disused engine.

The name flashed across Olive's mind, lighting a hundred other little fires—but the wind and the mud quickly blew them out again.

"We must get out of here, miss." Leopold's eyes were on the sky. What had been ash-gray was now inky black. The air above was nearly as cold as the water below. Olive's teeth were chattering, and the stinging in her hands had grown so deep that she could hardly feel it at all. The painted mud was beginning to trickle away from her body and flow back to its spot, but while this made her cleaner, it didn't make her any warmer.

Shivering, she scrambled to the muddy man's side.

"Can you walk?" she asked him. "Because we need to hurry!"

The man's brown eyes blinked back at her. Up close, she could tell that his woolen clothes were made of paint. His skin was swirled with faint streaks and was clammy and cold from being buried in that bog for who knew how long. Still, while Olive locked her arm through his, she felt a trace of warmth, as faint as one drop of blood in a bowl of milk.

"Mary," the man said again. "She didn't mean to do it. She would never have left me here." His rusty voice grew louder. "He forced her to do it."

"Who did?" said Olive.

"The old man. Next door. Al—"

A horrible roaring filled the sky.

"Run, miss!" Leopold shouted.

"Come on!" Olive yelled over the noise. "We'll get you out of here!"

With all the strength she had left, Olive hoisted the man's arm onto her shoulders. They staggered toward the frame. The wind lashed at them, howling. Mud and bracken struck their faces. But the man's legs seemed to be remembering how to hold up the rest of him, and the frame was growing closer.

"Take hold of my tail, miss!" Leopold yelled.

In a clumsy, muddy chain, Leopold, Olive, and the strange man clambered out of the bog and through the picture frame.

Olive tumbled to the museum floor. It wasn't a

comfortable place to land, but the air was warm, and the parquet was wonderfully clean and hard.

The man plopped to the floorboards beside her. He sat, gazing bewilderedly around. In the dimness, with his paint-shiny skin and antique clothes, he looked fragile and half-unreal, like a photograph that had fallen out of a very old album.

And Olive recognized the photograph. In it, the man was neat and smiling, his mustache combed and his eyes crinkly and warm. He was posing with the rest of his family: his sweetly smiling wife, his stiff, spotless daughter, and his son, who had a round face and tufty white hair.

Olive took a shaky breath. "Mr. Nivens?"

The man's eyes widened. "Yes?" he whispered.

"Um—my name is Olive. I know your son."

The man's eyes grew even wider. "Morton?"

Olive nodded. "I'll take you to him. He's safe, at your house."

"At *our house*?" Harold Nivens stepped forward. "He's all right? He's alive?"

"He's all right," said Olive hesitantly. "But he's not really—I mean—he's like *you*."

"Where was he? Did the old man have him? How did you—"

"Mr. Nivens?" Olive interrupted as politely as she could. "Morton can tell you everything once we get back to Linden Street. For now, we should probably get out of this museum." She straightened the knitted cap that covered her hair. It was still slightly damp, but most of the mud had stayed inside the canvas, where it belonged. "Should we take the same route home, Rutherford?"

Rutherford didn't answer.

Olive squinted through the dark gallery. The rest of the room was empty.

"Rutherford?" she called as loudly as she dared.

Still no reply.

"Do you think he ran for help?" Olive asked, turning to Leopold.

"No, miss." The cat's eyes were fixed on one small, dark object on the parquet floor. "I don't think that's what happened at all."

"**W**HAT IS THAT?" Olive whispered.

She and Leopold inched forward. Lying on the gleaming floor was a single black glove. It was made of leather, with a red dragon coiling across the backs of its fingers. Embroidered on the cuff, Olive could just make out the words *Salem Knights' Tournament: The Festival of Fights.*

"Rutherford's glove," she answered herself. "He must have dropped it."

"Master Rutherford isn't the type to be careless with his things. Especially when they involve the Middle Ages," said Leopold.

"So what do you think happened?"

"I believe he is giving us a sign." Leopold's eyes glittered in the darkness. "I believe he *threw down the gauntlet.*"

Thanks to Rutherford, Olive had heard this expression before. "You mean there was a fight?" She glanced around the cavernous room. "Do you think there's any chance that Rutherford won?"

"Actually, I would call it a draw," whispered a voice from around a corner.

Olive froze. Harold and Leopold whirled around.

A wiry, curly-headed shape crept out of the shadows. As it slunk across the room, Olive could just make out the green dragon emblazoned on its T-shirt.

"Rutherford!" she breathed. "What happened?"

"I was nearly apprehended by a security guard," Rutherford answered in a rapid whisper. "He was working late, apparently. I didn't even hear his footsteps, and suddenly a hand grasped my collar. I'm not ashamed to admit that I fled."

"You outmaneuvered him?" asked Leopold.

"I ran around the corner, but he was still hanging on to my coat, so I simply wriggled out of it. I managed to escape by dodging into the next hallway and hiding. However, I lost my gloves—oh, there's one of them—and my coat, and—"

"—And the spectacles?" Olive interrupted.

"Correct."

Olive pressed both hands against the sides of her head. Something tightened inside her, asking to be let out in one long, pressure-releasing scream.

"I realize that you are aggravated," said Rutherford calmly, "but a security guard will not know the value of the spectacles. If we're lucky, we may simply be able to find them again. And my coat. And my other glove."

"The guard may still be nearby," Leopold murmured, "but if we proceed with caution, I might be able to trace the scent of your belongings. Follow me."

"Mr. Nivens?" Olive whispered as the cat slunk off across the room. "Would you please hide right here until we come back?"

Harold nodded once before backing into the darkest corner.

Leopold glided through the hallways like a shadow. Olive raced behind him, trying to keep her eyes fixed on the sheen of his fur. Rutherford's footsteps trailed after her.

At one corner, Leopold halted, whiskers twitching. Then he crept to the right, leading them into a narrower passage. This hallway had no paintings along its walls, only doors—heavy gray metal doors, the kind that usually led to storage closets. Before the third door, Leopold stopped. He put his nose to the narrow gap beneath it. Reflected in his eyes, Olive could see the glint of electric light.

"Through here," the cat whispered.

Olive reached for the doorknob. It turned easily in her hand. The door opened inward, revealing a flight of cement stairs that plunged down into the museum's basement.

Leopold glided soundlessly down the steps. Olive and Rutherford followed him, bracing themselves against the cold cement wall.

The staircase ended in a wide gray chamber. Rumbling vents and long pipes crisscrossed the ceiling. One fly-specked light fixture hung in its center, giving off a reluctant yellow haze. To either side, sturdy wooden shelves stacked with cloth-wrapped canvases and empty frames, rolls of bubble wrap, and straw-filled crates dwindled away into the distance. Hooks on the wall held tools and brushes and security guards' uniforms. The air was cold and dim and dry. It was the perfect place to store paintings, Olive realized. *Any* paintings.

Beside the first row of shelves, Leopold froze. "Miss," he whispered, very softly. "I've been here before."

"*Here?*" Olive whispered back.

Leopold sniffed at the air. "Yes. I am certain. This is where Annabelle brought me."

Goose bumps rippled over Olive's body. When Annabelle had taken Leopold away—when Olive had lost him in an idiotic bargain—she had kept him blind and smothered, confined in a bag so he couldn't escape. Leopold hadn't known where he'd been taken;

only that he was underground, in someplace cold and dim, and that Annabelle had used him to free the last self-portrait of her grandfather. That *someplace* could certainly have been *this* someplace.

Olive backed toward the wall. The chill of the cement seeped through her winter coat, straight to her skin. "Do you think Aldous is down here right now?" she breathed.

Before Leopold could answer, Rutherford let out a gasp.

"Look!" he whispered, beckoning the others down one narrow aisle.

On the floor, between two pallets of cloth-wrapped paintings, there lay the black heap of Rutherford's coat. Rutherford picked it up. "My other glove is in the pocket," he murmured, rooting through the fabric. "And stuck inside the sleeve . . ." He held up something that glittered in the faint light.

"The spectacles!" Olive sprang forward, grabbing them gratefully with both hands. She threaded the ribbon around her neck. "Oh, thank goodness! I was sure—"

"Shh!" hissed Leopold.

Olive and Rutherford fell silent. In the stillness, Olive could hear the faint swish of fabric along the cement floor. A half second later, there was a soft, metallic jingle—like the clink of keys on a dangling cord.

Olive craned around the shelves. At the far end of the room, with her back turned and her kinky red hair swaying, stood Ms. Teedlebaum. The art teacher was busy packing a crate. Keys and pens clattered as she bent down, sliding a canvas into the waiting straw.

Without a word, Olive, Rutherford, and Leopold backed down the aisle. They tiptoed up the stairs and through the basement door, closing it with the softest thump they could manage.

"I thought we heard Ms. Teedlebaum leave!" Olive whispered as they hurried back down the hall.

"So did I," Rutherford agreed. "She must have gone back through the museum rather than out the front doors."

They streaked into the gallery where Mary Nivens's painting hung. Harold Nivens's tall, sturdy shape stood in the center of the room, gazing at the image of Morton. He wheeled around as they approached.

"There you are!" he said, much too loudly. "We need to get Mary," he announced. "She's in the other portrait, I'm certain of it."

"Other portrait?" Rutherford repeated, before Olive could ask him to keep his voice down

"*Her* other portrait," Harold boomed, rubbing his hands together energetically. "She painted both of them at the same time. It must be nearby!"

"But Ms. Teedlebaum said there aren't any other

portraits by Mary Nivens in the museum's collection," said Rutherford.

"Wait!" gasped Olive. Everyone turned to look at her. "I think—I think I know where we can find one."

In the moment of silence that followed her words, there was a soft, not-too-distant *thump*.

"Let's get out of here!" Olive hissed.

Grabbing Harold's painted sleeve, she charged into the hallway. Her boots squealed on the parquet. Harold's and Rutherford's feet pounded beside her. At that moment, she wouldn't even have heard another pair of footsteps running after them. They tore across the entryway, Leopold sailing ahead like the shadow of some huge bird, and burst through the museum doors.

The sunlight that had tinted the sky was long gone. Darkness hung over the town, thick and total. The streetlamps turned patches of snow from gray to blue.

"Stay to the lighted areas!" Olive called over her shoulder as they rushed down the broad stone steps. "Mr. Nivens, you should keep your face down. The light could hurt you. Leopold, lead the way!"

The black cat shot ahead.

The rest of them clustered tightly together, skidding here and there on the icy sidewalks.

The center of town was full of worn brick buildings that had been built for one thing and were being used for another. Some still had old-fashioned signs painted on their sides, reading things like *Northern Lumber Co.* and *Sip a Simpsons' Soda!* but now their plate glass doors glinted like mirrors, and neon signs flared in their windows. Harold winced at the lights, turning his face away.

At first, everyone kept quiet. Olive could hear her own heartbeat, and Rutherford's panting breaths, but Harold made no sound at all—until, at one corner, he let out a loud "Huh!"

Olive whirled around. "What is it?"

"The post office!" said Harold. "They've put some big metal doors along that side. And there used to be a hedge along the front walk. Now it's gone."

"Oh," said Olive. "Well—yes. I'm sure some things have changed since the last time you were here."

"And is that Harrison's Haberdashery?" Harold asked loudly, pointing at the windows of a Chinese restaurant.

"Um . . . maybe?" said Olive, who wasn't sure what a haberdashery was but assumed it had something to do with smashing things, possibly with hammers.

"And there's Mason's hardware store!" said Harold, even more loudly. "Now it says 'Laundromat.' Huh! Must be a family name. French, perhaps."

"Actually," Rutherford's nasal voice piped up, "Laundromat is not a French family name; it's the name of a place for doing laundry in coin-operated washing and drying machines."

Harold blinked at him.

"Hello," said Rutherford. "I didn't have the opportunity to properly introduce myself before. I'm Rutherford Dewey. I was named after Ernest Rutherford, the father of nuclear physics, not after the sixteenth president of the United States. This is slightly ironic, as physics is *not* among my main interests, while history *is,* although I'm far more interested in medieval history than American history, and in fact I'm an expert on the middle ages in Western Europe, primarily Britain and France, which is why I can say with reasonable certainty that *Laundromat* is not a French name."

"Ah," said Harold. "Well, it's a pleasure to meet you, Rutherford!" He gave Rutherford's hand a hearty shake. "A real pleasure!"

When they reached the foot of Linden Street, even Harold and Rutherford fell silent. Everyone seemed to know that if something terrible was going to happen, it would have to happen here, now, in the few remaining moments before they were safe on the other side of a locked wooden door.

The hairs on the back of Olive's neck prickled with little electric shocks. Her stomach swirled. Her legs ached from running, and her lungs were sore with the scrape of cold air. She glanced from one house to another, waiting to spot a pair of painted eyes staring back.

"There's Mr. Fitzroy's house," said Harold, in a softer voice, when they were halfway up the hill. "And the Smiths'. And the Gorleys' . . ."

They crested a curve in the sidewalk, and suddenly, the tall gray house loomed above them. Its rooftops sparkled with a delicate crust of snow, and its downstairs windows glowed, ruddy and welcoming.

Harold let out a gasp.

The front door flew open before them. Walter's water-bird-like body appeared in the doorway. "Olive!" he rumbled. His gaze traveled past her to the tall, mustachioed man. "And . . . oh. *Oh.*" Walter's eyes widened. "Mmm . . . Come in! Come *in!*"

Everyone rushed past him into the hallway. Rutherford hurried to the wall, snapping off the nearest lights.

"Morton!" Walter called, in a voice that was several registers higher than usual. "Mmm . . . I think you should come down here!"

There was the sound of small bare feet stomping along the hallway above.

"What?" called Morton, rather grumpily. His tufty head appeared at the top of the staircase. "I was busy fixing the shelf in my room, and now—"

He stopped on the second stair as if he'd been

caught in an invisible net. His eyes went from Harold
to Walter and back to Harold before landing on Olive
for a split second. Then they flew back to Harold and
settled there for good.

"Papa?" he whispered.

Harold charged up the steps. He grabbed Morton
in both arms and hoisted him up into the air, both of
them laughing until Olive and Rutherford started to
laugh too. Walter made a rumbling "mmm—hah—
hoom" sound, and Leopold turned away, clearing his
throat and blinking hard.

"Where's Mama?" Morton asked, when Harold had
finally set him down again.

"I think I know!" Olive answered.

Taking the steps two at a time, she raced up the creaking staircase, with the others right behind her.

They raced into the dimness of the third bedroom. Leopold and Rutherford blinked around, observing the place for the first time. Harold turned in a circle, his warm brown eyes growing misty.

"Our bed!" he said, patting the end of the mattress. "And Mary's wedding-ring quilt!" Harold flipped back the blankets. "Our sheets! And our *pillows!* It's all still here!"

"I kept it this way, Papa," Morton piped up proudly. "I knew you would come back."

Glancing up from the bed, Harold's eyes locked on the portrait above the dresser. "*Lucy!*" he cried. "That's Mary's other portrait! We must be close!" He smiled at the others. "Where *is* Lucy? Is she here too?"

Everyone looked at the floor.

"Um . . . That's a long story," said Olive, unable to meet Harold's hopeful gaze. "And I think Morton should tell it to you. *After* we look inside the painting."

Harold looked down at the tufts of Morton's bowed head. "All right."

"Walter, you and Rutherford and Morton should stay out here with the spectacles, just in case."

"*And* Morton?" Morton's head shot up. "*My* mama might be right there, in a picture of *my* sister, in *my* house, and I have to stay *outside?*"

"Morton . . ." Olive sighed. "It might be dangerous."

"I *know* it might be dangerous," said Morton, pulling himself up onto the dresser after Leopold. "I might be the one who saves *you*."

Leopold placed one paw within the picture frame. Lucinda's image began to shimmer and shift. "Ready, miss?" he asked softly.

Olive gave another sigh. "Ready." She passed Rutherford the spectacles, grasped Leopold's tail with one hand, and took hold of Morton's sleeve with the other. She saw Morton smile as Harold clasped his cold little hand in his larger one. "Let's go."

They clambered across the dresser. The room had been too dim for Olive to get a good look at the surface of this painting, but as she crawled closer, she could see the portrait's strange bumps and whorls, its brushstrokes hiding a second, secret image.

What might be enclosed behind Lucinda's chilly smile? Another quaking bog? A swamp full of snakes or poisonous spiders? A prehistoric jungle roaring with herds of hunting tyrannosaurs?

Whatever it was, it kept perfectly—almost menacingly—still as Olive crawled through the surface and tumbled inside.

LEOPOLD, OLIVE, MORTON, and Harold Nivens plunged through the picture frame.

They fell past the portrait of Lucinda, into something soft, and crisp, and icy cold.

Olive sat up.

The ground crunched beneath her. Cold burned against her bare palms. Tucking her hands protectively under her arms, Olive watched the divots in the snow where she'd landed hurriedly fill themselves again.

Beside her, Harold and Morton staggered to their feet. Leopold stood a few steps away, staring into the distance. Olive followed his glinting green eyes.

They were in a forest—a frozen forest. Heavy snow blanketed the ground, and a cold pewter sky arched above. Trees stretched away on every side, thick ice coating their wiry black branches. Each twig hovered within its glassy skin like bones revealed by an X-ray.

Snowflakes hung motionless in the air. As Olive stood up, she felt the hovering flakes brush her face, each one returning to its spot the moment she stepped out of the way.

"Mary!" Harold shouted, making Olive and Morton jump. "*Mary!*"

There was no answer.

"She's here somewhere," said Harold confidently. He scanned the trees, chin raised. "Sweetheart! Hallooo!"

Without even waiting for an answer this time, Harold charged forward. He took long, loping steps, swinging his arms. If he'd had an ax over his shoulder, he would have looked like a cheerful lumberjack heading off for a day in the woods.

Olive, Morton, and Leopold followed him into the crunching snow.

Even in her coat and hat, Olive was starting to shiver. Somehow this piece of Elsewhere felt even colder than the wintery world outside. She tugged the mittens out of her pockets and wriggled her shaking hands into the wool. Beside her, Leopold was marching along, looking unfazed by the chill. Harold probably couldn't feel it either, not being actually alive anymore . . . but Olive saw him flex his painted fingers and rub his hands together, as though the cold was affecting him too.

Olive glanced down at Morton. His nightshirt fluttered. His bare feet left small, vanishing prints in the snow.

"Morton," she began, "it's really cold in here. Are you sure you don't want to go back?"

Morton shook his head. "I'm going to help look." He walked even faster, short legs and skinny arms pumping, until he'd caught up with his father.

They wound between the frozen trees. The snow was deep. More flakes dangled in midair, never landing, like falling petals captured in a photograph.

"Mary!" Harold shouted, striding ahead. "Mary, my darling! It's Harold! *Halloooo!*"

The sound of Harold's voice made Olive recoil. It was too loud, too bright, too *alive* for this place. And what if there was someone—or some*thing*—near enough to hear him? Olive glanced over her shoulder at the white waves of snow. Their footprints had refilled themselves the instant they were made. There would be no trail to follow back to the picture frame—and the frame itself was already out of sight, lost between the petrified trees.

"Don't worry, miss," Leopold murmured. "I will remember the way."

"Mama!" Morton shouted. "It's us! We're coming to find you!"

"Mary!" Harold bellowed again. Brittle twigs snapped

against his broad shoulders, ice fragmenting and fusing as he lunged between the trees. "Whistle if you can hear me!"

Olive chafed her arms. Her teeth chattered. "What if we can't find her?" she whispered to the black cat. "What if she isn't *here*?"

Leopold's eyes narrowed. His whiskers twitched. "I think—" he began. "Perhaps I—" The cat stopped himself again. "No," he said. "No. I didn't."

"Mama!" Morton called.

There was still no reply.

The shadows thickened around them. At first, Olive thought this was because they had moved deeper into the woods, but when she looked straight up, she saw that the sky itself had darkened. Its steely blue had turned black. A hush thicker and colder than ice filled the painting.

"He's watching us, isn't he?" Olive whispered through the darkness. "But there's no wind. There's *nothing*."

Even in the shadows, Leopold's eyes were bright. He looked at Olive for a moment, not speaking, before turning back to the woods.

Over a swale in the snow-covered ground, they stumbled on a spot where all the trees seemed to lean sideways. Soon the ground began to lean too. First Harold, then Morton, and then Leopold and Olive skittered down the snowy slope onto a flat, smooth surface.

Olive threw her arms out for balance. Her boots skidded in opposite directions. She had slipped on frozen puddles often enough to know what this was: Ice. A lot of ice. It was an entire frozen stream.

Leopold halted next to her. His eyes widened. His ears flicked forward. The tips of his silver whiskers shook. Raising his head, he sniffed rapidly at the air.

"I think—" he said again. "Perhaps—"

And without saying anything else, he streaked forward along the riverbed.

"Morton! Mr. Nivens!" Olive called.

Harold halted. Morton skidded to a stop, arms windmilling.

"Follow the cat!" Olive yelled.

Leopold flew soundlessly over the ice. He glided beneath frozen branches and skimmed through drifts of painted snow. Harold ran behind him with long, heavy strides. Morton flapped after his father, his nightshirt billowing. Olive struggled to keep up. The chill of the air was taking root inside of her. Her fingers throbbed inside the mittens, and her toes felt wooden and numb. If they had been inside the painting too long, she wouldn't even be able to tell.

But Leopold was slowing down.

They had reached a fork in the frozen stream, where

one vast, leafless tree spread its branches all the way to the banks on either side. Its rough black bark glimmered with ice. Heaps of painted snow balanced on each limb. The tips of its twigs shone like blown glass.

And, at the base of its trunk, half-buried in a mound of snow, Olive spotted something else.

Her heart beat faster.

As she followed the others toward the tree, the body came quickly into focus. She could see its pale yellow hair, its waxy skin, its motionless hands.

"*Mary!*" Harold yelled, lunging up the bank. He skidded onto his knees beside her in a spray of painted snow. "Mary! Can you hear me?"

Morton had halted a few steps away. "Mama?" he whispered.

Olive and Leopold crouched beside him. Olive stared into Mary Nivens's face: the rounded cheeks, the snub nose that matched Morton's, the smiling blue eyes. Only now the eyes weren't smiling. They were frozen, keeping as still as everything else in this frigid world. But then, as Olive watched, Mary's eyelids trembled. Very, very slowly, they lowered halfway over her eyes, in a weak, unfinished blink.

"What's wrong with her?" she whispered to the cat.

"She must have turned to paint just in time," Leopold answered. "Otherwise she would simply have frozen to death. But she didn't." The cat shook his head. "Of course, if all of us had the foresight to be born with *fur* . . ."

Harold picked up Mary's hand. It sat in his grasp as stiffly as a china doll's. "Mary?" he whispered.

Morton stared, keeping silent.

"But if she's paint, why is she—like this?" Olive asked the cat.

"Do you know what happens to paint when it gets extremely cold?"

Olive tried to picture a can of paint freezing. She hadn't ever seen it happen, but she imagined it cracking open in a colorful, gooey burst, like a can of orange pop left in the freezer.

"It explodes?" she ventured.

"It thickens," said Leopold. "It grows viscous, or brittle."

"Oh." Olive sucked in a breath. She glanced at Morton. ". . . Like taffy when it cools?"

"Precisely."

Mary's eyelids twitched again.

"I don't think she can move," said Harold, throwing a worried look over his shoulder.

"You are correct, sir," said Leopold. "You will have to move *for* her."

In Harold's arms, Mary looked smaller and stiffer than ever. Her arms hunched around her body in a motionless shiver. Even her long gray dress had turned solid. Her petticoats crackled like a bag of potato chips as Harold hoisted her out of the snow. The drift re-formed behind her, each painted snowflake settling back in its original spot.

"We should get out of here before that thickening thing can happen to Morton and Mr. Nivens too," said Olive. "And before I start to change. Or my toes freeze off."

"Excellent points, miss," said Leopold. "Follow me."

The black cat streaked through the frozen trees. Running after, Olive breathed on her hands and wiggled her toes inside of her boots, trying to keep the ache at bay. Morton trotted next to her, his wide eyes fixed on the figure in his father's arms. At first, Harold Nivens strode steadily beside them, but as they moved on through the hovering snowflakes, Olive noticed that his steps were slowing down. Whether it was the cold affecting his body, or the fact that he was carrying a second person through the drifts, she couldn't tell.

Leopold seemed to be slowing too. In one knot of trees, he hesitated, ears twitching from side to side.

"Perhaps . . ." he said, half to himself. "I think . . ."

"Leopold?" said Olive through chattering teeth. "What's wrong?"

"It's very strange, miss." The cat's ears flicked again. "There is nothing to smell. Nothing to hear. There's only . . ."

"Nothing?"

"Precisely."

Olive glanced up at Harold. Mary lay in his arms, as motionless as ever. Something strange was happening to Harold's face too—the crinkly eyes looked duller, and the mustache that had curved with his smile now looked icy and stiff.

"Mr. Nivens?"

Very slowly, Harold's brown eyes moved to meet hers.

"Are you all right?"

Harold's mouth opened. No sound came out.

"Uh-oh." Olive turned and grabbed Morton by the shoulders. "Are you freezing too?"

Morton shook his head stubbornly, but he didn't speak.

Olive tugged the mittens off of her numb fingers and worked them onto Morton's little hands. Even in the dimness, she could see that her skin had become streaked and shiny. She whirled back toward the cat. "Which way should we go?"

"I think . . ." Leopold began, taking a few quick steps to the left. "Yes, I think . . ."

But there he halted again. Olive followed his eyes straight up to the black sky. There was no moon, no clouds, no stars. Snowflakes clotted the darkness like bits of floating ash.

With the four of them frozen in place, the world

inside the painting was utterly, terrifyingly still. In that stillness, Olive could feel Aldous watching them. *Observing* them. If it weren't for the air itself, they could have been underwater, trapped like figurines in a motionless snow globe, or like specimens in a jar.

"Perhaps we should split up to look for the frame," Leopold murmured.

"But what if one of us gets lost?" Olive scanned the forest. Glassy branches surrounded them on every side. "I don't even remember which way the riverbed was. Mr. Nivens, do you—"

The words turned to ice on her lips.

Harold Nivens stood, frozen, beside her. His painted skin was dull. His eyes stared straight ahead, unblinking. His bare white hands clasped the folds of Mary's dress. The two of them might have been some strange, painted statue; something molded in plaster, or carved out of stone. Morton stood a few steps away. His mittened hands clasped his arms. His nightshirt made a frozen pool around his feet.

"Oh no," Olive breathed.

She took a step toward Morton and stumbled, one deadened foot giving out beneath her. She landed on her knees in the snow. The burning numbness in her feet was climbing higher.

"I'll summon help," Leopold promised, lunging into the trees.

"Leopold, no!" Olive tried to get back to her feet. "Don't leave me here!"

"Soon it will be too late," the cat called over his shoulder. "Just stay right there!"

Panic lanced through Olive's body. She glanced from the frozen figures beside her to the shape of the dwindling black cat. She was going to freeze here too, she realized, with horrible, icy certainty. She would be like Morton and Mary and Harold: Ice-bound but conscious, unable to call for help or to try to find it, unable to move or even speak . . .

"Leopold!" she screamed.

"Leopold!" shouted another voice.

Rutherford and Walter barreled through the trees.

The spectacles were perched on Rutherford's nose, wedged awkwardly under his own smudgy glasses. Walter's baggy brown cardigan appeared to have shrunk upward, leaving only its collar behind. A strand of crinkly yarn trailed away from his neck, winding back through the frozen trees.

Leopold whirled gracefully around.

"This way, men!" he shouted, racing back toward the spot where Olive and the Nivenses were gathered.

Rutherford and Walter were already heading in the right direction. They stopped next to Olive in a swirl of quickly settling snow.

"It's awfully fortunate that I can read your thoughts even from a distance, Olive," said Rutherford, readjusting the spectacles and glasses and squinting at her worriedly. "That *is* you, isn't it? The transformation to paint is not yet complete?"

"No," said Olive, managing to get up onto both boots. "But it *hurts*."

"I'm sure we can get Olive out of here," said Rutherford. He nodded at the frozen family around her. "But what about these three?"

Walter gazed at the Nivenses. His bulbous eyes narrowed. He swallowed hard. Then, with a little shudder, he raised both hands and squeezed his eyes shut. Just above the surface of his palms, a soft, orange shimmer appeared.

Olive recalled Annabelle forming a ball of blue fire between her hands before hurling it at Morton, and started to take an instinctive step back. But the fire in Walter's hands wasn't going anywhere—and she could feel a comforting warmth radiating from it, making her take two clumsy steps closer instead.

Cautiously, Walter held both hands toward Morton. He moved them slowly from the top of Morton's head down to his ankles, as though he were drying him off with two invisible blow dryers. The painted snow on the ground melted into dewy beads, crystalized, and became snow again.

Morton blinked up at him. "Now do Mama and Papa," he demanded.

Walter aimed both hands at the Nivenses, starting at the top and working his way down. When he'd finished drying Harold's cuffs, Walter stepped back. The fire in his hands flared and vanished. Rutherford, who'd been watching this through both pairs of glasses with a look of bleary fascination, gave his head a shake. "That spontaneous spellcasting is truly impressive."

Harold's mustache twitched. His brown eyes blinked. In his arms, Mary blinked too.

"Harold?" she breathed, in a voice as small and fragile as the snowflakes.

"Mary!" Harold shouted back, beaming down at her. "I've got you! We're almost home!"

"And I suggest that we get the rest of the way there," said Rutherford, throwing one of Olive's tingling arms over his shoulders.

Walter kept a close eye on Harold, who was looking down at Mary. Morton trotted after them. Leopold led the way. Together, they followed the line of worn brown yarn all the way back to the picture frame.

Leopold stepped smoothly to the side as Walter helped haul Harold and Mary through the frame. They settled her stiff body on the bed as Olive, Morton, and Rutherford tumbled off of the dresser. Mary's eyes moved back and forth between Morton to Harold, and her mouth seemed to be trying to smile, but the rest of her remained perfectly still.

"Mama?" Morton whispered. "Is she . . ."

"She—mmm—she'll be all right. I think," said Walter, untying the crinkled brown yarn that was still knotted to the bedpost. "She was—um—frozen for a very long time."

Harold tugged the quilt up over Mary's ruffled dress. "There we are, my darling. All tucked in."

Morton patted the blankets. "So she was right there, all along." His eyes flicked to Olive. ". . . Do you think Lucy *knew*?"

Olive, who was flexing her fingers and breathing through her teeth, shook her head. Her toes still zapped and burned, but the invisible needles poking her hands were getting duller. "I don't know," she managed. "I guess we won't ever know."

Morton's eyes went back to his mother.

"We'll take good care of her," said Walter gently. He put one knobby hand on Morton's shoulder. "We should let her keep still until she . . . mmm . . . thaws."

Olive glanced from the two of them to the windows. Even through the curtains, she could tell that the sky had turned to tarry black.

"I have to go," she said, staggering toward the door on her numb feet. "I'm already late. My parents will be worried."

"It's all right. Mmm—come back tomorrow," said Walter. "Things might be better by then."

Olive looked at Harold and Morton, their heads bowed over Mary's face like two lamps over an open book. She hoped things would be better by morning too. And, for now, that was all she could do.

A suspicious orange face greeted them in the doorway of the old stone house.

"What have you two been up to?" Horatio asked as Olive and Leopold dove inside. Olive locked the door soundly behind them.

"I'll explain the particulars before returning to my station," Leopold murmured.

"Is that you, Olive?" Mrs. Dunwoody's voice called from the kitchen. "Dinner is waiting! And what did we tell you about being out after dark?"

"I'm sorry," Olive called back, tugging off her coat. "I just—I got held up a little bit."

She flung her jacket over the coatrack and turned toward the kitchen. Her feet and fingers still stung, but she was safe. They were *all* safe. Even Mary Nivens, as damaged as she was, would be watched over by Walter and her family. They were home, and they were safe, and this was . . .

Olive paused, halfway down the hall.

. . . This was terrifying.

Aldous McMartin had been with them inside the museum. He had hidden in that vast, dark basement. He had driven the wind inside the painting of the quaking bog. His darkness had filled the painting of the snowy forest, where he had watched them nearly freeze into a sort of living death.

Only *watched*.

Never before had he let Olive remove something— *someone*—from Elsewhere without giving any sign.

If he had simply let them go this time, then he must have some other reason, some other plan. Something slower, and sneakier, and much, much worse.

Olive crept back down the hall toward the windows that looked out over Linden Street. Aldous McMartin was out there still. He was waiting for something— and Olive knew, with a sudden, hideous certainty, that it could only be coming closer.

12

W AKING UP FROM a night of bad dreams is generally a good thing.

Being woken is another thing entirely.

And being woken from those bad dreams by a cat's
chilly paw poking you in the face when you've just
been dreaming about being drowned in cold, black
water that's plopping down onto your cheek drop by
drop might make you want to swat that cat straight off
of the bed.

"Leave me alone, Harvey," Olive muttered, burying
her head beneath her pillow. "We can play detectives
later."

"Thank you for that exciting offer," said a sarcastic
voice. "But as I am not *delusional,* I believe I'll turn it
down."

Olive shoved the pillow aside.

In the faint pre-dawn light that filtered through the windows, she could make out the shape of a large orange cat sitting on top of her bedspread. His green eyes stared down at her, bright and hard as gemstones.

"Horatio?" Olive yawned, dragging herself up onto her elbows. Beside her, Hershel flopped over on his fuzzy brown back. "What's wrong?"

"I need to speak to you. Alone."

Olive sat up straighter. "Is this about what I did yesterday?"

"It is."

"Maybe I shouldn't have snuck into the museum, but I was just—"

"You were just trying to help. And you did." Horatio's eyes glittered. "You reunited Morton and his parents. It was a brave and kind thing to do, and you did it without anyone getting hurt. For now."

"For now?" Olive echoed.

"Olive . . ." Horatio brought his nose closer to hers. The tips of his whiskers brushed her skin. "You cannot make a change like this without it having other, drastic consequences."

Olive gave Hershel a tight squeeze. "If you're talking about Aldous, I—"

"I am not referring to Aldous McMartin," said Horatio sharply. "I am referring to Mary Nivens."

"Mary Nivens?" Olive bolted upright. "Did something happen? Is she—"

"Nothing has happened, as far as I know," said Horatio, before Olive could leap out of bed. "My concern is what *will* happen when Mary becomes herself again."

Olive sucked in a breath. "I knew it! She has *powers,* doesn't she? She's secretly a super-powerful witch!"

"'A super-powerful witch,'" Horatio repeated dryly. "Yes, Olive. I'm sure she'll be back to fighting crime with her spandex suit and magic broomstick in no time."

Olive blinked. "But everyone says—"

"Yes, everyone says that Mary Nivens was a threat to the McMartins," Horatio interrupted. "She *was.* And now she threatens them again. There *is* something special about Mary Nivens," he went on, lowering his voice. "But I want you to remember this: Don't believe everything she tells you. Sometimes the truth is very different from the *whole* truth."

"What do you mean?"

"I mean that when something long-buried comes to light, it drags other things with it." The cat's eyes glinted. "Things we may be better off not knowing."

"Like what?" Olive asked.

Horatio's tail lashed softly back and forth across the bedspread. "You've already done so much, Olive.

You've rid this house of the shades. You've destroyed Annabelle. You've reunited Morton and his parents. Our trouble with Aldous isn't over—but it would be easier to handle if it was our *only* trouble. Don't you see?"

Olive rubbed her chin over Hershel's fuzzy head. "Horatio . . ." she said slowly, ". . . are you keeping a secret from me?"

For a moment, Horatio kept quiet. "It is my job to protect this house and everything in it," he said at last, in a voice that was so low Olive had to hold perfectly still to hear it. "I will continue to protect it for as long as I possibly can. That is why I am asking you: *Let some secrets lie.*"

With a swish of his feathery tail, Horatio turned and leaped to the rug. Olive heard the click of her door closing behind him.

Several minutes tiptoed past. Olive sat in place, listening to the hushed patter of snow against the windowpane, and the deep, grumbling growl of the furnace far below. Getting out of bed—putting her feet on that chilly floor and heading out into the big, dark house—lay somewhere between *unpleasant* and *impossible*. But waiting just next door were Morton and his parents, and inside of them were all the missing pieces of the McMartins' giant puzzle.

Simply visiting with the Nivenses, learning how

they had been trapped inside those hidden bits of Elsewhere, wasn't digging. It was just being neighborly. It was what anyone would do.

She didn't have to put the pieces together, Olive reasoned. She could just hold them up, and look at them, and *know* where they belonged. And once she was finished, she would let them go.

By the time Olive ventured out the front door, the world was washed with the lavender light of daybreak. Except for the bowl of Sugar Puffy Kitten Bits that sloshed loudly in her stomach as she ran through the snow, Linden Street was silent.

The silence didn't make her feel any safer.

The twigs of the lilac hedge looked like mummified fingers. The shadows behind each leafless tree seemed to bend and move on their own. The houses themselves seemed to be watching her, just like they did in the painted version of Linden Street. Olive could almost feel painted eyes following her, making the hair on the back of her neck twinge—but when she whirled around, no one was there.

The windows of the tall gray house were dark. As Olive edged across the yard, she got the sudden, stomach-twisting sense that there was something ominous within that darkness. Anything could have happened behind those heavy curtains and locked doors. And she could already be too late.

With one shaking hand, she tapped on the wooden door.

It flew open.

Olive took a startled jump backward.

Standing in the doorway was a smallish, youngish woman. Light blond hair bounced in ringlets around her head. Her cheeks were round and rosy, her blue eyes were clear and bright, and a huge, welcoming smile was spread across her face.

"You must be Olive Dunwoody!" she cried, throwing out both arms. Her long skirts swished as she wrapped Olive in a hug and dragged her over the threshold. "Please, come in! *Come in!*"

"I HAVE HEARD SO much about you!" Mary Nivens went on, pulling a stunned Olive into the hallway and kicking the front door shut. "We both have! Harold and I, that is. Morton told us how you found him, and how the two of you bested Annabelle McMartin, and how you figured out where Harold and I had been hidden—"

Mary's words were cut off by a resonant slam from upstairs.

"Found it!" shouted Harold's voice. A second later, he came jogging down the steps with a gourd-shaped suitcase in his arms. "Ah! Olive! Good morning!" he exclaimed. "Are you a banjo fan?"

"Am I a—" Olive shook her head dizzily. "What?"

"The banjo." Harold shook the gourd-shaped case.

Something inside made a twangy thump. "Just found mine, up in the attic. Looks like the bagpipes and the Victrola are up there too!"

"Oh, wonderful!" Mary clapped her paint-streaked hands. "If there was anything I missed—besides home and family, that is—it was music!"

Harold strode away down the hall. The next instant, Morton appeared at the head of the stairs. "Mama, watch!" he shouted. Nightshirt billowing like the sail of a very small ship, he glided backward down the banister and bounced to the floor.

"Very nice, pumpkin," said Mary. "Now why don't you go choose a game for us to play?"

"A game!" Morton yelled, rushing down the hall after his father. "Hi, Olive!" he added over his shoulder.

"Oh—I must see how my bread is rising! Excuse me for just a moment." Mary fluttered away as well, leaving Olive alone in the hallway.

Olive's head spun.

Around her, Lucinda's silent, coffin-like house thrummed with noise and motion. Voices laughed in the dining room. Cupboards banged in the kitchen. She stood perfectly still for a moment, digging her fingernails into her own palm to convince herself that she wasn't dreaming. She was just about to follow Morton down the hall when a deep voice behind her said—

"Hello, Olive."

Olive spun around. Walter had slipped into the hallway. Even in the dimness, Olive could see that his face was streaked with deeper shadows than usual. The hollows beneath his bulbous eyes looked like someone had carved them with a spoon.

"Would you—mmm—would you watch them for a while?" Walter yawned, his Adam's apple bobbing sleepily. "Spontaneous spellcasting wears me out. They've been up all night. And—mmm—they're so loud . . ."

"Sure," said Olive. "You should take a nap."

"They're not used to being paint, you know," said Walter, yawning again. "Harold keeps talking about driving some old car, and mmm . . . Mary's already tried to use the oven. Twice. And they don't even *eat*."

"I'll be careful," Olive promised.

Walter nodded. With a last glance toward the kitchen, he turned and trudged groggily up the staircase.

Olive followed the sounds of twanging and laughing down the hall to the dining room. By the narrow band of daylight that slipped between the curtains, she could see that the room had already been rearranged. Doctor Widdecombe's writing desk had vanished. The long wooden table that had been scattered with Walter's books and plants and bottles and other magical equipment was now completely clear, and a familiar pile of books and plants and bottles and other magical equipment waited just beside the door. A worn velvet couch stood beneath the windows. Harold sat at one end of it, plucking at his banjo, and Morton was jumping up and down on the cushions at the other end.

"I sure am rusty!" Harold announced, as Olive inched through the door. "And it's tough to pick with these slippery fingers!" He played something that sounded like two chickens pecking at an aluminum can. Morton laughed and bounced higher.

"The dough is rising!" said Mary happily, swishing through the door after Olive. "But my beautiful pantry is bare. We'll have to place an order with Mr. Kowalski."

Olive felt sure that Mr. Kowalski—whoever he was—wasn't around to take orders anymore. "Um . . . it probably isn't safe for you to use the oven, Mrs. Nivens," she began. "But I can put the bread in it for you this once. I mean, you don't need to eat, anyway."

"Oh." Mary's smile wavered like a beam of sunlight in a trembling glass. "I suppose you're right."

"You can always bake for that scrawny Walter," Harold suggested. "He could use some fattening up!"

Mary's smile straightened again. "It's so stuffy in here!" she cried, waving both hands through the dusty air. She hustled across the room and grasped the curtains. "Let's let in a bit of light, shall we?"

A streak of sun, honed to blade-like brightness by the snow, sliced across the room.

With a gasp, Mary dove backward. Harold and Morton cowered against the sofa.

Olive flew across the room and yanked the curtains shut.

"Oh," said Mary, sounding rather out of breath. She gave a little laugh. "Yes . . . I keep forgetting that light isn't so pleasant anymore. Well!" She turned to Morton, clapping her hands. "Have you chosen a game for us to play?"

"We could play checkers," said Morton excitedly. "Out here, the pieces stay right where you put them!"

"Wait," Olive interrupted, before Morton could charge out of the room. "Don't we need to talk about— I mean, don't you want to talk about everything that's changed, or about the McMartins and Lucinda, or . . ."

Mary glanced at Harold, who was avidly tuning his banjo. "Morton told us everything," she said softly. Then she turned toward the china shelves. "That plate doesn't belong there," she declared, beginning to rearrange the porcelain. "And I wonder where my German candlesticks have gone?"

"Morton and I will find them, won't we?" said Harold, dropping the banjo and hoisting Morton onto his shoulder. "It's a treasure hunt!"

"A treasure hunt!" Morton cried.

Olive wasn't good at being pushy. She was much better at un-pushy things, like waiting until all of your classmates have gotten their papers before tip-toeing up to the teacher's desk, or letting all the other kids rush into the cafeteria ahead of you and ending up with the smallest, squishedest piece of cake. But a thousand questions had piled up inside of her. Their collected weight pushed her forward.

"*Wait*," she said again. "I need to talk to all of you. It's important. *Please*."

Harold let Morton slide from his shoulder back onto the couch. Morton folded his arms and gave Olive an impatient frown.

"Mrs. Nivens," Olive began, "everybody says there was something special about you." She inched closer to Mary's turned back. "They say that nobody could lie to you. That the McMartins were afraid of you. And I think I know why." Olive wrapped her fingers around the back of a chair. "It's because you have powers. You're like *them*."

Mary whirled around.

At first, Olive thought she was angry. But then she saw that Mary was smiling—and not just smiling, but laughing, as though Olive had told a hysterical joke.

"*Me?*" she gasped between peals of laughter. She pressed one paint-streaked hand against her chest. "Oh, Olive dear, I'm afraid you are *utterly wrong!*"

"Utterly wrong!" Morton echoed, bouncing happily on the couch again. "Olive is utterly wrong!"

"But—but what about the paintings?" Olive stammered. "Weren't you trying to learn about Aldous's magic?"

"Yes," said Mary, "but not to use it myself!" She shrugged, still laughing, and the ruffles of her collar rustled prettily. "I have one teensy little talent. It's a family trait, really, like being double-jointed, or being able to curl your tongue."

Morton and Harold stuck out their curled tongues at each other and chuckled.

"I'll show you." Mary leaned over the dining table. "Have you ever stolen anything, Olive?"

Olive looked back into Mary's eyes. They were a very pale shade of blue, like a shard of sky-colored glass.

"I stole a library book once," Olive blurted. "But it was an accident. I lost it, and my mother told the library it was gone, but then I found it again, and it was already so late, and it was one of my favorite stories, so I just peeled the library cover off and kept it." She stopped, clapping both hands over her mouth. Thank goodness she'd caught herself before the story of the paint-making jars from the basement—and who knew what else—could come tumbling out too.

Mary straightened up, smiling widely. "You see? As long as I am looking you in the eye, you feel compelled to tell me the truth."

"You said it was a family trait?" Olive asked. "So other people in your family could—"

"Oh, families pass down all sorts of skills," Mary interrupted briskly. "Some can read thoughts, some can concoct potions. As talents go, mine is pretty unimpressive. Compared to some members of my family, I am a huge disappointment!" Mary let out another laugh, not looking disappointed at all.

"You mean, there were people in your family who—"

"My great-aunt Viola had all sorts of talents," Mary interrupted again. "She belonged to a group that tried to fight the use of dark magic. Her kitchen was always full of interesting ingredients."

"She sounds like Mrs. Dewey," said Olive.

"When I was little, I wanted to grow up to be just like Aunt Viola," Mary went on, as though she hadn't heard Olive at all. "But I just grew up to be me."

"And we are awfully glad you did!" said Harold, grabbing Mary by the waist and twirling her around the room in a lively polka. The dishes rattled on the shelves. Morton jumped higher. The squeaking couch grew louder.

"Wait!" said Olive for the third time. "Did your aunt

Viola know about the McMartins? Was she watching them, like Mrs. Dewey?"

Harold spun Mary in one last rustling whirl.

"Aunt Viola?" said Mary, looking momentarily confused. "Of course she knew about the McMartins. The whole town knew about the McMartins. Everybody could tell there was *something* strange about them. There were rumors about where they had come from, about the Old Man and his paintings . . ."

"But Aunt Viola was getting old," Harold put in.

"Yes," said Mary. "She helped us buy this house so that we could keep an eye on the McMartins for her. We were to get to know them, to learn if they were doing anything dangerous—but they were so *unfriendly!*" Mary's eyes widened. "Aldous, that silly Albert and his wife, their daughter Annabelle; all of them as cold and stiff as iceboxes. They wouldn't join us for picnics. They wouldn't let Morton play in their yard. They even complained about Harold's banjo! Can you imagine?"

"No," said Olive, who could imagine it very easily.

"They didn't even like my *cookies,*" Mary added.

Morton gasped. "Even the *molasses* cookies?"

"Even those," said Mary.

Morton's eyes widened.

"So, you knew Albert McMartin?" Olive asked.

"I wouldn't say we *knew* him," said Harold, picking

a little pattern on the banjo. "The unfriendliness, you see."

"Oh," said Olive. "Because—because later—Aldous killed him."

Harold stopped picking. Morton stopped jumping. Mary's eyes widened. "*Killed* him? His own son?"

Olive nodded. "Because Albert wasn't like Aldous. Eventually, Albert tried to work against him—and that's when Aldous turned on him."

Mary and Harold exchanged a look.

"They'll sacrifice anyone, won't they?" Mary murmured at last.

There was a minute of thick quiet in the room, while no one answered Mary's question, and the dusty mantel clock ticked patiently to itself.

"So . . . if the McMartins were so unfriendly," Olive picked up again, "how did you get Aldous to give you art lessons?"

"Oh, *must* we talk about this?" Mary's voice was suddenly angry. "It was all pointless. *Pointless.* A waste of a hundred years." Her voice brightened again—but now it was too light, too brittle. "My bread dough!" she exclaimed, rushing toward the door. "It must be overflowing the pans by now!"

"Wait! I'll help you!" Olive called, running out of the room after Mary's fluttering skirts.

She chased Mary into the kitchen. Three pans of bread dough, which were starting to look like three rectangular, helium-filled mushrooms, waited beside the oven.

"I'll put them in the stove," Olive offered, before Mary could reach for the handle. She opened the metal door, and felt a blast of hot air rush out to meet her. Inside her collar, the metal frame of the spectacles burned.

Mary turned to the sink, where a stack of doughy bowls was waiting. "I suppose I can't even wash the dishes without washing myself away too."

"Probably not," said Olive. "But I can do them."

She turned the hot water tap and added a stream of soap, watching Mary's face out of the corner of her eye. Mary looked surprisingly sad for someone who had a permanent excuse not to do dishes. Olive picked up the cloth and began to rub a slippery bowl.

"I saw your sketches," she said at last. "You were learning to draw from Aldous, weren't you?"

For a moment, Mary didn't answer. Olive began to worry that she had pushed too far, but then Mary leaned against the wall and let out a little sigh.

"That was my excuse," she said. "I was stubborn, turning up at his house, begging for lessons. Eventually he must have figured it would be easier to let me in than to try to keep me out."

Olive swished the bowl through the water. "What did you learn?"

Mary laughed shortly. "Nothing. He barely spoke

to me. He just seated me in his front parlor, watched me draw, and made little growling noises in his throat. I couldn't learn *anything* about his family, or what he was really doing in that big stone house. I'm sure Lucy knew more than I did, spending all that time with Annabelle, but at the time, I—" Mary stopped, her face working. "I just didn't realize. I didn't suspect. Not my own daughter."

"Then why did Aldous trap you and Morton?" Olive asked. "He must have thought you knew something."

Mary's lips tightened. "That was my fault too." She lowered her voice until the sloshing of the sink almost covered it completely. "I gave too much away. It's funny . . . No one can lie to me, and I'm always the one blurting out the truth."

Olive froze, mid-scrub. "What was it? What do you mean?"

"I—" Mary hesitated. There was the twang of a banjo from down the hall. "I don't want them to know, even now. They would be safer not knowing. *All of us* would be safer not knowing."

A soap bubble popped against Olive's elbow. "Knowing what?" she breathed.

Mary's eyes fixed on the curtained window. "It was one night in the early spring, long after dark," she said softly. "I could hear voices coming from outside. Harold stayed sound asleep, but I got out of bed and went to the window—we'd left it open, and I can still remember the way the curtains wavered in the breeze—and I looked out. I could see them down there, just over the lilac hedge, in the backyard of the big stone house . . ."

Footsteps thundered along the hallway.

"Mama," said Morton, bouncing into the kitchen, "why is it taking you so long? You said we could play a game!"

Mary's face brightened as suddenly as if someone had thrown a switch. "I certainly did. Harold!" she called into the hall. "Why don't you bring down the Victrola and give us some music while we play! I can't *stand* this quiet anymore!"

Hand in hand, Mary and Morton skipped out of the kitchen.

Olive dumped the bowl into the drainer. "Wait! What was it?" she called, hurrying down the hallway after the others.

Harold Nivens was clomping down the staircase, carrying something that looked like a huge metal morning glory attached to a coffee grinder. Morton and Mary were busily clearing a space in the parlor.

Olive followed them inside. "What was it?" she asked again. "Who did you see?"

Morton glanced over his shoulder. "See where?"

Mary tugged Olive to the side. Bending close to

her ear, she whispered, "I don't know what I saw anymore. And whoever it was—whatever it was—it wasn't worth losing all of this."

"See *where?*" Morton demanded again.

Mary gave him a sunny smile. "Nowhere, pumpkin," she said, patting his hair. "There!" she added happily as Harold set the Victrola on the cabinet top. She beamed around the room, her clear blue eyes flickering from Harold to Morton, her smile dulling for a split second as her gaze landed on Olive. She looked swiftly away again. "Soon we'll have everything back where it belongs."

14

O LIVE STEPPED OUT of the dark gray house into
the blinding winter sun. For a few seconds, she
stood on the stoop, squinting and blinking. The difference between indoors and outdoors seemed as vast
as the difference between Morton's house yesterday
and today, and all of the sudden changes were making
her mind feel rather blinded and blinky too.

So maybe it was her mind, or maybe it was her
eyes, or maybe it was the strange incompleteness of
everything Mary Nivens had said, but something kept
Olive from seeing the figure on the sidewalk until
she'd nearly walked into it.

Olive jumped backward.

The figure was about Olive's size. It wore a tailored
coat made of bright red wool. Its hair was long and

dark and shiny. And its faintly suspicious eyes were rimmed with thick black eyeliner.

"You don't live here," Olive blurted.

"I *know*," said the girl. "I know where I live." She pointed past Olive, at the tall gray house. "Who lives *there*?"

"Where?" asked Olive.

"That house. The one you just came out of."

Olive's throat tightened. "Nobody."

"Then what were you doing inside it?"

"I mean—not nobody," Olive amended. "Just . . . people."

"I thought it was empty."

Olive's throat tightened a little more.

"No," she croaked. "Not anymore."

The girl glanced from Olive to the curtained windows.

"Well . . ." Olive rubbed her hands together. "It's really cold out here! Brr! I'd better get inside!" She took a few rapid steps toward the old stone house. "Aren't you cold?"

"Not really." The girl's eyes drifted from the Nivenses' home to the rooftops of the old stone house. "So that's where the famous artist lived? The one Ms. Teedlebaum was talking about?"

Olive swallowed. "Yes. That's—that's my house."

She took another two steps up the slope. The girl didn't move.

"Brr . . ." said Olive once more, over her shoulder. Then she broke into a run.

She whirled through the front door of the old stone house and slammed it soundly behind her.

"There you are, Olive!" shouted her father's voice from the library. "Come and help us decorate the tree!"

"Just a second!" Olive called back.

Craning around the curtains, she peeped out the narrow hallway windows. The girl wasn't standing on the sidewalk in front of the Nivens house anymore. Olive scanned the street. The sidewalks were empty. The houses stood, muffled and quiet, on their snowy lawns. She thought she caught a flash of red behind Mr. Hanniman's house, but it was gone so quickly that she wasn't certain it had been there at all.

Olive straightened up. The girl had caught her and Rutherford with the portrait of Morton in the museum. What might she have overheard? And why was she here now, on Linden Street, asking questions, if there wasn't some—potentially dangerous—reason?

With worry writhing in her stomach, Olive tossed her coat over the rack and headed into the library.

A very tall, very wide pine tree had been stationed in the corner beyond the tiled fireplace. Mr. and Mrs. Dunwoody were opening boxes of ornaments beside it.

"Isn't it a beautiful tree?" Mrs. Dunwoody asked as Olive shuffled across the floor. "So symmetrical!"

"It forms a nearly perfect cone," Mr. Dunwoody added, patting the branches.

"It smells nice too," said Olive.

"Yes!" said Mrs. Dunwoody, as though this idea had never crossed her mind. "I suppose it does."

There was a very specific tree-trimming routine in the Dunwoody household. First, Mrs. Dunwoody hung the strings of little electric lights so that there was a perfectly even number on each part of the tree, while Mr. Dunwoody and Olive waited. Next,

Mr. Dunwoody hung the garlands of wooden beads so that each downward swoop was exactly the same size, while Mrs. Dunwoody and Olive waited. Then came the careful planning stage, when Mr. and Mrs. Dunwoody sorted the ornaments by weight and size, with the largest ones assigned to the lower branches, the medium to the middle, and the smallest to the top, while Olive waited.

Finally, there was the decorating free-for-all, when Mr. and Mrs. Dunwoody hung their ornaments with careful attention to spacing and branch size, and Olive hung hers with careful attention to color scheme, glittery-ness, and whether certain ornaments looked like they would get along with each other.

The whole process—with a break for sandwiches and cocoa in front of the fire—took the rest of the afternoon. The sky beyond the library's tall windows darkened to gray and then to blue-black. The lights of neighbors' trees and garlands and wreaths sparkled along Linden Street like fallen stars.

Safe inside the old stone house, with a project and her parents, Olive felt the worries of that morning back slowly away. She didn't know it yet, but they were just waiting for nighttime to return.

"Are you warm enough in here, Olive?" Mrs. Dunwoody asked, stepping through the door of Olive's bedroom. "I swear, this room stays at least two degrees colder than the rooms at our end of the hall." She frowned around at the dimness. "I would estimate it's sixty-three degrees in here. Sixty-three point five at the most."

"I'm all right," said Olive, wriggling her legs under the blankets. "I've got three quilts on top of me."

"Did you enjoy your first day of winter vacation?" Mrs. Dunwoody asked. "I noticed you spent a lot of it at the new neighbors'."

"Yes," said Olive, not meeting her mother's eyes. "They're nice. And interesting."

Mr. Dunwoody bustled through the door. "*Brr!* Is it sixty-three point five degrees in here?"

"That was my estimate exactly," said Mrs. Dunwoody. "But Olive says she has a sufficient quantity of quilts to keep her warm."

Mr. Dunwoody patted Olive's shoulder through the blankets. "Ready to catch some designations of the set of integer numbers?"

"What?" said Olive.

"In mathematics, Z designates the set of all integers."

"Oh," said Olive.

"If you're feeling bored without school or homework, Olive, we could all take a family outing together," said Mrs. Dunwoody. "We could visit the zoo, or the bookstore, or . . ." She inhaled like someone about to take a bite of extremely unpleasant vegetables. ". . . or the art museum."

"No," said Olive quickly.

Her parents sagged with relief.

"I got to spend plenty of time at the museum already." Olive's toes curled, remembering those dim corridors. "But thank you."

"All right." Mrs. Dunwoody drifted toward the door. "If you change your mind, just let us know."

"Good night, Olive," said Mr. Dunwoody, giving her shoulder another soft pat. "You know what they say about an object at rest."

"I do?" said Olive.

"An object at rest will stay at rest, unless acted upon by a force. That would make a better 'Good night' than that old 'don't let the bedbugs bite' rhyme, wouldn't it?" Mr. Dunwoody tilted his head thoughtfully. "*The sky is blacked, your quilts are stacked; do not let the forces act.*"

Olive smiled. "That's pretty good, Dad."

Mr. Dunwoody switched off the reading lamp. "Do not let the forces act," he murmured through the glowing band of the doorway. The door thumped shut behind him.

Olive lay in bed, staring up at the ceiling.

Be an object at rest, she told herself.

But the mention of the museum had let all her worries back in. Even with her body perfectly still, Olive's mind would not stop spinning. Mary Nivens's words from that morning tumbled around and around inside it, like a few mismatched socks in a dryer. What had she heard? Who had she seen? What secret was so big that it had consumed the entire Nivens family?

Olive remembered Mary Nivens's frightened eyes. *Long after dark, I could hear voices coming from outside* . . .

The minutes ticked by. Olive heard the sounds of her parents brushing their teeth and the click of a distant light switch, followed by a long and sleepy silence.

And then Olive heard it too.

Voices.

Coming from outside.

Prying off the quilts, Olive swung her legs out of bed. She padded across the floor to the windows. The panes were fogged with frost. The yard below was dim, but enough light fell from the winter sky that Olive could make out the lilac hedge, and the edge of the Nivenses' snowy yard—and, sheltered in the shadow of a huge oak tree, a dark figure wrapped in a long, rippling cloak. She pressed her ear to the cold glass.

Yes, there were voices. Two voices; one higher, one lower, but she couldn't quite make out their words. As gently as she could, Olive unlatched the window and pushed up the frosty frame. Cold air and whispered words rushed over the sill.

". . . as long as they will be safe. Just let me go!"

"*Shh!*" someone hissed.

The dark figure turned its head to stare up at Olive's window. Its face was hidden in shadow, but Olive felt certain that it had heard the window creak open; that it was staring straight at her, hidden in the darkness behind the glass. Then it whirled around and darted toward the street.

Olive bolted toward her door at the same time.

She flew down the carpeted steps, crammed her feet into her boots, and snatched her coat from the rack. She was still threading her arms into the sleeves as she zoomed out through the front door.

15

OLIVE'S FEET CRUNCHED down the icy porch steps.
A pounding mixture of curiosity and fear drove
her forward.

Linden Street was empty.

The cloaked figure—whoever it was—had already
vanished into the darkness and the snow. Panting,
Olive glanced back along the leafless lilac hedge.
Another figure still stood beneath the oak tree: a figure
with long, dark skirts and glints of moonlight on its
blond hair. It didn't move as Olive hurried toward it.

"Mrs. Nivens?" Olive breathed, stopping a few feet
away. "Who was that? What's going on?"

Even in the weak light, Olive could see that Mary's
skin looked strange. "Olive . . ." she whispered through
lips that barely moved. "Please . . . help me inside . . ."

Olive managed to pry one of Mary's arms up and around her shoulders. With Mary leaning on her side, she struggled toward the back door of the tall gray house.

Except for the moonlight filtering through the windows, the kitchen was dark. Olive pulled Mary through the door and shut it firmly behind them. She braced Mary against one wall. Then she turned on the oven and opened its creaking metal door. Soft electric light poured from its mouth. A tide of heat followed it, sweeping out to the corners of the room.

"That stove—that wasn't here before," said Mary stiffly. "We'll have to—replace it."

"Who *was* that?" Olive asked, placing a stool at a safe distance from the oven door.

Mary sank slowly onto the stool. She didn't meet Olive's eyes. "I don't know who you mean."

"In the yard," said Olive. "Who were you talking to?"

Mary gave her head a small shake. "I just . . . I wanted to look at the sky. I wanted to be outside without the light burning me. I forgot that the cold could be just as bad."

Olive glanced around the empty kitchen. "Where's everybody else?"

"Upstairs. Walter is asleep in Morton's bed. Harold and Morton are repairing Lucy's old room." Mary's eyes flicked to the hallway. "I didn't want them to hear."

"Hear what?" asked Olive. "Hear you and that person in your yard?"

Mary's mouth opened. One of her hands jerked rigidly in her lap. Her eyes moved from Olive to the hall to the blue-gray pane of the window. "There is something I should tell you," she said at last.

Olive sat down on the chilly floor. "What?"

"I wasn't honest with you this morning," said Mary, still staring at the window. "I'm not sure why; that house is *yours* now, after all. It's about the real reason the Old Man trapped us—our family and our neighbors. It was my fault."

"You said you heard something in the backyard . . ."

"Yes," Mary whispered. Her face was thawing, lines of worry forming on her painted skin. "That night, when I got out of bed and went to the window . . . the air was so clear and still, like warm water. I could see all of them down there, behind the stone house: a man and a woman and a big orange cat."

In spite of the heat from the stove, Olive felt a sudden chill. "A big orange cat?"

"I recognized the man, of course," Mary went on. "It was Aldous McMartin, with his gray hair and his tall, thin body. But I'd never seen the woman before." Her eyes flicked toward the hall again. "I'd rather Morton and Harold not hear about this, even now . . ."

"What did the woman look like?" Olive asked quickly.

Mary frowned, her eyes dimming. "She looked quite young; too young for the streaks of gray in her long red hair. And she was beautifully dressed, in a gray silk robe with a gold pendant."

The air stuck in Olive's throat. "A pendant—like a locket?"

"I suppose it could have been a locket," said Mary. "She was looking up at the sky, and I could see her face in the moonlight. She looked so *sad*. That was what haunted me. Her face was pretty, but much too thin, and her skin was like wax, and the way she stared up at the moon . . ."

"What happened?" Olive prompted. "Could you hear what they were saying?"

"I heard the woman say, 'Please, let me go.' The Old Man grabbed her by the hand and jerked her back to the house. He said"—Mary put on Aldous's deep, stony voice—"'*Do not ask me again, woman! Now, hold your tongue!*'

"Then he dragged her inside. The cat went with them, staying right at the woman's heels. I heard the door slam. And that was that." Mary shook her head. "I tried to go back to bed. But I couldn't sleep. Eventually, I got up and got my pencils and paper, and I did a sketch of the woman. I made it as real as I could."

Olive's mind flashed to the drawings piled in the upstairs drawer, the sad-faced woman tumbled between the studies of Morton and Lucinda. She nodded.

"I wondered what the Old Man could be doing to her up there in that awful stone house. Trapping her. Hurting her. Starving her." Mary's hands rose from her lap, clutching at each other. "But I wanted him to know that someone was watching. That someone else *knew*.

"The next day, I brought the sketch to my drawing lesson. I asked him how long he'd had a houseguest. 'Houseguest?' he said. 'I don't know what you mean.' He looked puzzled—or he pretended to be puzzled. 'But I *saw* her,' I said. 'Don't you recognize her?' And then I showed him my sketch. The look that came across his face . . ." Mary's back tensed. Her hands made little jittery motions, as if they were knitting an invisible scarf. "I almost turned and ran right then. But he erased the look as fast as he could. 'What do you think you know?' he asked, in his deep, slow voice. I didn't answer him. I just stared straight into his eyes—those awful, yellow eyes—and I said, 'She's still here, isn't she? In this house? Where you're *forcing* her to stay?'"

Olive held her breath as Mary paused, her eyes darkening.

"I think that's when he figured out the whole truth about me," Mary resumed. "That he couldn't lie to me.

That I was watching him *because* of who I was. And he stared straight back at me and said, 'Yes, she is in this house. She is safe. She is comfortable. It may not be what she would choose, but it is still life.' Then he moved toward me so fast I thought he was going to rip the sketch right out of my hand. But instead he just said, 'Come back tomorrow. I believe we are ready to start painting at last.'"

"Then what happened?" asked Olive.

"I went back the next day. He had set up an easel with a painting already on it. It was a landscape—a muddy brown field, with hills and birch trees in the distance."

The bog, Olive's mind whispered.

"He said, 'For your first attempts, you will reuse some old canvases of my own.' He watched me finish my portrait of Morton, keeping almost completely silent. And next he gave me a painting of—of an empty, snowy forest . . ." Mary's voice wobbled, growing even softer. "The day after I'd finished Lucinda's portrait, Harold and I woke up—and Morton was gone. Of course, we suspected the Old Man. We told all the neighbors, thinking we were warning them, when instead, we were dooming them too. He got back at all of us soon enough."

Mary's head drooped. Olive knew that paintings couldn't cry, not actual tears. She guessed that needing to cry and not being able to would probably feel much worse.

"So . . . did you ever find out what happened to her?" Olive asked after a moment. "Who she was, or why Aldous was holding her there?"

Mary patted absently at her dry cheeks. "I didn't get the chance," she said. "All this time, I've wondered who she was, or what she knew that made her so important. To the Old Man, she was worth all of our lives." She raised her head. Her ice-blue eyes honed on Olive. "Perhaps . . . perhaps you'll find out the truth. If you act *fast.*"

Mary glanced at the window again. Her worried frown shifted, a look of surprise taking its place. "Goodness!" she exclaimed in a brighter voice. "I can't *imagine* what time it is! If your parents find you missing, they'll be worried sick."

Reluctantly, Olive stood up. She shut the oven door and switched off the heat. "I suppose I should go."

"I'll walk with you to the hedge," said Mary. "But this time, I'll hurry back indoors!"

Trudging across the yard toward the street, Olive waited until she'd reached the misty halo of a streetlight before glancing back at Morton's mother. Mary Nivens gave her a little wave. Olive waved back.

She had just veered to the right, heading around the barren hedge toward her own front door, when something across the street caught her eye.

In one upstairs window of the Butler house—a house that was usually darkened and sleeping by nine o'clock—a dim light was burning. Olive squinted up at it. Inside the faintly glowing window, she thought she could see the outline of someone gazing back out at her. As soon as her eyes locked on it, the light vanished. Olive blinked up at the dark window, holding her breath. Whoever it was, it didn't reappear.

Looking over her shoulder at the Butlers' house, Olive crept up the steps of the front porch and slipped inside, locking the door behind her.

16

OLIVE HAD DONE a very bad job of being an object at rest. She woke up with a sniffly nose and cramps in her calves, feeling as if she'd hardly slept at all. She lay under the rumpled quilts, staring foggily across the room, while her mind crawled straight back to its pre-bed problem.

The puzzle she'd been assembling for months— ever since she had moved to Linden Street—scattered its broken pieces through her head. Now Mary's story and the hooded figure in the yard added themselves to the mess, holes filling, edges matching with edges. But one piece still didn't fit. It dangled just above the rest, sparkling and spinning like a gold locket on a chain. And there was one person in the house—one big orange furry person—who might know where it belonged.

Olive flopped out of bed and pulled on jeans and a sweater. From the doorway, she could hear her parents at work in the library, their computer keys performing a brisk percussion routine.

"Horatio?" she called, edging out into the hall. "Horatio!"

A cat's head popped through the bathroom doorway. Even from a distance, Olive could tell that it wasn't Horatio's. When it said, "Agent Olive! Enter the safe zone for debriefing! *Quick!*" in a faintly British accent, Olive knew just whose it was.

By the time she slipped into the bathroom and closed the door behind her, Harvey was hopping around the toilet in a frenzy of anticipation.

"Agent Olive! You received my transmission." The cat lowered his voice. "The game is growing risky. *Very* close."

"Close to what, Harvey?"

"*Agent 1-800*," the cat reminded her in an urgent whisper. "Do you want to breeze my blanket?"

"You mean, 'Blow your cover'?"

"I am *speaking* in *code*," said Harvey, eyes widening. "Listen: This is for your ears only. *The ant has entered the picnic basket.*"

Olive blinked. "What?"

Harvey's eyes got even wider. "*The raccoon jumped into the pool,*" he hissed. "*The BEANS are in the CAN!*"

"What can?"

Harvey let out an aggravated sigh. "I have managed to trap an intruding intelligence officer," he said, under his breath.

Olive's body tensed. "Really?" she whispered back. "Where?"

"*In there.*" Harvey gestured to the cabinet beneath the bathroom sink.

Olive pictured the living portrait of Aldous McMartin curled up inside that cabinet like a dollar bill in a wallet. That couldn't be what Harvey meant. But maybe there was something *else* that Aldous had sent in his place—something small, and vicious, with lots of crawling legs . . .

A muted rustling came from behind the cabinet door.

Olive swallowed. "Is it safe to open it?"

Harvey gave a nod. "The enemy agent is contained."

Carefully, Olive reached out and tugged on the cabinet's brass handle. Inside was the wastebasket where Olive threw strings of used dental floss, when she remembered to floss in the first place. Next to the basket, a stack of toilet paper rolls had been arranged into a small, quilted staircase. Olive pulled out the basket and peeped over its edge. Inside, hopping through a few strands of dental floss, was one tiny, frantic mouse.

"He had managed to infiltrate the most private of

properties!" said Harvey, glancing around the bath-room. "Who can tell what he's overheard?"

This thought *did* make Olive a bit uncomfortable.

"What do we do with him?" she asked the cat.

"I had assumed you would know," said Harvey.

Olive watched the mouse hop against the basket's walls. "Aren't cats supposed to eat mice?"

"*Eat* the counterspy?" Harvey's eyebrows rose. "I'm not sure that follows agency protocol."

"It would be mean to put him outside when it's so cold," said Olive as the mouse's miniscule paws scrabbled for a foothold. "I don't want to *hurt* him."

"Off the record, Agent Olive," Harvey whispered, "neither do I."

"So . . . should we let him go?"

Harvey paused, considering. "I believe it is our only valid option," he said at last.

Olive tipped the basket onto its side. The mouse shot across the floor and disappeared into a crack in the wall.

"We will meet again, my friend!" Harvey called after it. "Live to die another day!"

"Harvey," said Olive, pulling her thoughts away from undercover mice and back to the present, "do you know if there was a woman who Aldous kept prisoner in this house? Someone with long red hair and a silk robe?"

Harvey stared at her. ". . . A female prisoner in her nightclothes?" he said very slowly. "You *have* visited Elsewhere, haven't you?"

"No, I don't mean the neighbors on Linden Street," said Olive. "I mean—a woman who was here *before* any of them, even Morton. She might have been sick, and she wore a gold pendant, and . . ."

Harvey's body stiffened. Strands of splotchily colored fur rose along his back. When he looked at Olive again, his eyes were fragile and scattered, like the shards of a broken window about to fall from their frame.

"No," he said, in a voice that was also strange and fragile. "No. Aurelia is gone." He sidled past Olive, keeping both eyes on her face. "Long gone."

"*Aurelia?*" Olive repeated. "Was that her name?"

With his backside, Harvey bumped open the bathroom door. "Agent 1-800 out," he said shortly, before shooting off down the hall. By the time Olive stepped through the door, he had vanished.

Olive stood in the hallway for several seconds, chewing the inside of her cheek. *Aurelia.* Why had Olive's description made Harvey behave so oddly? Was this another secret the cats had been forced to keep?

Olive crossed her arms across her chest, feeling the spectacles dig softly into her collarbone. She gazed along the hall at the softly glimmering pictures. This was where Aldous had kept his other prisoners. He might have trapped Aurelia there too, concealing her in some well-hidden spot that Olive had never even noticed.

She scanned the nearest paintings. She had spent more time inside the misty picture of Linden Street than in any other painting in the house, and she hadn't seen anyone there who fit Mary's description of Aurelia. There were certainly no thin, sad-faced women in the painting of the bowl of strange fruit, or in Annabelle's deserted portrait.

With a tremor in her stomach, Olive strode back toward the painting of the moonlit forest and put the spectacles on. The painted trees shivered. The moon gleamed on the winding white path. Olive thrust her head and shoulders through the frame. A hard, cold wind whipped through her hair.

"Aurelia?" she shouted into the darkness. "Aurelia, are you here?"

She listened, her breath tight in her lungs. The wind seemed to still. The trees stopped their bony clattering. But no one answered.

Olive proceeded toward the other end of the hall. Just as she'd expected, there were no delicate, long-haired women to be found with the grumpy bird on his fencepost, or in the painting on her parents' bedroom wall, where the fake Olive waved eerily back at her from the deck of the ship on its purplish sea. There were no fluffy orange cats, either. In fact, the more Olive looked, the more cat-less the rooms seemed to be.

Well, thought Olive, raising her chin, if Horatio was hiding from her, then she would just finish her search on her own.

In the painting of the gazebo, things were quite a bit friendlier.

"Hello!" called the dapper man in the black suit, getting up from his seat in the shade. "Back to witness another feat of magic?" With a flourish, he pulled a skein of colorful handkerchiefs out of one breast pocket.

"Hi, Roberto," said Olive as the handkerchiefs snapped rapidly pocketward again. "Actually, I'm looking for someone. Have you ever heard of a woman named Aurelia, here, in Elsewhere?"

"I'm afraid not," said the magician. "I performed with an Astonisha once," he added, tapping his chin. "But she was a trained seal."

"Oh," said Olive. "Probably not the same person then."

"Come back anytime!" Roberto called as Olive turned back toward the frame. "All shows are free! Matinees are half price!"

Back in her parents' room, Olive paused, staring at the miniature image on the deck of the ship again.

That small, blurry portrait was only the bait in a failed trap, Olive knew, but the sight of it still made her want to scratch it away, like an ugly bug bite. She would have liked to cram the whole canvas into the parlor fireplace and watch it go up in a warm, cheery burst. If the painting wasn't magically stuck to the wall—and Olive pried on the frame, just to be sure—she would already have gotten rid of it for good.

But that was the way Elsewhere worked. Everything stayed the same, day after day, year after year. Like objects in a museum. Or a prison.

Aldous's words to Mary echoed in Olive's head: *She is safe. She is comfortable. It might not be what she would choose, but it is still life.* This certainly sounded like existence in Elsewhere. But there were parts of Elsewhere that weren't especially safe or comfortable—like the silvery lake, and the snowy village in the attic, and the moldy ruins of the castle hidden in the blue bedroom.

Safe . . . and *comfortable.*

It might not be especially comfortable to be stuck holding an instrument for eternity, but Olive decided to check the painting of the ballroom anyway.

"Olive!" shouted the musicians in the orchestra, blatting out a few last notes.

"Olive!" chorused the dancers, stepping on each other's toes.

"Hello," said Olive, feeling a bit warm and prickly

with so many eyes on her at once. "I was wondering . . . Do any of you happen to be named *Aurelia*?"

There was a beat of silence, as if everything in this already changeless world had frozen for a split second.

The musicians and dancers blinked at each other.

"I don't *think* that's my name," said the man with the tuba.

"You know, I'm not sure I *have* a name," the flautist spoke up.

"Me neither," said the man at the piano.

"Let's make up names for each other!" squealed a woman in a pink ball gown.

The throng of people, who had only the vaguest idea of what names should sound like, began shouting suggestions.

"Fredegar!" someone yelled as Olive scurried away again. "Eurasia! Pootis!"

Olive lingered for just a few moments in the painting of the Scottish hillside. Where Rutherford and the cats had destroyed the image of a young Aldous McMartin with a gush of paint thinner, a blurred, muddy spot remained amid the bracken. Olive stood beside it, feeling the gorse scratch against her ankles. Even without searching the hills or the wood beyond, she felt sure that there was no one here. Not anymore. But several yards away, among the blowing heather, Olive spotted a solid black lump.

She ventured closer.

Lying in the painted bracken was an old leather bag with rusty clasps. Olive recognized it immediately: The last place she had seen it had been in the young Aldous McMartins's hands. It must have been hidden here among the grasses ever since. Olive pried the clasps apart. Inside were several jars of Aldous's paint, a few stained brushes, and the yellowing sheets of paper scrawled with his paint-making recipes. The sight of them—and the memory of Aldous trying to use them to trap Olive and Horatio in a pit for all eternity—made her body twitch. She would have to find a safer place for this. Lifting the bag under one arm, Olive climbed carefully back out of the frame.

After stuffing the bag temporarily under her bed, Olive crept back down the stairs.

There were certainly no sickly women in the painting of the stonemasons, or with the towel-wrapped lady dipping her toe in a bathtub.

The soft whoosh of the coffee machine floated out from the kitchen. Before her mother and father could come back down the hall, Olive darted into the living room and plunged into the painting of the Parisian street.

Tubby pigeons clucked and hustled around her shoes. Red geraniums in window boxes bounced softly in the breeze of a passing carriage. The woman holding up a glass of champagne tossed it into her escort's face and flounced away.

"Um . . ." said Olive, who felt shy around strangers even when she *could* speak their language. "Excuse me?"

A few people at the café tables glanced up. Most of them didn't.

"Is anyone here named Aurelia?" Olive struggled on. "*Aurelia?*"

As one, everybody in the café froze. The geraniums in their window box stopped bouncing. The hooves of the carriage horse went still.

Still, no one answered her. A moment later, the café resumed its bustle. A pigeon pecked at the tip of Olive's shoelace.

She was close to something big, Olive could sense it—something that brought all of Elsewhere to a halt. Her heart thudding, Olive climbed out of the Parisian painting and rushed into the library.

Several dancing girls in gauzy dresses smiled down at her from their large canvas. They stopped smiling the instant Olive hauled herself through their frame.

"You again?" said the one with reddish hair, backing away.

"Get out of here," whispered the blond girl. "You'll get us into trouble!"

The knot of girls looked up at the painted sky. Olive followed their eyes. She wasn't certain, but it *could* have been growing darker.

"I won't stay," she promised, shrinking under the girls' unfriendly frowns. "I just—I just need to know if one of you is *Aurelia.*"

The name fell like a blanket of ice. The flowery meadow went still. Painted birds froze in midair. The dancing girls stared at Olive with wide, horrified eyes. Everything—the grass, the sky, the air itself—seemed to be listening.

"We're not *anyone*," snapped the tallest girl at last. "Now go away!"

"But do any of you know who—"

"No," said the girl. "Get out of here, before *he* comes!"

Her cold, painted hand gave Olive a shove.

Olive tottered backward, stepped on her own heel, plunged through the frame, and landed on her behind on the library rug.

Straightening the spectacles and rubbing her tailbone, Olive stalked out into the hall. She flumped down at the bottom of the staircase.

There was something hidden here. Something important. Something very close.

But Aurelia didn't seem to be Elsewhere at all. Maybe in the end Aldous had done something far worse with her. Maybe she'd been locked in a bedroom, or kept in a closet, or walled up behind the basement's chilly stones. This thought made Olive shudder.

But she was out of less gruesome ideas. There was no painting left in the house where a sick woman would be safe and comfortable and perfectly hidden. Therefore, there was no place in Elsewhere where Aurelia could be.

But there *was* someone else Olive could ask. And, Olive realized with a little flash, she had the perfect excuse for visiting him.

"Leopold?" Olive called, tugging at the chain of the basement's light bulb.

"Correct as usual, miss," said a voice from the shadows.

"Leopold, I was just passing the painting of Scotland, and I noticed that we left Aldous's paints and instructions in there." She crouched down in front of the trapdoor, setting the leather bag beside the big cat. "It's probably not the most secure place for such valuable items."

"Indeed, miss," said Leopold, wide-eyed. "I apologize for our oversight."

"And I thought: Who better to guard them than the one who guarded them in the first place? So I brought them back to you."

Leopold's chin rose. "Your trust is not misplaced, miss. I shall return these objects to their original location, and continue to guard them with my life."

"Perfect," said Olive. "And speaking of guarding secrets, I need to ask you something important."

The black cat straightened up at the word *important*.

His chest inflated like a furry beach ball. "I will answer to the best of my abilities," he said puffily.

"Thank you." Olive met Leopold's sparkling green eyes. "Do you know anything about a woman named *Aurelia?*"

Leopold started. "Oh. Her." The cat blinked rapidly. "That is to say, she was—or rather—she *is*—or, perhaps I should say—she *isn't* someone of whom I know nothing at all."

"Really?" asked Olive. "Because it seems like you might know something."

"A soldier tries to give the impression of competence," said Leopold.

"I'm worried about what might have happened to her." Olive shifted her feet on the freezing stone floor. "Can you tell me where she might have gone? Give me a hint? Anything?"

"I would not know where to begin, miss. It's a long and unpleasant story."

"So you *do* know the story."

"No," said Leopold quickly. "Only that it's long and unpleasant."

"Please, Leopold." Olive thumped forward onto her knees. "Aldous McMartin must have done something to her. Mary Nivens saw them in the garden—Aldous, and Aurelia, and Horatio—and Aldous was treating Aurelia like a prisoner. I just want to help her."

"Horatio?" Leopold repeated softly.

Olive nodded.

The cat released a quiet breath. "I can tell you this much, miss. To the best of my knowledge, Aurelia is *gone*. Gone forever. And that is probably a good thing."

"A *good* thing?" Olive echoed. "Why?"

"Did I say a *good* thing? I just meant a thing." Leopold nodded. "She's gone. It's a thing."

With a sigh, Olive got back to her feet. "Okay," she said. "If that's all you can tell me . . ."

"It is, I'm afraid," Leopold answered. "Yes. That is all."

In spite of the cold, Olive climbed very slowly up the basement steps. When she turned to close the door behind her, she could still see a pair of bright green eyes watching her, glittering steadily in the dark.

OLIVE STOMPED ALONG the first-floor hall and
turned back into the library. The rows of books
glimmered on their shelves. The piney scent of the
tree filled the dusty air, and its perfectly spaced lights
shone softly.

As she crossed the room, Olive could have sworn
that she saw the glint of a cat's eyes among its branches.

"Horatio?" she whispered. "Is that you?"

The tree kept quiet.

Olive crept closer, the spicy smell surrounding her,
until she could see that the green glints were just two
small blown-glass balls.

Still, as she turned away, she couldn't shake the
sense that she was being watched.

She headed toward the bookshelves behind her

mother's desk, taking frequent glances over her shoulder. A row of old encyclopedias with bumpy green covers stood on the lowest shelf. Olive pulled down the A volume. Then she plopped down on the nearest creaky velvet couch.

The dancing girls in their painted meadow hung just above her. They had resumed their usual pose, their heads thrown back, mouths smiling—but Olive thought she saw something tense and brittle in their expressions now, and their painted eyes were wary.

She flipped to the back of the heavy book.

AURELIA, she read, *also known as the MOON JELLY. A bell-shaped, translucent marine jellyfish of the order semaeostomeae.*

Well, that was no help.

Olive sighed.

The scent of coffee blended with the scent of pine, and Olive glanced up to see her father striding through the library doors.

Mr. Dunwoody's face lit up when he noticed the encyclopedia in Olive's hands.

"What are you researching?" he asked.

"Jellyfish," said Olive honestly.

"Ah. Fascinating creatures, gelatinous zooplankton." Mr. Dunwoody took a sip from his coffee mug. "Are you finding what you need?"

"Not really," said Olive.

"If you could use additional research materials, we could go to the university library later this week."

"Thanks, but I'm pretty sure what I need is right here in this house. I'm just not seeing it."

"Hmm." Mr. Dunwoody seated himself at his desk. "I don't know how likely you are to find any jellyfish in this house, Olive."

"It's not just the jellyfish," said Olive, letting the book thump shut in her lap. "It's a bigger problem, and I just—I can't put the pieces together in the right way."

"Hmm," said her father again. "Have you ever heard of the incubation effect?"

"Is that what doctors do to babies that are really small?"

"It's what happens when we step away from a problem temporarily. Studies have shown that often our unconscious minds will make connections between elements that were already there. Later, the solution seems to come to us out of the blue, but really, it's just our brain catching up with itself."

"Oh," said Olive slowly. "So I should just try *not* to think about it?"

"No. You should come to the kitchen and frost cookies with us. Your mother is currently calculating the surface area of each cookie in order to mix up the ideal amount of frosting." Mr. Dunwoody hopped eagerly out of his desk chair. "Let's go!"

Olive sighed again. But she got up from the couch, leaving the encyclopedia behind, and followed her father out of the library.

It was the part of the morning that is really still night when Olive's eyes flicked open.

In her dreams, she'd been back at the art museum. Ms. Teedlebaum was leading her on a tour. They were the only two people in the building, and their footsteps echoed through the deserted rooms like stones falling into a well. As they passed through the spotlights that illuminated each painting, Olive could see Ms. Teedlebaum's hair change its hue, going from red to purple, red to black, red to royal blue. *Oh,* Olive thought each time. *So that's her real hair color.*

Impasto, Ms. Teedlebaum said, stopping in front of a painting of a big bowl of pasta. *See how thick the noodles are?*

Dream-Olive had nodded, and they'd wandered on.

Pentimento, said Ms. Teedlebaum to a painted bowl of olives. *See how the pimentos are hidden inside the olives, Olive?* The art teacher giggled. *But there's no hidden painting inside you, is there?*

Dream-Olive shook her head.

And a still life, Ms. Teedlebaum announced.

They had paused in front of a large painting. Inside

the painting, there was only a tabletop and an empty silver bowl.

That's funny, said the dream-Teedlebaum, pushing back a hank of kinky green hair. *I wonder where the life went?*

Olive sat up.

Hershel toppled over on the pillow beside her.

She knew that still life. She knew that silver bowl, and the tabletop it sat on, and the room that table stood in. Even without the strange fruits filling it, Olive would have known that still life anywhere.

It may not be what she would choose, but it is still life.

It is still life.

The answer was right there. The whole truth, as it was told to Mary Nivens, straight from Aldous's mouth.

Olive kicked her legs out from under the covers.

The floor was icy cold. She tugged on a pair of thick socks and pulled a sweater over her pink penguin pajamas. Then she edged carefully into the hall, closing her bedroom door behind her.

The sky beyond the windows was just beginning to thin from black to blue. Faint hints of daylight stretched along the edges of hanging picture frames. Tiptoeing over the carpet, Olive headed down the hall straight to Aldous McMartin's still life.

She pressed her palms to the frame and leaned

closer. The strange fruits glistened in their silver bowl. The tabletop beneath them was shiny and bare. The walls, painted with panels of dark wood, looked as solid as ever. But there had to be something there. It was only a matter of looking hard enough. Olive slipped the spectacles out of her collar and balanced them on her nose. The painting shimmered.

Throwing her belly over the bottom of the frame, Olive tumbled forward into the painting, sliding across the polished table and hitting the floor hands first.

She hopped swiftly back to her feet. She had checked the bowl of fruit for clues once before, but she overturned it again, just in case. There were no keys or maps or secret buttons this time, either. The fruits flew back into their places before she'd even turned the bowl upright again.

Wheeling away from the table, Olive examined the wooden walls, running her palms over the panels. Each panel was larger than a door, heavy and shiny and identical. At least, they *looked* identical. But in the center of one panel, Olive's fingertips hit something small and sharp-edged—something made of metal. Olive bent down to look. Hidden in the painted shadow was a tiny brass keyhole.

An electric rush shot through Olive's body.

She wheeled around, eyes skimming the room.

There was a good chance that the key wasn't here, she realized, as the rush began to tingle away. It could be hidden somewhere—*anywhere*—in this huge, cluttered, secretive house.

Or . . . if she was really lucky, it might be waiting right under her nose.

Olive plunged both hands into the bowl of strange fruit. She picked up the cluster of aquamarine grapes, popping a few of them off of their stems. They popped straight back on again. These were too small to contain a key, anyway. But the cylindrical orange fruit was more than large enough. With her fingernails, Olive tore into its squishy body. Trickles of juice and bits of painted pulp slipped through her fingers before pulling themselves together again. Olive tossed the fruit back into the bowl. She squished her fists into the pink-peeled citrus fruit and ripped apart something green and spiny that smelled like clover.

Nothing.

With hope and exasperation tangling in her chest, Olive grabbed the teardrop-shaped fruit with the long, looping vine and dug into it with her fingers. She could feel its cold flesh fighting to rebuild itself, and its slick, painted peel tugging inward around its holes, and, far down at its core, something hard and thin and made of metal.

Like a dentist extracting a tooth, Olive yanked the

metal thing backward. The teardrop-shaped fruit sailed back into the bowl, leaving a tiny brass key in Olive's hand.

Blood pounded in her ears. The back of her neck zinged. Olive dove toward the paneled wall, fitting the key into the lock. There was a click.

The panel was even heavier than it looked. Clamping the key tightly in one fist, Olive pried the painted door open just wide enough to slip through.

The panel thumped shut behind her. The lock clicked again.

Olive whirled around, saw where she was standing, and let out a loud, involuntary gasp.

The room inside the still life was small.

The room hidden *behind* that room was not.

Its ceilings were high. Its floor was covered with soft gray carpet. Tiny-paned windows lined one long wall, letting in a summery view of trees and blossoms. The opposite wall was filled with shelves, and each shelf, in turn, was filled with books. A golden harp nearly as tall as Olive stood in one corner. A piano with a cushioned stool waited for someone to sit down and play in another. At the room's far end, between two grand vases full of blooming flowers, was a bed draped with dove-colored curtains. Rugs and cushions and overstuffed couches covered the floor like decorative bubble wrap.

And, a few steps in front of Olive, with its back to the wood-paneled door, there sat one grand velvet armchair.

At the sound of the closing door, the armchair gave a creak. A ripple of gray silk trailed over one armrest.

"Aldous?" whispered a voice that was as soft and brittle as a moth's wing. "Aldous? Is that you?"

O LIVE HESITATED, HER back pressed to the hidden door.

"Um . . ." she began. ". . . No. It isn't."

There was a rustle of silk against velvet. Very slowly, the head and shoulders of a woman rose up above the chair's high back.

The woman turned around, clinging to the armrests. Her hair was long and reddish brown, shot with silver threads. Her face should have been pretty, with features like an old ivory cameo, but her cheeks were sunken, and there were violet half-moons under her eyes. Her painted skin didn't look like either paint or skin, but even more lifeless, like melted wax. Actually, Olive thought, she looked like a moving, speaking corpse.

"Who are you?" the woman asked. Her voice came out in a raspy wheeze.

"I'm Olive—Olive Dunwoody," Olive stammered. "I live here now. In this house."

The woman's eyes flickered. One hand, long-fingered and spidery, clutched at the back of the chair. "I knew it had been a long time," she whispered. "But I was sure he would find a way."

"You mean . . . Aldous McMartin?" said Olive, taking a small step forward. "He's the one who trapped you here, isn't he?"

The woman's eyes widened in her otherwise motionless face. "You know about me?"

Olive swallowed. "I know your name is Aurelia."

The woman gave a little start, as though Olive's words had struck her. "Please," she whispered. "Come and sit beside me."

Hesitantly, Olive padded across the carpet. A second, smaller velvet chair waited beside the larger one, and Olive perched on its edge, keeping the key clamped in her fist and one eye on the hidden door. This woman seemed about as threatening as a wet sheet of paper, but Olive knew enough to be wary.

The painted woman sank back into her own chair. "Aldous was always so careful," she said, keeping her sunken eyes on Olive. "How did you learn about me?"

"One of the neighbors saw you," said Olive carefully. "A long time ago."

"And now you walk in here, wearing his spectacles," the woman rasped. "How?"

"Well—because Aldous is gone," said Olive. "My family moved into the house last summer, after Annabelle McMartin died."

The woman blinked. "Annabelle?"

"Aldous's granddaughter. She was really old. Really, *really* old."

"His granddaughter." One of the woman's bony hands rose, patting absently at her chest. Olive would have guessed that she was struggling to breathe—if she hadn't known that the woman didn't need to breathe at all. "And Aldous himself?" Her eyes focused on Olive again. "How long has he been gone?"

"He died a long time ago," said Olive slowly. "But he isn't—he's not *completely* gone."

"Of course not," the woman whispered, as though she were talking to herself. "He would never give up this place."

"He trapped lots of other people—just like you," said Olive, watching the woman's eyes. "Magicians. Neighbors who knew too much about him. Anybody he thought was his enemy. But I guess . . . I guess he trapped you first." She inched closer to the edge of her chair. "Why? Did you know something important about his family?"

The woman's eyebrows rose very slightly. "But I *am*

his family," she said. "I am Aurelia McMartin. Aldous is—or was—my brother."

"You're his *sister?*" Olive stared at Aurelia's waxy face. There was a hint of family resemblance in it, she realized—not so much to Aldous himself, but to Annabelle, with her soft, pretty features. Aurelia looked like an Annabelle who'd been dehydrated, frozen, and wrapped in gray silk. Olive swallowed. She clasped the key a little bit tighter. "Then—why would he trap *you?*"

"Oh, Aldous didn't think of it as a trap. At least, not at first." The woman glanced around the room. "He thought it was a place to keep me safe."

"Safe from what?"

"From everything. I was ill, you see." She pressed one corpse-white hand to her chest again. "Consumption."

Olive thought of the old novels she had found in the library, in which women coughed delicately into lace handkerchiefs and then keeled over dead. She nodded.

"For a long time, I was shut away in my bedroom, so as not to infect anyone else," Aurelia struggled on. "But I only grew worse, and soon everyone knew that there wasn't much time."

"Couldn't Aldous use magic to . . . *fix* you?" Olive asked.

"There are some things in this world that even

Aldous's magic cannot overcome." Aurelia gave Olive the hint of a smile. "As you can imagine, this made Aldous furious."

Olive nodded again.

"Instead, Aldous created a world of his own. A world where nothing would age, or get sick, or die. He learned to paint his living pictures. Next, he began to experiment, leaving real things inside of them." Aurelia's weak voice grew even weaker. "Finally, he left me too."

"So . . . *that's* the real reason for all of this?" said Olive slowly. "He started Elsewhere for *you*?"

Aurelia looked away. "Here, nothing would change. I would never get worse. I would never get better. I would be safely hidden, neither dying nor living, forever."

"That's awful," Olive whispered.

"Do you think so?" Aurelia's sunken eyes flicked to Olive's. "Then set me free."

A spike of fear plunged through Olive's stomach. She shouldn't have let her guard down, not even for a moment. She shot to her feet. "I thought Annabelle was nice, and sweet, and helpless too. But when I let *her* out, she tried to *drown me*." She backed toward the wooden panels. "I'm not letting you out. And don't try to make me. The cats know I'm in here, and my friends will come and find me, so don't come any closer."

But Aurelia hadn't moved. Only her eyes followed Olive, and they looked even sadder than before. "Olive," she breathed, "you misunderstand. I don't want to be free of this painting. I want to be set free for good."

"What do you mean?" Olive frowned, backing up until her spine struck the hidden door. "You mean . . . you don't want to *exist* anymore?"

Aurelia looked down at the little table beside her chair. Next to a heavy silver box, one white rosebud stood in its vase, ever blooming.

"I've already existed longer than any person should," she said. "All I want now is to rest." Her fingers settled gently on the lid of the silver box. "You know ways, don't you, Olive Dunwoody?"

Olive *did* know ways. She'd used a few of them already: Bright light. Paint thinner. Fire. She looked at Aurelia's waxy face, at her skeletal fingers and slumped shoulders, and forced back a wave of pity before it could come sloshing out in words.

"I'm not sure," she said. "I need to think."

"I understand." Aurelia's voice was gentle. ". . . In the meantime, there is something I could do to help *you.*"

"Really?" said Olive warily. "What?"

"There was a locket," Aurelia began.

The back of Olive's neck started to prickle.

"A beautiful gold locket," Aurelia went on. "Aldous

had it made for me. I thought it was a gift . . . but really, it was a leash, a way to control the one who wore it. Once I was shut away in here, he gave it to someone else." In the painted flecks of Aurelia's eyes, Olive saw a shimmer—whether it was hope, or cunning, or a deep-buried memory, she couldn't be sure.

"You know what has happened to it, don't you, Olive?" Aurelia whispered. "That's another of the locket's powers. Its true owner always knows where it is."

In the back of Olive's head, something began to clang. It charged forward, growing louder and louder, until Olive realized what it was: alarm bells.

"No," she said, working the key into the lock. "No *way*."

The shimmer in Aurelia's eyes died. Her face looked sad and hollow once again. "Of course," she said softly. "It is up to you. Perhaps you would like to keep the locket for yourself. Perhaps you have even decided to work *with* Aldous rather than against him, or—"

"No I haven't!" Olive shot back. "I would never work with him!"

"Then you must get rid of it," Aurelia whispered. "Please believe me, Olive. Let me destroy it before it hurts someone else."

The trusting part of Olive inched out, wanting to believe—but Olive could feel danger creaking beneath her, like the rung of a ladder about to snap.

"I'll think about it," she said at last. She turned the little metal key.

Behind her, Aurelia sighed. "Of course," she whispered. "I understand."

Olive pried open the hidden door. She glanced around, making sure that the outer room was clear. Just before she could step through, something on the painted shelves to her left caught her eye.

It was a book, bound in worn brown leather. Its embossed cover faced the room. Carved into that cover, with sharp angles and shimmering smudges of gold, was a large, elaborate letter *M*.

Horatio had hidden the grimoire, just as Olive had asked him to.

He had hidden it *here*.

Aurelia's voice suddenly sounded as though it had traveled through a mile of swirling gray fog. "Good-bye, Olive."

Olive didn't answer.

She lunged into the outer room. The paneled door banged shut behind her, throwing her forward. The key tugged itself out of her fingers and flew through the air, darting back into the strange yellow fruit.

Olive sprawled across the table and dove through the canvas, landing on the hallway carpet. Her mind spun with so many questions that she couldn't even see straight—which was why she nearly stepped on the huge orange cat waiting in the patch of early morning sunlight just below the frame.

Olive let out a startled squeak.

Horatio kept silent. His eyes moved from the painting to the spectacles on Olive's nose.

Olive tugged them off. She could hear her parents downstairs, the soft thump of footsteps in the lower hallway.

"You know what's in there, don't you, Horatio?" she whispered.

"Yes. I know *exactly* what's in there." Horatio's words were slow and deliberate. "But I am not sure that *you* do."

"I do too," Olive argued. "She told me herself. She's Aurelia McMartin, and she was going to die, so Aldous put her there. She's why he made Elsewhere in the first place." She folded her arms across her chest. "And you gave her the grimoire."

Horatio's eyes narrowed. "I did not *give* it to her. I left it where it would be hidden and guarded."

Olive dropped to her knees, bringing her face close to Horatio's. "But she's a McMartin! What if she *uses* it?"

"She doesn't *need* to use it." Horatio's eyes darted toward the banister. There was a muted creak from the foot of the stairs. "Believe me, Olive, that book is in the safest spot in this house."

Olive sank back against her heels, feeling suddenly sad. "Why didn't you tell me about her?" she whispered. "How could all three of you have kept this big secret?"

"All *three* of us *didn't*," the cat snapped. "*I* was the lucky one who had to keep it—and *her,* and *you*—safe." Horatio padded closer. "Olive, for the sake of everyone in this house . . . leave Aurelia alone. Promise me, no matter what happens, that you *will not let her out.*"

"I wasn't going to," said Olive. "Probably."

At that moment, Mr. Dunwoody's head appeared between the rungs of the banister. He was climbing the stairs very slowly, because he was reading a book at the same time. He reached the top of the steps, spent a few moments searching blindly with one foot for a stair that wasn't there, and drifted to the right. In the door of Olive's bedroom, he looked up. A puzzled expression floated across his face.

"Your room is the other way, Dad," said Olive.

"Oh. Thank you, Olive." Mr. Dunwoody gave her a smile. "I just can't think about directions and self-consistent recursive axiomatic systems at the same time." Raising the book again, her father shuffled off through the correct doorway.

Olive glanced down. The fluffy orange cat had vanished too.

Before Olive could trace him, there came a loud, rapid knock from the front door.

Olive hurried down the steps. She tugged the door open, and a blast of frigid air swept into the front hall, nearly tearing her breath away.

Rutherford stood on the porch, wrapped in layers of scarves that coiled around his head like a knitted boa constrictor. His glasses were fogged, and he was jiggling quickly from foot to foot, but Olive could still see the worry in his dark brown eyes.

"Olive," he said, "I'm afraid we have a problem."

19

ANOTHER KNOT ADDED itself to the tangle in Olive's mind. "What's wrong?"

"It's Walter," Rutherford answered, through the layers of scarves.

"Walter?"

Rutherford nodded urgently, still jiggling. "Can you come next door? Immediately?"

Olive glanced along the hall. Her mother was in the kitchen, arguing with a TV program. Something sizzled on the stove.

"I can come for just a minute," she said, grabbing her coat. "If it's so urgent."

"It is," said Rutherford, jiggling even harder.

"I'm *coming*." Olive squished her feet into her boots. "You can stop jiggling now."

"The thing is . . ." said Rutherford. ". . . Mm . . . Would you mind if I used your restroom?"

"Oh," said Olive as Rutherford jiggled past her into the entryway. "Sure. Go ahead."

"No need to wait for me." Rutherford hustled toward the stairs. "I've started to pick up Walter's thoughts even when we're not face-to-face. I'm afraid something very bad is beginning to unfold."

In the thin morning light, Olive dashed across the lawn. Last night had been even colder than the one before, and a new, rock-like crust had formed over the surface of the fallen snow. Her boots crunched with every step.

As she approached the front door of the tall gray house, she caught a strange sound coming from inside. It was a violent pounding sound, like someone kicking a wall with a steel-toed boot. Olive's heart clenched. What could be happening in there? The pounding grew louder and louder, ending in a sudden bang as Olive threw open the front door.

Even with the lights dimmed and the curtains drawn, Olive could tell that something had changed inside the tall gray house. She looked around at the floors scattered with freshly unrolled rugs, and the walls hung with unfamiliar pictures, and the rooms stuffed with rearranged furniture, and realized that the *something* that had changed was *everything*.

Lucinda's perfect white furniture had disappeared, replaced by older, cozier chairs. The bare walls were decorated with black-and-white photographs. Every modern appliance and electric lamp had been whisked out of sight.

Gathered in a heap at the foot of the stairs were all of Walter's possessions. Olive took in the crates of old books and brass tools, the bags of unusual plants, and the limp brown sack full of Walter's limp brown clothes. Standing beside the heap, looking even limper and browner and sadder, was Walter himself.

"Hi, Olive!" Morton crowed as he and Mary trundled down the stairs with an old steamer trunk. It gave a final bang as it slid from the bottom step to the floor. "Look! Everything's the way it was!"

"Good morning, Olive!" said Harold, emerging from the dining room with another stack of old books. "Back again already?"

Olive looked from the Nivenses to Walter's hanging head. "What's going on?"

"We're changing it *back*," said Morton proudly. "We're changing everything back!"

Mary beamed, dusting off her smooth white hands. "I just wish I knew where my cuckoo clock went."

"I couldn't find my pliers, either," said Harold, dropping the books into the heap. "You leave home for a little while, and everything gets turned upside down."

"You did all of this in just one day?" Olive asked.

"One day and one night!" Harold whistled a happy tune.

"You get so much done when you don't need to *sleep!*" Mary sang, adding another book to the pile.

Olive watched the book slide to the floor, its pages crumpling. "But why is all of Walter's stuff in the hallway?"

"Because Walter is leaving," Mary chirped.

Olive turned to Walter. "Are you?"

"Well—mmm—" said Walter, shuffling uneasily. "See—they're putting everything back the way it was. Before. And the problem is—mmm—*I* wasn't here. Before."

"We are so grateful that you've watched over Morton, and that you've taken such good care of the house." Mary gave Walter a perky pat on the arm. "You are always welcome to visit. And I'll need you to come over and eat my baking!"

"But you need Walter here for other things too," said Olive as a worried knot in her mind began to tighten. Behind her, Rutherford slipped in through the front door. "He's the one who saved you from that snowy painting. He can *protect* you."

"With this stuff?" Harold gave the heap a skeptical look. "I don't know about all these charms and potions and dead birds and such. Frankly, we would rather not keep any magical trash in our house."

Rutherford stared at Harold as though he had just

declared that the Battle of Hastings had never happened. "*Magical trash?*" he repeated.

"Preparing yourself for battle often invites it," said Mary, before Rutherford could explode. "And a battle with *him* is the last thing we want. Don't you understand?" Mary turned back to Olive, smiling sweetly. "We just want to get back to our normal lives."

But you're not *normal,* Olive wanted to shout. Something in Mary's blue eyes made her stuff the words back inside just in time.

"In that case, Walter," said Rutherford loudly, "I hereby invite you to come and live with me and my grandmother. In fact, I have a project which will require your expertise. The armory can be turned back into a guest bedroom. The replica broadswords and falchions are—"

"Mmm—are you sure?" asked Walter, blinking down at Rutherford.

"I give you my word." Rutherford bowed. "As emissary for the House of Dewey, I give you my grandmother's word as well. I'm sure she would say the very same thing. In slightly different terms."

Walter looked around the hallway. "Maybe I *will* stay with you," he said, pushing his sleeves up his spindly arms. "At least for now."

While Olive, Rutherford, and Walter picked up the first armloads of Walter's stuff, the Nivenses got back to their noisy work. Harold hammered a nail in the hallway. Morton kicked his striped ball through the parlor. Mary's happy humming came from the dining room. When Olive opened the front door, letting Walter and Rutherford out before her, Morton and his parents didn't even say good-bye.

By the time Olive ran from Mrs. Dewey's place back to the old stone house, the sky was a pale, dirty gray. Thick flakes were starting to fall. Wind moaned above the house, carrying the promise of a dark, snowy day. Olive scurried across the porch, threw open the door, and slammed it shut behind her.

Her parents' voices murmured in the distance. A light glowed in the kitchen, sending its warm gold streak along the polished floor. Olive knew that breakfast would be waiting for her. But she didn't feel hungry. She felt heavy, and tired, and too full of problems to fit anything else inside.

Flicking on the stairway light, Olive trudged slowly up the steps.

There was no sign of Horatio anywhere. Harvey seemed to be making himself scarce. Olive was paying such close attention to the shadowy doorways, watching for glittering green eyes and twitching tails, that she didn't glance at the paintings at all.

She didn't notice that she sky above the silvery lake

had darkened to inky black, or that the frozen waves seemed to be rippling a bit more urgently toward their painted shore. She didn't notice that the moonlit forest was no longer moonlit; that the white path had turned gray, and the trees had become one thick black mass, like a wall of thorns. She didn't notice that the candles in the windows of Linden Street had winked out.

Olive turned into her bedroom and plopped down, face-first, on the rumpled blankets. For a while, she slept, as the sky beyond the windows lightened and then darkened again. She woke up feeling completely exhausted, as though all her bones and muscles and blood had been replaced with lukewarm dishwater.

There were too many problems left to solve. And with each one she fixed, another three popped up to take its place.

Aurelia. Horatio's secrecy. Walter and the Nivens family.

And, worst of all, Aldous himself. Aldous, who was still out there, watching and waiting.

What else was he waiting for? What was he going to do next?

Olive flopped onto her back, feeling the dishwater slosh. Across the room, her collection of old pop bottles winked in a beam of window light. One dust-free oval still marked the spot where the filigreed locket had hung. Olive got up and dragged her feet across the floor. She opened the top vanity drawer and reached inside, all the way to the back, where she'd thrown Aldous's locket.

Her fingers rattled over old pens and pencils, pieces of hard candy, and several plastic figurines from the dispensers that always stood in grocery store entryways, but there was no locket. Olive yanked the drawer out as far as it would go. She couldn't see the locket any more than she could feel it.

Breathing a bit faster now, she pulled open the next drawer, tossing out the socks and stockings and one partnerless blue slipper. No locket. She rooted through the other drawers, spilling her collection of smooth rocks decorated with fingernail polish and her sacks of interesting coins. No locket.

By the time she'd dug through the jumbled drawers of her dresser, torn apart her closet, and peered into the darkness under the bed, Olive's skin was prickling with a panicky fever.

The locket was gone.

Not just gone—*taken*.

This wasn't a case of accidentally throwing it across the room in her sleep, as she had done with her retainer, or daydreamily leaving her latest mystery book inside the microwave in place of a plate of leftovers. She'd put the locket with Aldous's portrait in the top vanity drawer, she was certain, and someone else had taken it out again.

And Olive knew who that someone might have been.

She sank down in a heap of strewn clothes, feeling too shaky to think and stand up at the same time. How could Aurelia have gotten out of the locked room, escaped from the painting, and taken the locket? There were so many things she would need: the key to the hidden door, a chance to slip through the house unnoticed, another pair of spectacles or one of the cats . . .

. . . and only one of the cats knew Aurelia was there.

Olive stuck a hank of hair in her mouth and chewed it.

Horatio had brought Aurelia the grimoire. Might he have given her the locket too, to keep it safe? Did he trust her that deeply? Olive chewed faster. And if he was keeping *another* secret, did he trust Aurelia more than he trusted Olive?

This thought made Olive's stomach ache.

One way or another, she needed to know the truth.

Tucking the hank of damp hair behind her ear, Olive peered out into the hallway.

She'd been asleep for longer than she'd realized. Afternoon was already dwindling away. The light that pressed through the windows was the color of tarnished silverware. Suddenly, the entire house looked darker—the lightbulbs dimmer, the doorways blacker, the carpet a bloodier shade of red.

"Horatio?" Olive whispered.

Downstairs, a door opened and closed. Adult voices blended and faded away.

Olive crept out into the hallway.

Horatio wasn't on her parents' bed, or under it. He wasn't in the white room, or the green room, or the chilly, tiled bathroom. As she slunk back around the corner of the hall, Olive got the distinct sense that something was watching *her*—something hidden and silent, something that wouldn't reveal itself until it knew the game was won.

"Horatio?" she whispered again. No one answered.

Olive tiptoed into the lavender room and switched on the light. Across the room, just above the dresser, Annabelle's empty portrait hung, staring back at her. The painting looked darker now. Much darker. Inside the parlor where Annabelle had posed at her tea table, afternoon had turned to midnight. Silverware glinted like weapons in the dark.

The strangled shriek of the teakettle came from downstairs, making Olive jump. She scurried back out of the lavender room and stopped in front of Aldous McMartin's still life.

A shadow had fallen over the bowl of strange fruit. The wood-paneled walls had turned black. Olive leaned closer, staring at the hidden door. Perhaps Aurelia was sitting in her room right now, holding the locket in her cold, waxy hands. Perhaps she truly *did* want to destroy it. Or perhaps that had been one more lie. Perhaps—

"Olive!" Mr. Dunwoody's voice rang up the staircase. "Would you come down to the kitchen, please?"

With a last look at the darkened still life, Olive turned and trudged slowly down the steps.

She had expected to find her parents making dinner, measuring precise ratios, discussing boiling points of various sauces. What she found instead made her stop with a jerk.

Ms. Teedlebaum was seated at the kitchen table. The kitchen light in its stained-glass shade burned above her, catching on her bushy hair and leaving the rest of her face in shadow. Mr. and Mrs. Dunwoody sat like smiling bookends on either side. All three of them looked up as Olive froze in the doorway.

"Come in, Olive," her father said brightly. "Have a seat."

Olive inched across the floor.

Ms. Teedlebaum's faceted green eyes followed her.

"I was just telling your parents what a promising young artist you are, Olive," she said.

Olive perched on the empty chair as if it were upholstered with cactuses.

"Her work in class is always exemplary." Ms. Teedlebaum's voice sounded even sparklier than usual. "She seems to have a real passion for art."

"Olive has always been very creative," said Mr. Dunwoody, in a but-we-make-the-best-of-it tone.

"Yes, she started asking for sketch paper instead of graphing paper by the time she was four years old," Mrs. Dunwoody added with a little sigh.

"During our trip to the art museum, Olive impressed me again," said Ms. Teedlebaum, leaning forward over her steaming mug of tea. "She identified a very rare two-layered painting, all on her own. She has a gift for spotting hidden truths, doesn't she?"

Olive swallowed. Sitting across the table from Ms. Teedlebaum felt like standing too close to a splattering frying pan. She looked down at the art teacher's fingers wrapped loosely around the mug.

"You're right, Florence," said Mrs. Dunwoody. "Olive often notices things that we don't. Isn't that true, dear?"

"Hmm?" said Mr. Dunwoody, who was counting the crystals of sugar falling from his spoon into his cup.

Olive went on staring at Ms. Teedlebaum's hands. They looked strangely clean. Even the art teacher's fingernails, which were usually tipped with little half-moons of brightly colored paint, were spotless.

"I certainly understand her fascination with the museum," Ms. Teedlebaum was saying, taking her hands off the table and clasping them in her lap. "I share it myself. But I'm afraid I have one problem to temper all this praise."

Mr. Dunwoody looked up from his mug.

Olive held her breath.

Ms. Teedlebaum let out a sad little sigh. "It seems that Olive sneaked back into the museum after it was closed on Saturday."

The breath in Olive's lungs turned to ice.

"If she'd just been exploring the place after hours, I wouldn't even have come here tonight," said Ms. Teedlebaum, sounding almost apologetic. "I would believe that she'd just gotten carried away by the artworks and lost track of time. But I am quite certain that wasn't what happened. You see—she was spotted by a security guard, not long after closing. He says that she was clearly trying to hide from him. And just a little while later, I saw her myself, in the basement's storage room."

The ice in Olive's lungs splintered into shards.

"We could have reported this to the police, of course, but I didn't think there was any need for that kind of trouble." Ms. Teedlebaum gave a little cough. "Not when a friendly visit over a cup of tea would do."

There was a moment of silence while everyone stared at Olive.

Olive couldn't speak.

Her parents didn't have this problem.

"Is that true, Olive?" Mr. Dunwoody asked.

"Did you stay at the museum after closing?" asked Mrs. Dunwoody at the same time.

Olive blinked from one parent to the other. She nodded reluctantly.

"Was it simply a mistake?" Mr. Dunwoody sounded hopeful. "Maybe you didn't know that you weren't supposed to be there?"

Olive shook her head even more reluctantly.

"I wish that were the case, Alec," said Ms. Teedlebaum. She looked straight into Olive's eyes. "But you see, it seems that Olive stole something—something of value—from the museum's collection."

Olive felt her whole body freeze, from the toes inside her socks to the hairs on the back of her neck. Every tiny, terrified cell was waiting for Ms. Teedlebaum's next words. Because Olive—and all of her cells and toes and hairs—had just figured out the truth.

Ms. Teedlebaum *knew.*

She knew about the Nivenses. And if she knew about them, she knew about Elsewhere. And if she knew about Elsewhere, she knew about Aldous McMartin, who had been hiding in the museum's dim, dry basement. And if she had learned the truth about Aldous without getting trapped or destroyed in return, then she was working *for him.*

And now she would say, with perfect honesty, *Olive stole a painting* . . . and the Dunwoodys would make Olive give it back.

"What is she believed to have stolen?" asked Mrs. Dunwoody.

"It was a pair of antique spectacles," said Ms. Teedlebaum.

Something shot through Olive's body with the speed and ferocity of a firework. She felt the ice shattering, the petrified pieces of her heart threatening to explode.

"*What?*" she choked.

But she didn't need to hear Ms. Teedlebaum's words again. Her mind had already flashed from one truth to another.

Ms. Teedlebaum wasn't going to stop with the Nivenses. She was after an even bigger secret.

"They are extremely valuable," the art teacher was explaining to the Dunwoodys. "Their age and their history make them most unusual, and they belonged to one of our greatest local artists." Her spotless hands floated back to the tabletop, fingernails tapping against her mug. "I must ask for them back."

Mr. Dunwoody looked confused. "Did you take a pair of spectacles, Olive?"

"I—" said Olive.

"I believe they are hanging around her neck right now," said Ms. Teedlebaum.

The Dunwoodys looked at Olive's collar, where Ms. Teedlebaum's gaze was already locked. Reluctantly, Olive reached into her sweater. She tugged out the spectacles on their purple ribbon.

"I—I didn't steal them," said Olive, managing to force out a sentence at last. "I *found* them. They were—"

"I understand," said Ms. Teedlebaum, tipping her head sympathetically to one side. "They were just lying there, and no one was using them—but they are not *yours,* are they?"

"Well—no, but—"

"Olive appears to have a fascination with eyewear," said Mrs. Dunwoody.

"Yes," Mr. Dunwoody agreed. "Wasn't she playing with another pair of old glasses that she found last summer?"

"I wasn't *playing* with them," said Olive. "I was—"

"Maybe she simply needs glasses of her own." Mrs. Dunwoody gave Olive an encouraging nod. "We'll take you to the optometrist first thing this week, Olive."

"No—I don't need glasses, I—"

"Then you won't mind quite so much when I ask you to return them." Ms. Teedlebaum held out her hand, palm up, over the kitchen table. "If you just give them back to me now, Olive, we can forget that this whole thing ever happened."

Olive caught her lip between her teeth. Panic and anger and confusion spiraled inside of her like the sharp metal bit of a drill. Her parents watched her. Ms. Teedlebaum waited, wearing a forgiving little smile.

Very, very slowly, Olive pulled the ribbon over her

head. She folded the spectacles with a click. Fingers shaking, she set them down in Ms. Teedlebaum's cold, smooth palm.

"Well done, Olive," said Mr. Dunwoody.

"You can pick out glasses of your own at the optometrist's," said Mrs. Dunwoody.

"Thank you so much, Alec and Alice," said Ms. Teedlebaum, rising to her feet. To Olive, she looked suddenly, terribly tall. "And thank *you* most of all, Olive," she went on. "You've done the right thing."

Olive swallowed.

Ms. Teedlebaum wrapped her sparkly cloak around her shoulders. "If you don't mind, might I have a word alone with your daughter?" she asked, looking from Mr. to Mrs. Dunwoody. "Perhaps she could walk me to the door?"

"Certainly." Mr. Dunwoody picked up Ms. Teedlebaum's cup of tea. "Thank you for stopping by personally, Florence."

"Yes," added Mrs. Dunwoody. "You're welcome in our house anytime."

Olive walked ahead of Ms. Teedlebaum through the darkened hallway. No one had turned on the sconces, and the light through the windows was wintery and pale, leaving most of the hall in blackness. Olive could hear the gentle clink of Ms. Teedlebaum's necklaces, but the teacher didn't speak.

Olive yanked open the heavy front door. The snow was falling fast and hard, thick flakes blotting out the streetlamps. Cold air rushed into the hall.

Olive shuddered.

Ms. Teedlebaum didn't. "Step outside with me, will you, Olive?" she murmured.

Olive slunk to one side, waiting for Ms. Teedlebaum to step through before following her onto the snowy porch. She kept one hand on the doorknob, just in case.

A few quiet seconds passed. Olive shivered. Ms. Teedlebaum kept perfectly still.

Finally, Olive whispered, "You're working for *him,* aren't you?"

The cold wind tugged her words away, but she knew Ms. Teedlebaum heard. Her eyes fastened on Olive's, light green and glittering.

"Maybe you met him at the museum," Olive went on. "Maybe he promised to teach you about his paintings. Maybe he promised to make you like *him.* You just had to help him first."

For another instant, Ms. Teedlebaum was quiet. Then a slow, snaky smile spread across her face. "Oh, Olive," she said, in a voice that didn't sound like Ms. Teedlebaum's anymore. "So close, and yet so completely wrong."

Ms. Teedlebaum lifted one long-fingered hand to

her head. She gave a strong, steady pull, and her mass of frizzy red hair slid from her scalp. Olive couldn't hold back a gasp. Ms. Teedlebaum wore a wig! But why would anyone choose hair that looked like it belonged to an electrocuted clown? Then she saw that it wasn't just the hair that had peeled away. Part of Ms. Teedlebaum's face had come with it.

A limp, bloodless strip, like a piece of very thin leather, had torn from her forehead. Another shade of skin—paler and rougher—glimmered beneath. Olive stared, frozen to the floorboards. The long-fingered hand went on pulling. The art teacher's cheek stretched and split. The rip plunged downward, streaks of fleshy color glinting, as her shoulder and chest and arm tore away. Ms. Teedlebaum reached up with her other hand, tugging down the sparkly cloak and the long, flowing dress and the skin beneath it, until the layers of her body—kinky red hair, flowing dress, empty skin—lay in a heap on the icy porch floor.

Nausea flooded Olive's stomach.

She stared from the scraps of Ms. Teedlebaum to the body now standing in their midst. It was dressed in a dark suit. Long legs led up to a bony chest, a pair of wide, humped shoulders, and a craggy, sunken, horrible face.

Olive tried to step backward, but her legs had turned to lead. She could only stand in place, breathing hard, staring up at a pair of eyes that burned against the swirling snow.

"Pentimento," said Aldous McMartin, in his own deep voice. "One painting hidden inside another."

Rutherford, Olive thought. *Get your grandmother, get Walter, and—*

Aldous stepped forward. "Too late, Olive Dunwoody," he said. A smile hovered on his face, as faint and impermanent as dew on a stone. "I am home at last."

A blast of wind swept across the porch. Flying snow stung Olive's skin. She tried to lunge into the house, but Aldous's bony hand lashed out, knocking her backward

A cascade of blackness dropped over her. It shut out the snowy street, the freezing air, and, finally, that pair of burning eyes. Olive felt herself dissolving. With one last hiss of frigid wind, the spark of her mind winked out.

O LIVE'S EYELIDS FLICKED open.

She was lying on her back. A deep violet sky floated above her.

She twitched her legs and wiggled her fingers. Nothing hurt. Nothing seemed to be missing. As she moved, she could hear the sleepy sound of long grass whispering against her ears.

Grass?

Olive sat up.

She was lying on her own front lawn. The old stone house loomed above her, a few gold lights gleaming in its windows. Morton's house stood next door, and Mrs. Dewey's cozy white house nestled on its lawn just down the street.

Olive glanced down. The ground where she lay was

dewy and cool, and soft mists were pillowed on the curve of the hill. How had she closed her eyes in wintertime and opened them in spring? Had she fallen off the front porch and slept through an entire season?

She patted the front of her sweater. And where had the spectacles gone?

Olive clambered to her feet. In the spot where she'd lain, the grass rustled as it straightened itself.

She took another look around. She knew this misty hill, and this empty, car-less street. She knew the houses that waited here in frightened silence.

This wasn't her front lawn at all.

This was Elsewhere.

And the old stone house was towering above her.

On the whole painted street, this had been the one house that was missing. The space beside Morton's house had been noticeably bare, *disturbingly* bare, like a socket without an eye.

But now, here it was. The old stone house.

The swing hung on its porch. Ivy tendrils climbed its walls. Lush baskets of ferns dangled above its front steps. It was captured in every perfect, painted detail.

Olive's mind whirled. She stumbled backward, looking around for anyone who could explain. Through the mist, she spotted three blurry figures in front of Mrs. Dewey's house. Olive lunged toward them.

The mist thinned as she ran across the lawns. Soon

she could see that one of the figures was long-legged and knobby, like a water bird wearing a baggy sweater. One was short and round with tiny feet. And one was wiry and quick-moving, with a head of very messy hair.

"Rutherford?" Olive shouted. "Walter! Mrs. Dewey!"

"Well, hello, Olive," said Mrs. Dewey pleasantly, straightening up from a patch of leafy shrubs. Behind their tiny wire-rim glasses, her eyes were the same color as the mist. "A lovely evening, isn't it?"

"Lovely—what?" said Olive. "You . . . What *happened?*"

Mrs. Dewey blinked. "What do you mean, dear?"

Olive gestured around the quiet street. "How did we get here?"

"Well, *we* came out to gather Drowsy Grayleaf," said Mrs. Dewey. "It only unfurls at night."

"I—mmm—I think I found some," said Walter, who had to fold his long legs nearly up to his ears in order to reach the ground.

"Very good, Walter," said Mrs. Dewey over his shoulder.

"You might think that something called Drowsy Grayleaf would be used in sleeping spells," said Rutherford to Olive, "but that is not the case. It got its name because the leaf itself acts drowsy."

"No—but—" Olive spluttered. "I mean, how did you get *here?* Elsewhere?"

Mrs. Dewey and Walter looked up, puzzled.

"Elsewhere?" Rutherford repeated.

"You're in a painting! *This* is a painting!" Olive burst out, flinging her arms through the misty air.

The other three glanced at one another.

"Mmm—I think—" said Walter, looking worried. "I think you might be—mmm—"

"Hallucinating," Rutherford supplied. "Or sleepwalking. Or you're having another experience of pareidolia. Maybe you saw the water vapor re-form itself, and *assumed* this was Elsewhere."

"*Rutherford.*" Olive released an exasperated breath. "Look!" She kicked a pebble on the walkway as hard as she could. It bumped weakly across the lawn before flying back to its original spot.

"I'm not sure what you're trying to demonstrate, except that you should not plan on a career in professional soccer," said Rutherford.

Olive grabbed him by the arm. "Read my thoughts. Please. *Believe me.*"

Behind their lenses, Rutherford's brown eyes were paler and softer than usual. "I believe that *you* believe it," he said.

"Olive," said Mrs. Dewey, picking droopy gray leaves that flew straight back to their stems, "why don't you come inside with us? There are infusions I could make that might—"

"No." Olive took a step backward. Her eyes followed Mrs. Dewey's hands, plucking the same leaf over and over again. "That's—that's okay."

"Come back if you change your mind!" Mrs. Dewey called as Olive turned and bolted away.

She ran across the Nivenses' front yard, stopping suddenly at the sight of a glimmering candle in the parlor window. As Olive veered up the walkway, more lights came into view: a burning lamp in the living room, another candle flickering upstairs. She'd never seen so many lights in Morton's quiet house.

The painted front door tried to pull itself shut again, but Olive managed to pry it open just long enough to slip inside.

Morton, his mother, and his father were gathered around a piano in the living room. Mary was playing a loud, lively tune that Olive didn't recognize, and Harold and Morton were singing along in one deep bass voice and one light squeaky one.

They all looked up as the front door slammed.

"Olive!" said Mary, swiveling around on the piano stool. "How nice to have a visitor!"

"Come sing with us!" said Morton.

"We could use another treble voice," Harold agreed. "Do you know 'Oh, I Could Pull a Trolley in my Jolly Holley Motor Car'?"

"Um . . ." said Olive.

"Or how about, 'She May Be Homely, but her Apple Pie's a Beaut'?"

"What? No," said Olive. "Do you know what's going on?"

"Going on?" Mary echoed.

"How did he get all of us into the painting?"

The Nivenses looked perplexed.

"Morton," said Olive desperately, "you've been here. You were stuck here for *decades,* remember? You must recognize all of this!"

"Of course I recognize it." Morton folded his skinny arms. "It's my house."

"But it's different," said Olive. "The stone house just *appeared* in the spot that was empty before, and—"

"The stone house?" Mary's eyebrows drew gently together. "It's always stood right next door, Olive."

Harold gazed out the window, at the twilit slope of Linden Street. "Yes," he said, nodding. "Everything looks shipshape to me."

"Morton." Olive stared into his eyes. "We're *Elsewhere.* I don't have the spectacles, and Aldous is somewhere nearby, and—"

Morton's cloudy eyes suddenly focused. "Shh!" he hissed. "Don't say his name!"

"Let's all change the subject, shall we?" Mary turned back to the keyboard. "Why don't we sing—"

"'Flapjacks in My Belly and a Song in My Heart'?" suggested Harold.

"That's just what I was about to say!"

Mary pounded the piano. Morton and Harold began to sing.

Feeling dizzier than ever, Olive staggered back out of the house, through the slamming front door.

She paused beside the lilac hedge. The stone house loomed above her, as solid and sudden as a wall of rock rolled downhill by an avalanche. She didn't want to venture inside of it alone, without any friends or neighbors or cats to help her find another way out.

But perhaps the cats were already inside, waiting. Perhaps there was something else that she was meant to find. Whatever it was, Olive could feel the house drawing her forward.

The air turned cold as she climbed slowly up the porch steps. Ferns rustled in their hanging baskets. Ivy whispered against the windows.

The doorknob was shinier than Olive remembered. When she turned it and pushed the door open, the hinges were oddly quiet—just like Olive's footsteps when she stepped across the threshold into the long, dim hallway.

Olive looked around. There was something wrong with the house. Every trace of the Dunwoodys had vanished: the family photographs, the math books, the winter coats and purple backpacks. But that wasn't all. Each surface and line looked vaguer, blurrier, as though the interior had been created with hurried brushstrokes. The polished banister was a streak of brown. The wood panels of the walls were one solid, oily line. The paintings on the walls were mere suggestions of paintings, blots of color closed inside the ghosts of golden frames. The whole interior was like something seen through a frost-covered window, or through a pair of very bleary spectacles. Instinctively, Olive touched the empty spot around her neck. Nothing here felt real at all.

Except . . .

. . . Except for the whisper of pencils that came from the library.

Olive edged between the streaked wooden doors.

Mr. and Mrs. Dunwoody sat at their desks, or at the streaks of paint that looked vaguely like their desks, their heads bowed over stacks of paper. Their computers had vanished. Mr. Dunwoody's special high-efficiency reading lamp was gone, and the chandelier that dangled above them was dimmer and simpler than it had been before, with just a few yellow bulbs burning among its brass scrolls.

A cold, sloshing lake filled Olive's stomach. When she stepped forward, its icy weight came with her.

"Mom?" she called, in a very small voice.

Mrs. Dunwoody glanced up. "Oh, hello, Olive. Having a good day?" Her head snapped back down.

Olive inched across the blurry rugs. "Not really."

Mrs. Dunwoody didn't reply. Neither of her parents looked up as Olive moved closer. The book-lined walls glimmered around them, like the mother-of-pearl inside a sealed shell.

Olive stopped beside her father's desk. He was grading a huge stack of papers. He took the topmost sheet, scribbled a mark that immediately vanished, and set the paper aside. It glided straight back to the top of the stack.

"Dad?" Olive whispered.

Mr. Dunwoody went on scribbling, turning, and scribbling again.

"Dad?"

This time Mr. Dunwoody paused. "Oh, hello, Olive," he said. "How was school?"

Olive looked hard into her father's face. His eyes seemed faded, as if the irises had been dusted with silvery powder. His skin still looked alive; there were no streaks or swirls of paint on his hands. But Olive didn't know how much longer this would last; she could have been lying on the front lawn for minutes or hours.

"Dad," said Olive as Mr. Dunwoody's eyes wandered back to his work. "Dad, we have to get out of here."

"Certainly, Olive," her father answered. He scribbled on the top paper once more. "Just as soon as I finish grading these tests."

A soft creak came from above. Her parents didn't seem to hear it, but Olive's entire body stiffened. There was someone upstairs.

She backed out of the library. With one hand on the streak of paint that served as a banister, she climbed cautiously up the steps.

The upper floor was even dimmer than the one below. Olive swept one hand across the chilly wall, but there were no light switches. The sconces were missing too. Where the still life usually hung, she could make out the outline of a frame. Olive touched the muddy blur inside. It was smooth, and solid, and very, very cold.

There was another creak overhead. Keeping one hand pressed to the wall, Olive moved along the upper hallway and through the door of the very last bedroom.

By the twilight that breathed through the foggy curtains, she could see that the pink room had changed. The walls were darker and streaked now. All the furnishings were gone. And where the picture of the ancient Roman town should have been, there was only a door.

An open door.

Its warped black wood swung outward, waiting, like a beckoning hand.

Olive tiptoed through it.

She paused in the dark attic entryway, blinking and

listening. From above came a soft, whispering sound, almost like a human voice. Olive recognized it. It was the sound of a moving paintbrush. Shakily, she climbed the narrow stairs.

The attic was strangely empty. The piles of old luggage and jumbled antiques had disappeared—or had never appeared to begin with. Its angled walls were only half complete. Streaks of paint hung in midair. In the gaps where the rest of the walls should have been, patches of blue-black night sky peered through.

The rest of the attic was so dim that the sky seemed bright by comparison. Olive squinted, trying to pinpoint the source of the whispering sound, but the blurry darkness gave no clues.

She was just about to edge away from the staircase when a deep, stony voice said, "Stop."

Olive froze.

"Do not move."

Before Olive could decide whether to obey or not, something damp and slick moved around her wrist. It tightened like a coiling snake. Olive gasped. Through the dimness, she saw that a dense black rope had knotted itself around her wrist—a rope that hung from the rafters, made of swiftly drying paint. She tugged at it with her free hand, but the strands tightened again the second she'd loosened them.

The floor creaked. Something tall and dark and

bony peeled away from the shadows beside her. Olive struggled, but the rope held tight. She could only cower in place as Aldous McMartin stepped nearer, dabbing his brush against a palette of glinting paint.

He was so tall, his head nearly brushed the unfinished ceiling. His face was a smear of shadows and crags. Even in the darkness, his eyes gave off a yellowish light, like those of a huge, predatory cat.

Even though she'd known she might find him here, the sight of the old man made Olive's skin swarm with goose bumps. Her memory shot back to the moment, months before, when she had faced Aldous in the icy black attic of the real house. Here, the attic was cool and misty, and the warped, unfinished walls made everything feel like a horrible dream.

"Olive Dunwoody," Aldous said. His voice made the skin of Olive's neck crawl. "You may be irritating . . . infuriating, even . . . but at least you are predictable."

Olive forced down the fluttering panic that threatened to block her throat. "What do you mean?"

Aldous twirled the brush through a pool of paint. "I never have to pursue you. You walk straight into my traps." On the rafter above Olive's head, he painted the first silvery strands of a spiderweb. "Dressed as a security guard, I watched you make your visits to the museum. There I reclaimed my own spectacles and used them to enter my latest portrait: one of a certain museum volunteer named Florence Teedlebaum. In that disguise, I was welcomed into your home . . . *My* home, that is." Aldous's brush drew another thread on the air. "And now, you come to me once again. You clomp up these steps to confront me in my own house, in my own world." Aldous gave an amused little snort. "There are all kinds of creatures in the world, Olive Dunwoody. But it is the clever, patient ones who win." Aldous dipped his brush in a darker color and returned to the web. In its center, a large black spider began to form.

"But—how?" Olive kept her eyes on the growing spider. One angular leg, now two, now three, jutted from the tip of Aldous's brush. "How did you get everybody in here, without them even realizing? Did you use a Calling Candle, or—"

"There was no need," Aldous interrupted. "I had help."

Olive felt as though she'd plunged into the bog once again. A cold, hopeless fear surrounded her. He must have forced someone to turn on her. "Who?" she whispered. "Who was it?"

The pale light from the sky illuminated Aldous's face as he turned to dip his brush. It was so stiff and still, it could have been a mask—or the face of something already long dead. "Perhaps someone you thought was your ally does not want what *you* want at all," he said. "It would not be the first time, would it, Olive Dunwoody?"

The last flicker of warmth in Olive's heart sputtered out. *Not the cats,* she thought. *Not Horatio. Please.*

Aldous's brush made a final stroke. The spider twitched to life.

"I have such respect for the spider," Aldous murmured. "An artist among predators."

On its long, spiky legs, the spider crawled across the web. It was nearly the size of a rat. Its body was sleek and pointed. Glints of light shivered in the facets of its eyes.

Olive dragged her own eyes away. "What are you going to do?"

Aldous dipped his paintbrush in a paler color. He drew a fine line through the air. "Your neighbors will remain here for good. That's what Elsewhere is for, after all. It is just like a spider's web. A perfect creation. A beautiful trap. A home that protects itself from intruders. A place for dead things to stay, as long as the spider collects them."

Aldous painted one more delicate downward stroke, ending right in front of Olive's face. The spider crawled down it. There it hung, so close that Olive's breath made the thread tremble. One of its six-jointed legs whispered over her cheek like a loose hair. "Are you fond of spiders, Olive Dunwoody?"

Olive was shaking too hard to squeeze out an answer, but Aldous seemed satisfied by the look on her face.

"A terribly misunderstood creature," the old man added. "The spider is not evil. It only does what it must do to survive. It feeds itself, it keeps its home and family safe." His yellow eyes stared into Olive's. "It cleanses the world of a few irritating, over-populous insects in the meantime."

"But—" said Olive. "But you—"

The puff of her breath set the spider in motion. It swung nearer, another needle-thin leg brushing her skin. Olive shuddered.

Aldous brought his face close to Olive's. The spider twisted on its thread between them.

"You still see yourself as the heroine." Aldous's voice was soft. "And in this picture, I am the villain. But let us reverse the image for a moment. Imagine that someone invades your home—the home that you built yourself, where all that remained of your family lived and died. Imagine that this person plays with and breaks your precious possessions. She damages your life's work. She turns your associates against you." Aldous's voice grew deeper. "She desecrates your family's graves. She destroys the person you loved most in the world. Now, tell me, Olive Dunwoody . . ." Aldous drew so close that Olive could see the yellow flecks of paint that made up his eyes. ". . . *Who* is the villain?"

"But—I was—" Olive stammered. "I was trying to make things *better.*"

"For whom?" Aldous asked. The spider swung close again, and Olive felt one of its legs grasp for a foothold on her cheekbone. "Who have you helped?"

Olive took a breath that sounded like a sob. "I helped Morton."

"*Morton* is where he was to begin with," said Aldous. "Yes, you reunited him with his family—apart from the sister you helped to incinerate, of course . . ."

"That wasn't my fault!" Olive protested.

"Is that so?" Aldous's voice was taunting now. "Tell me how you did *not* spy on her, sneak into her home, and try to steal her possessions?"

Olive's mouth fell open, but nothing came out.

"The troublesome Nivenses are right back where I put them. Safe inside the web." Aldous stared into her eyes. "Try again, Olive. Who have you helped? Whose life have you made better?"

"The cats," said Olive, wishing her voice sounded steadier. "You hurt them. You made them do things they didn't want to do." A thin flash of hope streaked through her mind. "You've probably trapped them somewhere right now, so they can't come and help me!"

Aldous's eyebrows rose. "You have hurt and trapped them yourself," he said. "I swear to you, I have done nothing to the cats. Right now, they are hiding, waiting to see who emerges from this frame. When they see that I am master of this house again, their loyalties will return. It will be as though you were never here at all."

A choked sob escaped from Olive's mouth. "My parents . . ." she said weakly.

"You think you have made their lives *better?*" Aldous's sunken eyes shimmered as he shook his head. "Your parents are trapped here *because of you.* If you had never come stumbling into my secrets, your parents would still be alive tomorrow."

Aldous rose to his full height again. Olive had to tilt her head back to stare up at him, a black silhouette against the strips of night sky.

"Their lives would have been better had you never entered them in the first place," he went on. "They have each other, their shared work, their shared talents. You are barely part of their lives at all. And I know just what they feel. I felt it myself, for my only child. *Albert.*" Aldous almost spat the name. "He was a traitor. A thing of disappointment, humiliation, disgust. In the end, I couldn't stand the sight of him. I had to remove him myself." Aldous's voice rasped like iron. "If someone had ripped him from my path, as I am about to do for your parents, believe me, I would have been *grateful.*"

Olive yanked at the rope around her wrist until her skin burned. It was no use.

"I could simply keep you here," said Aldous, very softly. "Tied to the rafters, alone. Stuck forever in my trap. But I will not." He stepped closer. "Because I do not want *you* in my home. Not in this world or in any other." He bent down again, lifting the spider gently in one palm and setting it back in the heart of its web. "And when I destroy you, it will mean less to the world than the crushing of one little spider."

Olive felt her lips start to tremble. She bit the inside of her cheek, forcing the tears backward. "That's not true."

Aldous turned away. With two quick brushstrokes, he formed the outlines of a simple table to set down his palette and brush. Then he opened his empty hands. All the light that remained in the attic—the glimmers of fresh paint, the misty twilight slipping through the unfinished walls—dripped downward like melting wax. Rivulets of light ran into Aldous's cupped palms from every direction. The attic turned black. Above his palms, a poisonous green fire began to flicker.

"Let us see who comes to help you now," he said.

The streak of green fire seared through the attic and landed on Olive's tied hand.

In the first instant, there was only a crinkling, tickling warmth. Olive stared at the ball of fire, wondering why she didn't feel anything worse. . . until an instant later, when the flame had already dug into her skin, and the pain opened like a burst balloon.

Olive screamed. She tried to jerk her hand away from the burning ball, but the rope held tight. Aldous watched her writhe, his face as calm as if she were a piece of meat in a skillet.

He was right, Olive realized, through the terror and the pain. No one was coming to save her. They were too far away, or too muddled by magic. Or maybe everything Aldous said was true. Maybe they didn't even *want* her to be saved. Maybe she hadn't helped anyone at all. A fresh spike of pain reached all the way to her heart.

But I tried, she thought. *I tried so hard.*

And then another thought floated up from the very back of her mind. It was foggy at first, and it seemed to shift from her very first glimpse of Morton's frightened, moonlit face, to Horatio's bright green eyes when she'd pulled him out of the sack where the young Aldous had trapped him, to her parents' sleeping selves slumped in the depths of Dr. Widdecombe and Delora's closet. It spoke with a voice that was very small and very soft, and yet it seemed to contain the voices of her parents, and the Deweys, and the Nivenses, and the cats. In a whisper, it said—

Try harder.

Olive forced her arm forward, straight into the fire. The painted rope slid through the flames. There was a rush of heat followed by a soft sizzle—and then the rope dissolved.

Olive yanked her arm free.

She cupped her burned hand to her chest as the flame melted away, its dissipating brightness drifting back up into the night sky.

Olive's hand shook with pain. The skin itself seemed to be shrieking. The sounds that came from her mouth were only an echo.

Aldous leaned over the spot where Olive was huddled. "Once you have turned to paint, you will burn far more easily. But you know all about that, don't you, Olive Dunwoody?" His voice was a freezing whisper. "Weren't you surprised at how fast my Annabelle burned?"

There was a moment of quiet as Aldous straightened up again. Olive rocked in place, gasping through her teeth.

"You don't deserve such a quick ending. Not yet," said Aldous at last. "You deserve a bit more fear. A bit more pain. You deserve to see the lives of those *you* love destroyed, while you watch, unable to save them." His craggy face twisted into a smile once again. "You have kept so many secrets, Olive Dunwoody. Now you are desperate to tell the truth . . . *and no one will believe you.*"

Olive staggered backward, tumbling over the first step. She caught herself with her uninjured hand just in time to keep from falling down the rest of the flight.

"Go on," said the old man. "Try to warn everyone. Find the truth for yourself: You cannot save them, and they will not save you."

Whirling dizzily around, Olive stumbled down the attic steps, through the dim and empty bedroom. Aldous's laughter floated after her.

OLIVE THUNDERED BACK down the blurry stair-case. Her mother and father sat in the library, just where she'd left them. Olive tore across the room.

"Mom, come on," she begged, grabbing her mother's arm with her good hand. "We have to get out of here. *Please!*"

Mrs. Dunwoody might as well have been carved out of marble. "Just a minute, Olive," she murmured. Her cloudy eyes coasted across Olive's face. "As soon as I get this work done." She jotted down a row of symbols that quickly erased themselves.

"Oh, hello, Olive," said Mr. Dunwoody as Olive streaked past his desk again. "How was school?"

Olive bolted through the front door and staggered onto the dewy lawn. Tears left itchy trails on her skin. Her hand throbbed with each beat of her heart.

She raced across the empty street to the house that would someday be Mr. Hanniman's. "Hello!" she shouted, pounding on the front windows. Her voice dissolved into the twilight. "Is anyone in there? I need help! Please!"

No one answered.

Olive charged toward Mr. Fitzroy's empty porch. His windows were dark, his house hushed. "Mr. Fitzroy!" she yelled, kicking the door. "Mr. Fitzroy, help!"

Olive wrenched at the doorknob. It didn't budge. She stared along the row of lightless, silent houses. They seemed to be shutting their eyes and holding their breath, like creatures trying not to be seen.

Turning back toward the deserted street, Olive felt a tide of despair turn with her. It wound around her, spiraling and pulling, nearly dragging her to the ground.

No one would help her. No one would believe her. No one would see the truth.

Olive's eyes swept up the row of houses, with their locked doors and curtained windows. In the tall gray house, one cheery light still burned.

Wait. There *was* someone who would see the truth.

Olive tore back across the street and up the steps to the Nivenses' front door. Without knocking, she wrenched it open and lunged inside.

The living room was empty now, the piano quiet. Olive could hear Morton's and Harold's laughter drifting in from another room.

Mary's blond head appeared around a hallway corner.

"Oh, Olive!" she exclaimed. "How lovely! Come and join us for a guessing game!" Her smile faded. "Is something wrong?" She glanced at the hand that Olive held awkwardly to one side. "My goodness. Come to the kitchen, quickly!"

"Mrs. Nivens," Olive panted as Mary dipped a cloth in a jug of water, "you know what's going on here, don't you? You know the truth?"

Mary looked faintly puzzled. "Why, Olive, what do you mean?"

"You know that we're *trapped* here!" Olive winced as Mary patted the cloth against her hand. "You know *he* did it, and he—"

Mary's eyes widened. She put a finger to her lips. The sound of Morton's and Harold's laughter went on.

Pulling Olive by the arm, Mary stepped into the corner by the closed pantry door. The damp cloth, already dry, flew from her grip back to its spot by the sink.

"Now," she murmured, still holding Olive's wrist, "calm down, and tell me what you are so upset about."

"He's *here!*" Olive burst out. "This is Elsewhere, and my friends and my parents are dying, and *Aldous is here!*"

A sudden silence swept through the noisy house. Harold and Morton went quiet.

"He trapped us—all of us," Olive rushed on. "My parents. Rutherford, Walter, Mrs. Dewey. You. But nobody realizes it. And soon we're all going to be stuck here forever. You know I'm telling the truth, don't you?" she pleaded, looking up into Mary's clear blue eyes. "You believe me, right?"

Mary let out a soft breath. "Yes, Olive," she whispered. "I know you're telling the truth."

Olive rocked with relief. "So you'll help me?"

"No, Olive," said Mary smoothly. "I won't help you."

For a second, Olive was sure that her ears had malfunctioned. "What?"

Mary's blue eyes were clear and bright. "I won't help you," she repeated. "Why would I help you to get everyone out? I'm the one who helped get them in here in the first place."

"*What?*" said Olive, a bit more loudly this time.

"Keep your voice down," said Mary. "No need to get everyone upset." She took both of Olive's hands, making Olive flinch. "There's no point in trying to fight Aldous McMartin," she went on, staring straight into Olive's eyes. "He's stronger than we are. I know what he can do when he's angry, and I will *not* spend another hundred years away from my family." Her face curved into a smile. "I made a bargain with Aldous instead. I promised to help bring you and your allies here, and *he* promised that we could all stay together."

"So—it was him," Olive choked. "That night in the snow, he was—"

"All it took was asking Mrs. Dewey to bring Rutherford and Walter to your house, saying something had gone wrong—which was perfectly true!" Mary interrupted with a little laugh. "In return, Aldous will let us stay here together, in peace. *Forever*. Don't you see how wonderful this is, Olive?" she asked, her voice bubbling with stifled happiness. "We have our very own houses. Our very own street, just the way it was. Even our own neighbors! Maybe one day, Aldous will paint a portrait of Lucy to join us." Her eyes shone. "I know it won't be exactly the same, but we're safe. We're together." She gave another laugh. "As Aldous said, it is still life!"

"But—but it *isn't!*" Olive spluttered. She shook her head so hard that the dim, painted kitchen became a blur. "It's not life. It's *fake*. You and your family are already paint, but everybody else—they're *dying!*"

Mary pursed her lips. "Oh, don't be so dramatic, Olive. You sound just like Morton. Don't you realize how lucky we are?"

"No!" Olive clenched her teeth. "If you won't help me, I'll keep trying on my own. I'm not just going to let him win!" She took a step toward the kitchen door.

Mary's grip on Olive's hands tightened. "I'm sorry, Olive, but I can't let you do that."

Olive tugged, but Mary's fingers were like painted handcuffs. "Let go," she said, trying to sound bold and firm but sounding rather wishful and wobbly instead.

"Oh, Olive!" Mary sighed. "Don't spoil it for the rest of us!" With her spare hand, she reached for the hook where a key hung just outside the pantry door.

Olive made a grab for it, but Mary was stronger. Before Olive could catch her balance, Mary had opened the lock and whipped her through the darkened doorway.

The painted door slammed, sealing Olive inside.

22

Trapped in the unlit pantry, Olive heard the rasp of the closing lock. There was a click as the key flew back to its spot.

She hammered at the door. "Let me out! Morton! Harold! *Help!*"

Footsteps whispered across the kitchen.

Olive heard Morton's high-pitched voice. "What happened, Mama?"

"Olive was going to do something that would make the Old Man very angry," Mary's sunny voice answered. "And then he wouldn't let us be together anymore."

"We don't want that, do we, son?" asked Harold's deeper voice.

". . . No," said Morton after a moment. "I just want to stay with you."

"Morton, please!" Olive shouted. "Let me out!"

"Let's go back to our game, shall we?" Mary asked brightly. "I believe it was Morton's turn!"

Three pairs of footsteps moved out of the kitchen and dwindled into the distance.

Olive grabbed the heavy brass doorknob and wrenched at it so hard she thought her fingers might break. The door didn't budge.

Blindly, she pawed through the darkness. The pantry shelves were bare. There were no windows to break, no vents to pry open, and nothing to light on fire, even if she'd had anything to light a fire *with*. Olive shoved her hands gingerly into her pockets. People in books always picked locks with hairpins, which they seemed to carry with them everywhere they went. Olive didn't wear hairpins, so the fact that there weren't any in her pockets wasn't a surprise. She let out a desperate growl anyway. Time was dwindling, and she was wasting her last living, breathing seconds inside an empty pantry—

Wait. There was one more person who might help her, even if he didn't know the whole truth.

Rutherford. I am locked in the Nivenses' kitchen pantry. Olive thought the words as clearly as if she were dictating a letter. *Mary trapped me here. The key is hanging by the door. Please come and let me out.*

Then she just thought *please please please please* for several seconds, followed by *hurry hurry hurry,* and then she heard the most beautiful of sounds: a sharp, clear knock on the far-off front door.

Olive held her breath, listening.

The door creaked open.

"Hello, Mrs. Nivens," Olive heard Rutherford say in an extremely loud voice.

"Good evening, Rutherford," Mary answered. "What can I do for you?"

"May I please come inside?" Rutherford blared, as if he were reciting Shakespeare to a crowded auditorium. "I would like to speak with Morton for a minute."

"Is that truly why you've come here?" Mary asked.

Olive pressed her ear against the door.

"Why don't you look at me, Rutherford?" Mary asked sweetly. "Now, tell me what you were *really* planning to do."

"I was going to go to the kitchen and take down the key and let Olive out of the pantry," Rutherford announced.

"That's what I thought." Mary clicked her tongue. "I'm afraid I will have to ask you to leave."

There was a slam.

Olive listened, her ear pressed like a suction cup against the painted door.

Rutherford didn't knock again. Maybe he was running home to tell Mrs. Dewey and Walter what had happened. Maybe they would believe him.

And maybe they wouldn't. Maybe Rutherford hadn't really believed her himself.

Olive flexed her fingers. Her burned hand still felt tender, but the raw pain had begun to fade. Tentatively, she ran the fingers of her other hand across her palm. Her skin was perfectly smooth. There were no blisters, no cracks. It was already healing.

Oh no.

The repair hadn't been instantaneous, but it was abnormally fast. She must have already begun to change. Olive wriggled her stinging toes. The transformation always started at the extremities, nibbling patiently inward, like frostbite. If she didn't get out soon—*very* soon—it would be too late for everyone.

She sank down on her knees against the painted door. *Rutherford!* she thought. *Please help me!*

Outside the pantry, the big gray house was silent. Inside, there was only the sound of Olive's teary, ragged breathing, and the stubborn beating of her heart.

Mary's words spiraled in her mind like a firefly caught in a jar. *We are safe. We are together. It is still life.*

But for Olive, it wouldn't be life for long. Once they had all turned to paint and it was too late to save anybody, Mary would hand her over to Aldous. Aldous would form another little orb of fire, and the painted version of Olive would vanish in a quick, quiet burst.

She could bear this, Olive thought, if she knew that her life had meant anything at all.

But . . . as much as it made her entire chest ache to think about it . . . Aldous might have been right.

Her parents were trapped because of her. Walter and the Deweys were stuck here because of her. Even Ms. Teedlebaum—wherever she was—had gotten tangled up in this mess because Olive had made the mess in the first place.

And the cats . . .

What if Aldous had spoken the truth about them too?

What if she had only been a temporary tenant, a caretaker who'd disappointed them and hurt them and wasted their time, while they waited in dread for the *real* master to return?

Had she made anyone's life better *at all?*

Olive pressed her face against the wooden door. She could have been better. She could have been smarter, kinder, more loyal, more unselfish. She had tried, and she had failed. She couldn't undo her mistakes. She couldn't start over.

This was where all her trying would end.

And then, even though she hadn't turned the doorknob again, Olive heard a tiny click, as delicate as a snapping thread. The door swung open. A band of light fell into the pantry—and in it, she could see the outline of a small, round, worried face.

"Morton?" she whispered.

"Shh!" Morton whispered back. Standing on his tiptoes, he slipped the key back onto its hook. "Mama and Papa are upstairs. You can get out, if you run fast."

Olive hesitated. "But your mother said—"

"I *know* what she said," Morton interrupted. "But I don't think it's fair," he said. "I don't think it's fair to trap you here, when you untrapped all of us. Now, get out of Mama's pantry."

"But I *didn't*," said Olive as Morton grabbed her arm and pulled her out onto the floor. "You're all right back where you started. I didn't do *anything*."

Morton gave Olive an *are-you-crazy?* look. "You found *me*," he said. "You found *Mama* and *Papa*. You made me a *Halloween costume*."

"But what if there's no way to beat Aldous?" Olive whispered. "What if just giving up and doing what he wants is the only way your family can be safe?"

Morton gave Olive a funny look. He shrugged his knobby shoulders. Then he looked down at his toes. "Mama and Papa aren't my *only* family," he said.

"Here," he added, still looking down. "You should take this with you." From somewhere in the folds of his nightshirt, he pulled out a small, slightly battered flashlight.

"Where did you get that?" Olive asked.

Morton's eyebrows rose. "*You* gave it to me," he said. "Remember? It was the first time you visited me in here. We drew on the sky."

"That's right . . ." said Olive, remembering whirling with Morton through the mist, their dancing flashlight beams making the darkness withdraw for just a moment. "We wrote our names."

"You let me keep it." Morton pushed the flashlight into Olive's hand. "I tried not to use it too much. There should still be plenty of batter in it."

Olive let out something that was a mix of a laugh and a sob. "Good," she whispered.

There was a faint creak from above.

"Hurry!" Morton breathed. "Run!"

Olive tried, but her feet wouldn't take her to the door yet. Instead, they took her closer to Morton. Her knees bent themselves, and her arms threw themselves to either side, and Olive gave Morton a huge, tight hug.

"Thank you, Morton," she whispered into his tufty hair.

Then she spun around and tore down the hall toward the front door. She was already halfway across the lawn when she heard it slam itself behind her.

Olive flew down the hill. Beneath her feet, the green grass looked black. The mist had turned from silver to lead. Ahead of her, hanging in midair, she could make out the flinty edges of the picture frame.

Olive skidded to a stop.

Through the frame, she could see that the house was dark. A whisper of snowy moonlight reached through the windows, revealing the empty hall. Olive smacked her palm against the surface of the painting. It was like pounding on foot-thick glass. There was no way she could get out on her own.

She had just one chance: That Aldous had been wrong about the cats. That they weren't merely waiting for him to regain control. That the friendship between Olive and the three of them was stronger than their fear.

Olive flicked on the flashlight. Aiming it at the painting's surface, she moved her hand back and forth through the beam, making it flash like a distress signal.

Flash. Flash.

The light shivered on the carpet, on the polished banister, and on one tiny fleck of green in a distant doorway.

Olive's heart surged. She flashed faster.

The green fleck grew. It became a glint, and then a streak, and then a huge black cat was landing on the edge of the frame as though it were the sill of an open window.

"Leopold!" Olive gasped. "I'm so glad to see you!"

Leopold nodded briskly. "This may not be the appropriate time to say so, miss, but I am utterly delighted to see you too," he murmured back. "Now come with me!"

OUTSIDE THE PAINTING, the house was dark. Aldous's presence had chilled the air, leaving the hallway as black and still as the deepest chamber of a cave. The moment she slipped through the frame, Olive's hands and toes began to sting, and the cold covered the rest of her body with goose bumps—but there was no time to think about that, or even to feel it.

She chased the glints of Leopold's eyes into her own bedroom. The light switch clicked uselessly under her fingers. Olive tugged out the flashlight, slashing its beam warily around the room. In the center of the bed, a tuna can breastplate glittered.

"Milady!" cried Harvey, darting out of a fortress of Olive's pillows. "You are safe!"

"Sir Lancelot! Thank goodness!" Olive leaped onto the mattress. "Where's Horatio?"

"We 'ave not seen heem," the cat answered. "Sometimes, when you hide, neizer friends nor foes can find you."

"Well—we'll have to think of a plan without him. *Fast*. Because Aldous is already here."

"We are aware," said Leopold, with a stately bound onto the bed.

"He trapped everybody in the painting—my mom and dad, and—"

"And *you*, miss," Leopold pointed out. "And he will already know that you got *out* again."

For the space of a breath, they sat perfectly still. Olive could almost feel the walls of the old stone house leaning in around them. Watching. Listening.

"He also knows I won't just leave everybody in there," Olive whispered. "We have to do something he *won't* expect."

"Unfortunately, a sneak attack is impossible," said Leopold. "He oversees all of Elsewhere."

"And 'e has already reclaimed zee spectacles and zee paints," Harvey pointed out. "We 'ave no weapons left to draw him out."

"*Wait!*" Olive's gasp made a frozen puff in the air. "There *is* something he might want—the grimoire! It's with *her!*"

"Whom are we discusseeng?" Harvey asked Leopold out of the corner of his mouth.

"*Her,*" Leopold answered.

"Ah." Harvey inclined his head. "Her who?"

Leopold blinked. "Who?"

"Aurelia!" said Olive.

Both cats stiffened. Leopold's ears flicked like black switchblades. Harvey's splotchy fur rose, tufting around the edges of his breastplate.

"Aurelia . . . is *here*?" asked Leopold.

"Hidden inside Elsewhere," said Olive, already jumping off the bed. "Horatio knew all along. Come on!"

The cats exchanged a look.

"What do you think?" Harvey murmured to Leopold.

Leopold's whiskers twitched. "If it is the *only* way . . ."

"Do you have a better plan?" Olive asked urgently. "Because we're running out of time!"

The cats gave each other one more look.

"Please," Olive begged. "They need us. *Let's go.*"

Leopold let out a soft breath. "Lead the way, miss."

With the flashlight shoved back into one pocket and a book of matches from the bathroom wedged into the other, Olive charged toward the still life. In the darkened house, its frame shimmered like mist on cold water.

They tumbled through the jellyish surface. The two cats watched, keeping mum, as Olive ripped the key out of the strange yellow fruit and pried open the paneled door.

Aurelia struggled to her feet as Olive and the cats burst in. Her hands trembled against the arms of her chair like withered leaves in a strong wind.

"Olive Dunwoody," she whispered. "And . . . is that Leopold? And little Harvey?"

"Sir Lancelot," Harvey mumbled, ducking out of sight behind Olive's shins.

Leopold pressed close to Olive's side, his eyes fixed on the shaking woman before them.

"Have you come for me?" she asked, in a hopeful whisper.

"No," said Olive. "We need to take the spellbook back."

Aurelia took a step forward. "Is that so?"

Olive edged toward the shelf where the McMartin grimoire glimmered. The cats followed her like two furry magnets. "But we're not going to use it, I promise. We just need it for—"

"I know why you need it." Aurelia glided closer to Olive. Something strange flickered in her sunken eyes. "Because Aldous is here, and he is going to destroy something you love. Now you need something *he* loves. But you're choosing the wrong thing."

Before Olive could reach for it, Aurelia's hand flashed out and grasped the spellbook. "I know how he thinks, Olive. I know what he truly loves." She tucked the book under her arm. "I can help you . . . if you take me with you."

Desperation beat in Olive's chest like a swarm of wasps against a windowpane. There wasn't time to argue, or to bargain, or even to think.

"Fine," she blurted. "But we have to go *now*."

The strange, flickering thing in Aurelia's eyes grew brighter.

The cats watched, as still as gargoyles, as Aurelia glided back toward her armchair. She lifted the heavy silver box from the tabletop. Very gently, she cradled it against the thick leather book, inside the crook of her arm.

"We're ready," she said. "Now, take me to him."

Crouched in the painted grass below Linden Street, Olive made sure the matches and flashlight were secure. The sky above them had grown blacker still. Thick, ashy clouds billowed through the darkness, erasing the painted stars. A frigid gust of wind swept down the hillside. The cats flanked her, pressing closer as the wind whipped by.

Beside them, Aurelia stood, staring up the hill. The look on her face was both intent and dreamy, as if she were trying to recognize a far-off song. Cradling the book and the silver box, she started up the slope.

Olive was about to follow when a voice behind her shouted—

"Olive!"

She whirled around.

A huge orange cat leaped from the picture frame into the misty grass.

"Horatio!" Olive dropped to her knees, reaching out for the cat. "Where have you been?"

Horatio let Olive give him a quick stroke. "I've been searching for the locket. It seems to have gone missing."

"But—" Olive stammered "—but you were the one who took it out of the drawer in the first place!"

Horatio's eyes widened. "How on earth did you arrive at *that* conclusion?"

"You were the only one who knew where it was!" Olive gestured up the hill, where a pale form was dwindling into the distance. "Just like you were the only one who knew where *Aurelia* was!"

Horatio's eyes grew wider still. "You let her out?" he asked, very softly. "You brought her *here?*"

"She said she'd help us with Aldous. And I *had* to let her out, because *she* had the spellbook, which *you* gave her in the first place!"

"I *gave* it to her?" Horatio exploded. "Leaving it with

her was like locking it in a vault! If there is anyone on earth who has no interest in that book—"

"Because she already knows everything in it!" Olive interrupted. Harvey's and Leopold's eyes zoomed from Horatio's face back to hers. "Because she's a McMartin!"

"*Exactly!*" Horatio shouted. "Because—"

"Because she's his sister!" Olive yelled.

Horatio gave a start.

Harvey and Leopold inched backward.

Another sudden wind tore down the hillside. Through the swirls of mist, Olive could see Aurelia's frail, fluttering shape vanish over the crest of the hill.

"No, Olive," said Horatio, his voice so low that the rustle of the grass nearly buried it completely. "She's not his sister. She is *his wife*."

"H IS WIFE?" OLIVE repeated dizzily. "But why would she lie to me?"

"I suppose she thought you'd be more likely to free her if you didn't know she'd made a vow to love and honor Aldous McMartin for as long as she lived," said Horatio sharply. "And look! It worked!"

"But she said she wouldn't let him hurt anyone else!" Olive cried as Horatio raced toward the hill.

The cat glanced back over one shoulder. "We'll see."

Olive, Leopold, and Harvey tore after him.

The closer they came to the crest of the hill, the harder the wind blew. Olive's hair lashed across her eyes. Her cuffs twisted around her ankles. The air was full of a thousand icy hands, all shoving her backward. By the time they reached the pavement of Linden

Street, the towering trees were lashing nearly to the ground. Branches scraped the cowering houses like warped, furious claws.

In the dimness, the stone house looked nearly black. Aurelia stood before it, a glimmering, moon-colored splotch against the dark. Her silk robes billowed. The grimoire glittered in the grass at her feet.

As Olive and the cats struggled toward her, Aurelia raised her chin. Her gray-streaked hair whipped in the wind.

"Aldous McMartin," she said.

The hush that fell over the street was so sudden and total, they might all have been trapped beneath a huge glass lid. The wind died. The trees ceased thrashing. The grass straightened itself.

Silent seconds tiptoed by.

Across the street, doors inched open and neighbors peered out. The Nivens family crept onto their porch. Beyond them, Rutherford, Walter, and Mrs. Dewey ventured toward the sidewalk, their eyes fixed on the huge stone house.

Olive felt the reverberations of her heart against her ribs, its pounding beats making her whole body tremble. Where were her parents? Why hadn't they come outside?

At last, the door of the stone house creaked open.

What stepped through it wasn't Aldous McMartin.

It had Aldous's shape—the bony shoulders, the long arms and hands—but nothing else: No colors, no features, no face. As it slid silently across the porch, Olive saw that it was Aldous's own painted shadow. It was taller than Aldous, stretched out in the way that a shadow stretches as it angles away from its source, and it moved with a sort of flickering smoothness, gliding down the steps like a pool of oil—or like an insect with so many legs that each one hardly seems to move at all. That first shadow was followed by another, and then another, and then another, until a nest of freshly painted shadows filled the porch, their eyeless faces flicking from side to side.

The cats huddled against the ground, their fur rising. The hairs on Olive's skin rose too.

Can those shadows see? she wondered. *Can they think?*

She reached toward the flashlight in her pocket. The shadows turned their blank, black faces toward her, one after another, like a hive operating with a single mind.

Olive froze.

There was a soft thump, and Aldous McMartin himself stepped through the front door.

He strode to the top of the steps where the knot of shadows was thickest, and there he stopped. His eyes fixed on the painted woman. His face was cold and calm, without a flicker of surprise. He had known they were coming, Olive realized. Was that why he had painted this swarm of shadows? But why did he need all of those slippery, warping, writhing things to face his own fragile wife?

"Aurelia," he said softly.

The shadows shifted, tensing. A single one of them slithered out over the lawn, reaching toward Aurelia with its long, boneless arms.

Aurelia's waxy face didn't change. "Aldous," she whispered back. "It has been a long time."

The shadow's snaking fingers stroked the hem of her robe.

"It has," said Aldous.

"When you left me there . . ." Aurelia paused. ". . . I thought that I would never forgive you."

Out of the corner of her eyes, Olive saw the Nivenses moving nearer. Mary's face was a frightened mask. Walter and the Deweys crept to the edge of the lawn, the cloudiness in their eyes beginning to thin. Olive inched her fingers toward the flashlight again.

"You did not understand," said Aldous sternly.

"But now I do." Aurelia spread her hands. "You were only trying to save me. You wanted to give me eternity. An eternity with you."

Olive saw Aldous's jaw clench. "You spoke very differently once."

"So much can change in a hundred years." Aurelia's

voice was wistful. "At last, I can see that everything you did, every choice you made, was to save our family. To save our home."

She took a step closer to the porch. A few more of the shadows left Aldous and inched toward Aurelia, their eyeless heads following her every move.

Aurelia opened her arms, tilting her waxy face up toward the spot where Aldous stood. "I forgive you, Aldous McMartin. I will gladly wear your gift once again."

Horror poured through Olive's body. Aurelia wasn't going to destroy the locket. She was going to side with Aldous to take the house *back*.

Without thinking, Olive lunged forward. She whipped the flashlight out of her pocket, her thumb searching for the switch. But before she'd taken a second step, two shadows streaked across the lawn. Their fingers stretched to the length of arms, and their arms grew longer than Olive's entire body. They coiled around her, pinning her arms, ripping the flashlight out of her fist. The flashlight shot through the air and disappeared over the hillside. One of the shadows dragged Olive to her knees. Another loomed above the cats, keeping them at bay.

Meanwhile, Aurelia turned toward Rutherford. She pointed, and two more of the shadows elongated to grab him, their limbs wrapping around and around his body like spiders' thread. Behind their smudgy lenses, Rutherford's eyes widened with fear.

"Give it to me," said Aurelia gently.

The shadows' fingers lengthened and groped, and Olive saw the gold pendant flash from Rutherford's pocket to Aurelia's hand.

"*Rutherford!*" Olive burst out. "*You* took it?"

"I knew you were considering giving it to this woman, which I believed to be a risk," said Rutherford very rapidly. "I believed that Walter and I could destroy the locket instead, but it resisted our attempts."

"But you didn't *ask!*" Olive shouted back.

"Would you have said yes?"

Olive threw out both arms. "*No!*"

"*My point EXACTLY!*" Rutherford shouted.

"*Enough!*" roared Aldous, through his teeth.

A rush of cold wind blasted the street. Everyone but the McMartins and the shadows was flattened to the ground. The wind seemed to rip the air out of Olive's lungs. Cold pressed down on her like a physical weight. Gasping, she forced her head up from the grass. Two shadows crouched over Rutherford's prone body, and behind them, Walter and Mrs. Dewey were struggling closer. Olive thought she saw flames beginning to flicker in Walter's hands—but then another knot of shadows streaked forward. Walter and Mrs. Dewey were thrown backward into the street, pinned by a web of writhing black arms. Mrs. Dewey let out a shriek that made Olive's stomach twist.

Aurelia turned to Aldous, the locket dangling from her fingers, and lifted the silver box from the crook of her arm.

The wind softened. "What is that?" Aldous asked suspiciously.

"My gift in exchange for yours." Aurelia's voice was more delicate and raspy than ever. She set the box on top of the spellbook.

Olive heard the click of its lid.

A sudden, instinctive dread sizzled through her body. She craned forward, peering through the dimness, but the surrounding shadows and the freezing wind hid whatever lay inside.

"You will see in just a moment," Aurelia whispered, almost as if she had read Olive's thoughts. "But first . . ." She turned to gaze across the lawn. Her sunken eyes glittered as they hooked on Olive's. Very slowly, she lifted the locket chain toward her head. "Well?" she murmured. "Aren't you going to stop me?"

Olive lurched forward. "*Stop!*"

The wind redoubled. It forced her eyes shut, plugging her ears with its howl. The shadows whipped around her legs, dragging her back to the ground. Kicking and clawing, Olive writhed toward the flickering gray blur. "*Stop!*" she screamed again. The wind ripped her voice away so swiftly that Olive herself couldn't hear it.

But then, behind her, another voice gave a shout.

"*Foul sorceress!*" A splotchily colored blur soared toward Aurelia's chest. "Face zee righteous wrath of Lancelot du Lac!"

One black and one orange blur shot after it.

Olive squinted upward, fighting the wind and the thrashing black limbs. Shadows had grasped both Leopold and Horatio. She could see the cats' mouths opening, letting out furious hisses, but the sound was lost in the shriek of the wind. Aurelia's hands were clamped around Harvey's throat. His claw raked a deep slit in her arm.

"Let him go!" Olive screamed. She thrashed one arm free of the entwining shadows and yanked the book of matches from her pocket. With one last desperate lunge forward, she opened its cover.

Aurelia threw Harvey aside. Her hands lashed out and wrenched Olive upright, locking her in a stony embrace. Olive felt the matchbook slip through her fingers.

Icy lips moved against her ear. "Thank you," Aurelia whispered.

Then, shoving Olive backward, Aurelia turned toward the house. Olive stared, pinioned to the ground by a cocoon of shadows, as Aurelia extended her scratched arm over the open silver box. Beads of painted blood fell into the darkness.

Aldous had been overseeing his shadows, but now he turned suddenly toward his wife. His voice was tense and low. "What are you doing, woman?"

"Oh, you know this spell, Aldous," said Aurelia, in a voice that wasn't weak or raspy at all. She dropped the locket into the box's open mouth. "You wrote it in the spellbook yourself." She struck a match. Its flame winked once against the wind before falling out of sight.

Inside the silver box, something ignited—something small—something made of a fire so bright that it didn't have any color at all.

"What is that?" Aldous whispered. "What have you done?"

The strange little smile still clung to Aurelia's face. "Why, these are the ashes of our son," she said, slowly and clearly. "Our only child. The one that you killed."

Out of the silver box, a bright spiral began to rise. It twisted into the air, its coils widening, its light intensifying. The shadows tangling with the cats began to give off wisps of smoke. Olive felt the limbs around her loosen.

"Do you think you can act against me alone, here, in my own home?" Aldous demanded. His face was warped with fury, and his voice was a roar that made the ground itself shake. "In my own *world?*"

"I am not alone," said Aurelia. "You are in this as well: Your portrait. My blood. And our child." Her smile widened. "And he does not fear you anymore."

Olive's mind locked these words together. In the painting of the moonlit forest, she'd watched Annabelle combine Morton's blood, Aldous's ashes, and the portrait from the locket into something made of pure and powerful darkness. But the thing that rose from Aurelia's silver box was something very different. It was *someone* very different.

The fiery spiral continued to grow. Already, its brightness illuminated the whole lawn, making the painted neighbors dart back toward their houses. The Nivenses vanished through their front door. The Aldous-shaped shadows thinned and dissolved like mist at sunrise, leaving nothing behind. The cats hesitated, looking slightly dazed, still scratching at the air. Their green eyes glittered in the strengthening light.

"Did you think I would never know what you had done?" Aurelia asked. "What you had done to our son, because he wasn't like you? Because he was weaker, and softer, and *kinder* than you?"

The glowing spiral wheeled against the night sky, black clouds fizzing and fading around it. Olive watched it, her eyes watering. It flickered with soft white ash, and streaks of fading ink, and with something that looked almost like a person—or like a shadow made entirely of light. It spun through the darkness as if it were dancing

Even Aldous had to back away. He crouched behind the pillars of the porch, his burning eyes glaring from the shadows.

"I did this for you!" he shouted over the lawn. His voice was like broken stone. "I created this entire world for you! I only wanted to keep you safe, forever!"

Aurelia stepped forward. Her robes trailed softly over the grass, their silk edges already beginning to fuzz and dissolve. The light from above illuminated her face. Olive could see that it wasn't just brightening her, but *bleaching* her, erasing the shadows in her cheeks and under her eyes, lifting away her features, stroke by stroke.

"Everything changes, Aldous," she said softly as the light in the sky tightened into one flaring streak. "Even you and I."

"Look out!" Olive heard Harvey scream.

"Miss, back away!" Leopold shouted, flying past her side.

Olive scrambled backward. In the distance, she could see Rutherford and Mrs. Dewey and Walter doing the same. She glanced up again just in time to see the spiral of white fire streak down from the sky.

It seared toward the stone house like a silvery comet. There was no crash as it struck—just a soft puffing sound, as if someone had blown the seeds off a massive dandelion.

A blinding flash filled the air.

Linden Street was washed with light. Dew sizzled on the painted grass. The darkness in the sky seemed to vaporize. Knocked backward, her eyes stinging, Olive squinted up at the stone house.

In the spot where the McMartins had stood, nothing remained but a white burst of fire. Flames unfurled from its center, lashing across the porch. Floorboards split and bubbled. The scorched leaves of hanging ferns drifted down like black snowflakes.

"Olive!" Horatio shouted over the crackling fire. "We have to get everyone out of here!"

A wave of heat rolled toward her, making Olive's eyes water. She squinted through the wavering air. The flames weren't just climbing the house's stone walls; they were spreading outward in every direction at once. The grass, the earth, the sky—everything made of paint—crackled with threads of fire. Already, flames had swept across the lawn, surrounding the silver box and the McMartin spellbook. A bright flower of light shot up as its pages ignited. Olive felt another burst of heat, this one strong enough to suck her breath away.

"Quickly, Olive!" Horatio's voice rang in her ears. "She's destroying it all!"

And suddenly Olive realized just what the cat meant.

Aurelia hadn't merely destroyed Aldous.

She was going to destroy Elsewhere itself.

OLIVE KNEW THAT she was running—she could hear her feet hitting the painted grass, and the smoky air around her had become a grayish blur—but the rest of her mind had switched off. Her body had taken over, flying her toward the back of the stone house.

Behind her, Horatio's commanding voice rose above the fire. "You two, split up and evacuate the Deweys and as many other neighbors as you can find. *Run!*"

Olive's heart was a hot stone at the base of her throat. Choking for air, she leaped up the back steps and through the painted door.

The roar of fire grew louder as she tore from the empty kitchen into the hallway. With each step, she pushed deeper into the crackling steam. Her eyes stung. Her lungs burned. She lurched forward until she reached the spot where the front of the house should have been.

All that remained of the entrance was a wall of strangely colored flames. The painted stones were trying to re-form themselves, but the heat was too fast and strong. Green streaks exploded from the bubbling paint, sweeping inward. The wooden floor had begun to boil.

Mr. and Mrs. Dunwoody were still scribbling away as Olive raced through the library doors.

"Dad!" Olive grabbed him by the sleeve. There was something strange about its fabric; something slick and slippery. "Mom! We have to get out of here! The house is on fire!"

Mr. Dunwoody looked up at the library's farthest wall. The glimmering books were puffing into flame one by one, like fiery kernels of popcorn. The haze in his eyes seemed to thin.

"You appear to be correct, Olive." He pushed back the desk chair. "Funny—I didn't hear the smoke detectors."

"That *is* funny," said Mrs. Dunwoody, whose eyes were also looking clearer. "Especially as I recall you changing the batteries when we moved in, which leaves us well within the recommended twelve-month usage limit. Perhaps we should—"

"We can check batteries later," said Olive, hustling both parents toward the double doors. "Let's go."

"Is there any chance that the batteries *themselves* weren't new?" asked Mr. Dunwoody as they hurried along the hallway. The rug burst into flames behind them.

"I doubt it, dear, as we've only owned this house for six months, and I don't believe we packed old batteries in order to bring them here with us," Mrs. Dunwoody answered.

"Ah, yes," said Mr. Dunwoody. Blue-green fire snaked along a brushstroke in the plaster just to his left, opening the wall like a zipper. "A logical point, darling."

Olive managed to get both of her parents through the back door just before a gust of flame ripped down the hallway, tearing open the painted ceiling. Jets of blue fire rippled along the edges of the rooftops.

A huge orange cat met them in the yard. "There you are!" he cried. "Let's get your parents out of here quickly!"

"Shh!" Olive hissed. "They'll *hear* you!"

"Yes," said Horatio shortly. "Well, they are going to have to climb through a picture frame while holding my tail in a moment. We've got larger concerns ahead." With a sharp look at the Dunwoodys, Horatio bounded ahead of them down the misty hill.

Olive ran after him, dragging her parents by their smooth, slippery hands.

They all tumbled through the frame into the unlit hallway. Leopold and Harvey waited on the carpet. Walter, Rutherford, and Mrs. Dewey stood beside them, their milky eyes now clear and intent. Huddled in the shadows several steps away were Mr. Fitzroy, the old woman with the nightcap, and several other neighbors in nightclothes.

But Olive wasn't paying attention—not to the people around her, not even to the burning sensation in her own fingers and feet. She was watching her parents.

The moment they were through the frame, Mr. and Mrs. Dunwoody had crumpled to the floor. Their eyes were closed, and their teeth were gritted. Mrs. Dunwoody let out a muffled scream. Olive had never seen her parents in such pain—not even two years ago, when Mr. Dunwoody had been so preoccupied by an algorithm that he'd walked straight into the coffee table and broken two toes. She knew what they were feeling. She'd felt it herself when she'd stayed Elsewhere too long and her body had begun to turn to paint. It was like having your skin skewered by a swarm of icy needles. And the longer you'd stayed, the deeper the needles went.

She dropped to her knees next to her mother. "Are

they going to be all right?" she asked, her voice wobbling.

Mrs. Dewey knelt down beside her. "That they feel pain means they're still *able* to feel," she said firmly, before pressing her head to each of the Dunwoodys' chests. Olive noticed that Mrs. Dewey kept clenching her own shiny hands. Nearby, Walter was chafing his arms, and Rutherford was jiggling anxiously from foot to foot—but with Rutherford, this could have meant almost anything.

"I hear heartbeats," said Mrs. Dewey, straightening up at last. "It's not going to be pleasant, but they're alive, and they'll stay that way. Help me move them into Olive's room," she told Walter and Rutherford. "We'll make them as comfortable as we can."

Starting with a moaning Mr. Dunwoody, Rutherford, Walter, and Mrs. Dewey struggled off through the nearest bedroom door.

Olive glanced around the chilly hallway. "Where are Morton and his parents?" she asked, squinting into the shadows.

"We could not find zem, milady," Harvey spoke up. "We searched zair house, and we called to zem—but zey did not emerge. We could not delay saving zee othairs."

Olive turned toward the painting of Linden Street. Even without the spectacles, she could see the fire rippling within the canvas. It wasn't just in the distance anymore. It was surging outward, its reaching green-gold limbs grasping each house, climbing each painted tree.

From the corner of her eye, Olive caught another flicker. In the painting of the bowl of strange fruit, a tongue of fire was licking at the table. A crackling grass fire was sweeping toward the trees in the painting of the moonlit forest. Down the staircase, the first hints of smoke were coming from the silvery lake.

"Oh, no," she whispered to the cats. "It's spreading."

"Elsewhere has many pieces, but they are all connected," said Horatio quickly. "Aldous could move between them. *Magic* can move between them."

"So what do we do?" Olive watched a ribbon of flame climb a painted tree. "How do we stop it?"

The cats exchanged a look.

"It's too late to stop it, miss," said Leopold. "Even if it were an ordinary fire. Which it isn't."

Olive grabbed a hank of her own hair and pulled. "Maybe Walter or Mrs. Dewey could—"

"Zat would be like a duel between a broadsword and a begonia," said Harvey.

Olive whirled back toward the burning painting of Linden Street. There might still be time to find Morton and his parents, if they were lucky. But what about the three stonemasons and Baltus in the kitchen downstairs? What about the friendly orchestra, and the castle porter, and Roberto the Magnificent, and the dancing girls, and the Parisian pigeons? What about everybody else?

She spun toward the cats. "We need to get everyone out. *Everyone.*"

Horatio's eyes widened. "And then what? We can't simply let them roam free; they won't be safe!"

"They won't be safe in burning paintings either," Olive pointed out. "They *need* us." She crouched down in front of the cats. "All this time, you've protected this house. Now you can protect the people *in* it instead."

The change in Horatio's face was tiny, but Olive knew him well enough to see it. She turned to the others. "Leopold, Harvey: Go and get everyone out of Elsewhere. People. Animals. *Everyone.*"

Leopold straightened to his fullest height. "Aye, aye, miss!"

"Oui, milady!" Harvey added.

With a salute and a bow, the two of them flew off into the darkness.

Olive met Horatio's eyes. "Let's find Morton."

Back inside the painting of Linden Street, the cool, misty air had turned hot. The oily stench of burning paint hung in the air. Olive and Horatio tore up the hillside, avoiding the ripples of fire that flowed down it, leaving only greasy ash behind.

They raced along the deserted street. The fire had nearly finished with the old stone house. A sooty smudge marked the spot where Aldous and Aurelia had stood. The rest of the house was a heap of smoldering, sizzling black. The fire had moved onward, climbing from one treetop to another, swallowing the next houses in the row. Mrs. Dewey's house was in flames. And the Nivenses' tall gray house was a tower of writhing light.

"Morton!" Olive yelled. "*Morton!*"

There was no answer but the roar of fire.

Horatio streaked ahead. "I'll check inside!"

"Horatio, no!" Olive panted after him. "It's too dangerous!"

"Go to the backyard," the cat shouted over his shoulder. "I'll look for another way out!" With a bound, he disappeared through a hole in the flames.

Olive trampled a patch of grass that was still struggling to repair itself and skidded to a stop in the backyard. She stared up at the tall gray house. One small portion of the upper story was not yet on fire. Below the still-solid rooftop, an open window exhaled streams of smoke. The wall below the window was a mass of flames.

"Horatio!" she shouted, between coughs. "There's an open window back here!"

There was no answer, whether Horatio heard her or not.

Olive looked desperately around. As she surveyed the scorched yard, she noticed something she hadn't spotted before.

The fire wasn't just eating the objects in this painted world. It was eating everything behind them: air, earth, canvas. What was left after even the paint and ash were gone was *nothing*—just blackness, like a hole without any bottom.

A gap was opening in the earth before the old stone house, where the fire had begun. As Olive stared, the gap widened into a trench large enough to swallow a person whole. And as for what would happen if a person fell *through* that trench—

"Olive!" shouted a voice.

Olive glanced up at the burning house. A round, pale face had appeared in the only remaining window.

"Morton!" she shouted. "Is Horatio with you?"

"Yes!" Morton shouted back. "And Mama and Papa too!"

"Then jump! You can make it!"

Morton shook his head wildly. "Mama won't *leave!*"

"Mrs. Nivens!" Olive shouted, raising her voice even higher. "If you hurt anything, it will fix itself!"

"No," Morton yelled. "She doesn't *want* to leave!"

Fresh streaks of fire rose toward the window like the fingers of a groping hand. The air thickened with the stench of smoke. Olive coughed, each breath scraping her throat like steel wool.

"You're going to have to throw her," Horatio's voice commanded from inside the window. A flash of orange fur appeared in the opening. "Harold, Morton: Pick her up."

Mary's struggling form appeared on the sill. Her sweet, pretty face was twisted with fear. "No!" Olive heard her shout. "There's nothing out there for us! We *belong* here!"

"Ready?" Harold's voice boomed. "One . . . two . . . three!"

With a shriek, Mary flew through the window and plunged to the lawn below.

"Sorry, Mama!" Morton called after her.

Morton leaped next, his nightshirt billowing, and landed with an almost-proud bounce on the grass. Harold dove after him. The moment he crossed the sill, a gust of flames poured through it, nearly catching the tail of his jacket. The wall crackled. The painted glass dissolved in a burst of smoke. The flames slithered upward, groping for the rooftop.

Horatio halted on the sill. His eyes flicked from the house's interior to the disappearing lawn below. "Get them away!" he shouted down to Olive. "I'll be right behind you!"

The roof tore open with a fountain of blue flame. The upper floor sagged. Olive heard Mary's and Harold's gasps, slashed by the pitch of her own shriek.

"Run!" she screamed, shoving Morton and his parents ahead of her.

They raced down the smoking hillside, leaping over the widening chasms.

In the scorched lawn where the stone house had stood, Olive spotted one small, terrified spider scuttling over the grass. She swept it up into her palm before running on.

At the picture frame, Olive stopped. She glanced over her shoulder, looking for a flash of orange fur, but all she could see was a row of fiery coals where Linden Street's grand houses had stood.

She banged at the surface of the painting. Her hands stung so badly that she gasped. When she glanced down at her palms, she saw that the skin was perfectly smooth—too smooth. Her feet were numb. Of course they were, Olive realized. She had been inside Elsewhere much too long. Even with Aldous gone, some wisps of its power clearly remained.

Her body flared with panic. Her breaths came faster, each one dragging in a prickly swirl of smoke. She banged at the surface again.

Out in the dim hallway, one of the painted neighbors looked up. She turned to another person, speaking quickly. Olive watched the message travel along the hall until suddenly a black cat leaped into the frame.

"Leopold," Olive choked, "please take the Nivenses

out." She set the frightened spider on his back. "And this spider too."

"What about you, miss?"

"I—" Olive stopped, coughing. "I'll wait for Horatio."

Leopold nodded once. "Be careful, miss."

Olive watched Leopold, then Morton, then Harold, and finally reluctant Mary disappear safely through the frame. Then she turned back toward what remained of Linden Street.

As Olive ran up the hill a final time, the air was growing hot and thin. Smoke coated her mouth and throat. The ground beneath her felt brittle; her feet crackled in the burned brushstrokes, sending flakes of oily ash into the air.

Cracks had appeared all around, leading down to nothingness. Olive leaped over them, skirting the huge, scorched hole that had emerged in the McMartin yard, racing with a new burst of panic toward what remained of the Nivens house. Her numb legs just managed to keep her upright.

The tall gray house was only a black heap. A few embers still glowed in its foundations. The walls had collapsed into ashy lumps, where wisps of paint undulated gently in the rising air.

"Horatio?" Olive called, running toward the back.

The window where she'd glimpsed the orange cat

had dissolved into the smoking rubble. Burned paint bubbled where the back door had been. Another black crevasse was widening across the yard.

"Horatio!" Olive called again.

A cloud of smoke rushed into her open mouth. She doubled over, coughing, inching closer to the embers. Her legs and arms could barely feel the heat. Her fingers might as well have been made of plastic. Olive wondered if a spark from the fire would incinerate her as quickly as Lucinda and Annabelle, making her vanish in one sudden, blazing streak.

But she wasn't going to turn away. Horatio was here somewhere. She couldn't abandon him, frightened or trapped or hurt, or wondering why she had never come back.

She crept into the sizzling remains of the house. Her eyes fogged and watered. Itchy sweat dribbled down her collar. Her lungs gave an angry throb as she inched forward into the heat's core.

Something that had been a wall fizzled away as Olive moved closer. Through the smoke, she could see another bottomless hole where the staircase had stood, and a black smudge that had once been the hallway floor . . . and, half buried in a pile of ash, its rich orange color dimmed to gray, one long, thick, motionless tail.

Horatio.

Olive plunged forward.

The painted ground snapped under her weight. She leaped as the floor crumbled beneath her, landing beside the big orange cat. The smoke was thick, and the stifling air was warped with heat, but she could see that the cat didn't move.

He didn't open a bright green eye, or twitch a whisker, or stir one single strand of fur as Olive dragged his limp body out of the ash and into her arms.

Clutching Horatio's body to her chest, Olive lunged back out of the burned house. The black fissures in the earth were widening, and she had to veer left and right to avoid the dissolving spots, once slipping and catching herself on one rubbery hand just in time to keep from plunging down a cliff that had no bottom. Her other hand was wrapped tight around Horatio, holding him close.

By the time she staggered down what had been the grassy, misty hillside, the air was nearly black. Even the smoke that filled her lungs was burning away, replaced by nothingness. She was running out of air. The painted world crumbled behind her as Olive placed one numb hand on the picture frame.

The surface of the painting didn't budge.

With Horatio in her arms, it should have softened, letting her through . . .

But instead, her hand pounded against the barrier as though it were made of glass.

Olive's heart tightened.

This meant the cat in her arms was—

He was—

"Milady?" Harvey's splotchy body appeared in the frame. "Take hold of my tail and—" His eyes caught on Horatio, lying limp in Olive's arms. "Oh," he whispered.

With her free hand, Olive grasped the cat's tail. She crawled through the frame, lifting Horatio as gently as she could. As her feet kicked through the surface that final time, Olive felt a stiffening around her, the jellyish surface of the painting turning brittle and thin. Then, with an explosion of vaporous shards, the last fragments of the painting dissolved.

Olive threw a glance over her shoulder. Where the painting of Linden Street had hung, there was now only an empty gold frame. She turned away.

For several minutes, she merely crouched against the hallway wall, cradling the huge orange cat and taking deep, raspy breaths. The bristles of invisible hairbrushes were pounding at her foot soles, and her hands felt like they'd been stung by a hundred tiny bees, but Olive didn't make a sound. She knew if she even opened her mouth, all that would come out would be one long, hopeless scream.

The house around her kept silent too.

At the edges of her bleary vision, Olive could see Harvey and Leopold standing guard. The painted faces of neighbors and musicians and dancers encircled her, worried and watchful. Morton inched through the crowd. He hesitated next to Olive for a moment. Then he touched Horatio's side very gently, running his small fingers over the thick orange fur.

"Good kitty," he whispered.

Horatio didn't move.

"Grandma?" Olive heard Rutherford's voice coming from somewhere that seemed very far away. "Can we do anything?"

Mrs. Dewey's round form bent down next to Olive. "For a creature like this . . . For a *problem* like this . . ." She examined the cat's limp form. Then she shook her head. "That would take more powerful magic than any witch possesses." She patted Olive's shoulder. "Olive dear," she murmured. "I am so sorry."

Still cradling Horatio in her arms, Olive rose slowly to her feet. She carried him across the hallway. Harvey and Leopold flanked her. Morton and Rutherford followed them as far as the head of the stairs. There they stopped, letting Olive and the cats continue down the steps alone.

At the bottom of the staircase, Leopold and Harvey stopped too. They seemed to know that Olive needed these few moments with Horatio. They stood at attention on either side of the steps, their eyes watchful, but a bit dimmer than before.

Olive trailed through the darkened lower hall. To either side of her, paintings were turning to ash and dwindling away, leaving only their empty frames behind. She carried Horatio past the parlor doors where a collection of Parisians and pigeons had gathered. They watched her pass, keeping still.

Olive thought of the dozens of times she'd slammed through the front door and seen Horatio's wide orange face appear in the very same spot, making sure that she was securely inside.

"Look at everything you kept safe," she whispered to the cat.

The three stonemasons and Baltus sat in the kitchen. They all hopped to their feet as Olive entered.

"Miss Olive!" said one of the men. Then his eyes landed on the furry lump in her arms. All of them went silent. Even Baltus stopped jumping. One of the masons took off his dusty black cap and held it quietly in his hands.

Olive carried Horatio through the family room,

past the windows that looked out into the backyard. The winter wind had died away. Snow fell, soft and thick, outside the panes. It was very late, Olive could tell, but the moon cast its sheen over the snow, turning everything to silver.

"We're really safe, Horatio," Olive whispered. "My parents, and Leopold, and Harvey, and the Nivenses and Deweys, and all the people from Elsewhere. The whole house. You kept us all safe."

The cat didn't stir. A beam of moonlight fell across his face, revealing his closed eyes.

Olive turned and headed back down the hall.

A knot of girls in gauzy dresses stood between the open library doors. They had been whispering together, but they hushed as Olive approached. As one, they stepped back, their dresses rustling, to form an aisle for Olive.

Olive passed through.

Inside the library, the huge frame that had enclosed the painted meadow hung empty, its corners blackened with soot. The books gleamed softly on their shelves. The pine tree, its limbs hung with pearly glass balls, breathed its spicy sweetness into the air.

Olive carried Horatio to the worn velvet couch and sat down. The cat sagged in her lap, cold and heavy. The springs in the ancient cushions creaked.

Then that sound died away, and the entire house was still.

It wasn't the stillness of sleep, or of danger, or the lonely stillness of a place where no one lived. It was a different kind of stillness. It was the stillness of a moon-bright night in midwinter, when everyone is safe indoors.

"We did it, Horatio," Olive whispered into the cat's ear. "The McMartins are gone for good. You kept the house safe all along." Her eyes filled with tears. She rubbed her chin against Horatio's furry forehead. "You did such a good job. And now your job is done."

Then, for a while, Olive cried.

She sniffled, and wiped her nose on her cuff, and she sobbed out loud once or twice as the dancing girls squeezed each other's hands and watched, hanging their heads.

Olive sniffled again. One teardrop plopped from the tip of her nose to Horatio's ear. The ear twitched, flicking it away, but Olive was wiping her face and didn't notice.

Something soft and furry bumped at her arm. Olive jerked upright, her heart leaping with hope, but it was only Leopold and Harvey settling on the couch beside her.

They gazed down at the cat in Olive's lap, their faces solemn.

"I didn't get to thank him." Olive's throat tightened again. "He warned me not to let Aurelia out, but I didn't listen. And he was right."

"Perhaps," said Leopold, very softly.

"I should have told him I was sorry. And I should have told him how thankful I was."

"He knows," said Harvey, in his own quiet voice.

"I hope so." Olive blotted her eyes on her sleeve and stared down at the motionless cat. She gave his fur a stroke. "Maybe it's silly, but I didn't—I didn't think you *could* die."

"Whatever gave you that idea?" said a dry, slow voice from Olive's lap.

Olive froze.

"We live until something stops us," said Horatio, in a voice that was much softer than usual.

"And then . . . ?" Olive breathed.

"And then, if we have a very good reason, we can *start* living again."

Olive grabbed Horatio in both arms and squeezed him as hard as she could.

"Considering that I *wasn't* breathing a moment ago, you might allow me to do it now," said the cat, in a voice that was muffled by Olive's neck.

Olive loosened the squeeze a teeny bit. "But I'm part of your reason, aren't I?" she whispered into his ear. "At least a little part?"

"Yes, Olive," said Horatio's muffled and grumpy voice. "You are more than a little part of the reason."

By the time Olive stepped back through the library doors with Horatio at her side, word had spread. Perhaps Leopold and Harvey had carried the news up and down stairs, or perhaps the house itself had sensed it, but its wintery stillness was thawing fast.

The orchestra had moved downstairs to the formal parlor. As Olive crossed the entryway, she could hear them launching into an out-of-tune waltz. The dancers swayed in the hallway, spinning in small circles and bumping into one another, and the Parisian café patrons joined in, the fat pigeons waddling between their feet.

"This way, this way . . ." The castle porter's lantern bobbled as he led a flock of geese from the attic's painted farmyard safely through the crowd.

Behind Olive, there was a rush of giggles. She turned to see the dancing girls flit off toward the family room, with Harvey hurrying behind. "Fair maidens!" he cried. "You need not run from zee chivalrous Lancelot!"

In the bathroom doorway, the bathing woman tightened her towel. The bird from the fencepost perched on a wall sconce, looking crankily down at everyone.

The painted neighbors had gathered on the staircase. Roberto the Magnificent stood above them, spreading his skinny arms. "As you can see, my hands are empty," he announced. "But watch closely . . ."

A furry blur shot past Olive's legs. Leopold, followed by Baltus, charged up the stairs into the crowd.

"Voila!" shouted Roberto as a bouquet of roses that *didn't* shoot right back into his sleeve appeared in his hand. At the same instant, Leopold took a graceful leap, landing safely on the magician's shoulders, and Baltus took a much less graceful leap straight at the magician's stomach. Roberto, cat, dog, and several neighbors toppled in a squealing, kicking heap.

It was at that moment that the Dunwoodys emerged from Olive's bedroom.

They blinked around at the people in old-fashioned pajamas and the magician who'd just wrestled a dog to the floor.

Mr. Dunwoody leaned toward his wife. "What door did we just step through?" he murmured.

"Mom! Dad!" Olive hurried up the stairs. "Um— all the power went out on Linden Street. It must have been the snow or something. Everybody's heat turned off, except ours—so, to be safe, they all came here."

The pajama-clad people nodded. Baltus gave Roberto a slobbery lick on the face. Downstairs, a goose honked.

Olive swallowed. "These are our neighbors."

Mr. Dunwoody's eyebrows rose. "Oh, I see!" he said cheerily. "In that case, welcome, everyone! Make yourselves at home."

"Alice Dunwoody," said Olive's mother, holding out her hand to the old woman in the nightcap.

"Alec Dunwoody," said Olive's father, shaking Mr. Fitzroy's hand.

The Dunwoodys made their way through the hall and down the stairs, greeting neighbors on every side.

"Excellent thinking," said Rutherford as the stonemasons appeared to haul Baltus away. "A reasonable and almost truthful explanation."

"They'll be all right," Mrs. Dewey promised, nodding at Olive's parents. "And don't worry; I'll whip up something that will erase their memories of most of this."

"What about everybody else?" Olive asked. She watched the castle porter set down his lantern to shake Mr. Dunwoody's hand. One of the dancing ladies was teaching Mrs. Dunwoody the two-step. "Can you fix them?"

Mrs. Dewey let out a soft sigh. "They're not *alive*, Olive. And making something not alive be alive again is beyond any magician on earth."

"Oh." Olive took another look at the Nivens family. Morton had left his parents to watch Roberto's magic show, but Mary and Harold still stood apart, Mary's face buried in Harold's old-fashioned jacket.

"And Horatio was correct: They won't be safe in the real world," added Rutherford. "There are too many dangers, on top of the threat of exposure. You saw what a struggle it was for the Nivens family, and they were only out for a few days."

Olive looked around at the hollow picture frames. Silvery water, rolling hills, blooming flowers, eternally glowing moons: Everything had vanished. There was nothing left to fix. There was only emptiness.

Meanwhile, filling the house were dozens of friends and neighbors and not-quite-animals, all needing someplace safe to stay. As Olive gazed at the empty frames and the unused bedrooms and the faces of the painted neighbors and Walter and Rutherford and Mrs. Dewey, a brand-new plan began to sketch itself in her mind.

She sucked in a breath.

"I think I have an idea," she whispered.

It would be a lie to say that the old stone house returned quickly to normal.

Mr. and Mrs. Dunwoody thought it did, but they had both eaten double portions of Mrs. Dewey's Crunchy Caramel Coffee Cake, and woke up the next day unable to remember their own middle names.

"The long-term memories will return," Mrs. Dewey assured Olive. "But for the next couple of days, keep a close eye on them. Make sure they turn off the oven, take the keys out of the ignition before locking the car, and so forth." She opened a dusty jar, sniffing carefully at its contents. "Walter, hand me that blue glass bowl, would you?"

Olive, Walter, and Mrs. Dewey stood in the stone room at the end of the basement tunnel. On the shelves around them, ingredients winked in their dusty glass jars. Sheets of yellowed paper, crisscrossed with tape and scrawled with Aldous's handwriting, were arranged on the high wooden table. Leopold sat beside them, keeping watch over the goings-on. It was freezing in the underground chamber, so everyone— except for Leopold, who was equipped with his own fur coat and mittens—was bundled up in winter jackets and hats and gloves. Two cheery gas lamps burned on the table, making the air bright enough to reveal their puffs of breath.

While Mrs. Dewey filled the blue glass bowl with a stream of white liquid, and Walter ground what looked like glossy beetle shells in the big stone mortar, Olive bounced up and down, rubbing her arms with a mixture of impatience, cold, and excitement.

"She'll be here soon," she said, watching Walter mash the gleaming black powder. "Are we almost ready?"

"Almost," said Mrs. Dewey. "Just one more shade to go."

Between her bowl and Walter's mortar, a beaker of bright yellow juice bubbled over a candle. Feathers and petals and leaves and tiny bones waited on little brass trays. A row of jars already filled with vivid pigments stood along the table's edge.

"You can take these upstairs with you now and see

how things are progressing," said Mrs. Dewey, loading the full jars into a basket. "It took us three tries to get that red shade to work, but I think we finally did it!"

Holding the basket carefully, Olive tiptoed back along the tunnel, up the rickety ladder, and out of the basement.

The empty spot on the kitchen wall where the painting of Baltus and the stonemasons should have hung made Olive pause, even though she had gone through the entire house herself, removing the hollow picture frames. With Aldous and Elsewhere gone, they had dangled on their hooks in a perfectly ordinary way. Olive guessed that even Alec and Alice would notice if their house was suddenly decorated by a collection of empty frames. Besides, looking at them had made Olive's chest ache.

Elsewhere had been dangerous and strange, but it had also been beautiful. Sometimes it had even been wonderful. And, for a while, it had been hers.

Giving the empty spot on the wall one last glance, Olive headed onward down the hallway. The jars in their basket clinked softly.

Inside the pink bedroom at the end of the upper hall, Olive set down the paints. The painting that had decorated this room—an ancient town somewhere in Italy or Greece—had burned away like all the others, revealing the attic's hidden entryway. Olive opened the heavy door and hurried up the steps.

All the inhabitants of Elsewhere had been packed into the attic. The neighbors from Linden Street were settled comfortably on the old sheet-draped furniture. The orchestra and dancers had made themselves at home in a corner. The castle porter and the stonemasons were building a fort out of boxes. Baltus was tied securely to the leg of a hefty wooden bureau, where he bounced and barked at the splotchily colored cat who sat on the rafters, just out of his reach.

"That's right, me old matey," Harvey growled, watching Baltus with the eye that wasn't covered by a patch. "Ye can caterwaul till the ocean echoes, but ye will never catch the wily Captain Blackpaw!"

Baltus made a jump so high that it jerked the entire bureau forward. Harvey shot across the rafters and hid behind the sewing dummy.

"How is it going?" Olive asked Morton and Rutherford, who stood together in the center of the room, their heads bowed over an open notebook.

"Very well," said Rutherford.

"Very *very* well," said Morton.

"I believe we've spoken to everyone," said Rutherford, leafing through the notebook's pages, "and we've managed to collect all viable requests."

Olive looked over the list, reading aloud. "'Daytime, nighttime, a circus, a castle, a meadow full of flowers . . .'"

"And a pond!" said one of the dancing girls.

"And chairs," said another. "Soft ones."

"'A café beside the Seine,'" Olive read on. "'A stage under the stars, a spiderweb, snow and sleds, houses, moonlight, a five-foot bathtub with gold taps . . .'"

The woman wearing the towel gave an emphatic nod.

"'A library, farmland, a hedge maze, bricks and mortar, a bone to chew on . . .'" Olive paused. "Who asked for an Apatosaurus?"

Morton raised his hand.

"You know about Apatosauruses?"

Morton glanced at Rutherford, who was looking at the floor. "Apatosaurus *was* first described by paleontologists in 1877," Rutherford murmured.

"You thought a dinosaur was a viable request?" Olive asked.

"They're herbivores!" said Rutherford defensively. "It would be passive. Whatever it tried to eat would just grow back, anyway. And we'd have the chance to see an *almost* living dinosaur! It's every paleontologist's dream!"

"No dinosaurs," said Olive, drawing a line through the Apatosaurus.

"Olive," said a voice from the attic steps.

Olive turned around.

Horatio's fluffy orange head peered over the top of the staircase. "She's here," he announced.

"Let me know if you think of anything else!" said Olive, ripping the list out of the notebook and flying down the attic steps behind the cat.

The front door was just creaking open as Olive and Horatio reached the top of the main staircase. A blast of cold, sunny air whooshed up from the entryway. Standing in a patch of sun, her necklaces glittering and keys jingling, was the genuine Ms. Teedlebaum.

"Florence!" said Mrs. Dunwoody, ushering the art teacher into the house. "What a nice surprise. Is there something we can help you with?"

"She's helping *me,* Mom," said Olive quickly, bounding down into the entry. Behind her, Horatio slunk out of sight. "Remember? You said I could paint a mural in one of the guest bedrooms, and you suggested asking Ms. Teedlebaum to help me?"

Mrs. Dunwoody blinked. "I did?"

"Yes," said Olive rapidly. "And you promised to make a big donation to the art museum in exchange."

"Oh," said Mrs. Dunwoody. She looked from Olive to Ms. Teedlebaum, who both beamed brightly back at her. Mrs. Dunwoody gave them a tentative smile. "I don't know where my mind is today. I think I could use another cup of coffee. What about you, Florence?"

"Oh, I never know where my mind is," said Ms. Teedlebaum, setting down an armload of paper bags and unwrapping herself from the sparkly shawl that spiraled around and around her body. "I'm lucky if I can find both hands in the morning." She pulled her arms out of her sleeves. "Look! There they are!"

"Let me hang that up, Ms. Teedlebaum," Olive offered, tossing the shawl onto the coatrack. "Then we can head upstairs and get started."

"Wonderful." Ms. Teedlebaum picked up the bags again. "Lead the way!"

Mrs. Dunwoody watched them climb up the staircase, smiling a confused but happy smile.

"Honestly, Olive," Ms. Teedlebaum said as they turned the corner and headed down the upper hallway, "I'm just delighted to have this distraction today. It's been a traumatic week." She let out a sigh. "First, it appears that the museum was broken into, although we haven't been able to figure out if anything is missing. And then one of our security guards simply *vanished.*"

"Really?" said Olive. "That's weird."

"Yes," Ms. Teedlebaum agreed. "And he was such a talented artist himself—very quiet, very reclusive, very gifted with paint. He asked me to model for a portrait once."

"Really?" said Olive again.

"It was an excellent likeness. Well—the proportions were a little off, but I doubt most people would even notice." She shrugged. "Honestly, I'm not a fan of that old-fashioned, realistic style."

"Oh, good," said Olive, leading the way into the pink room. "Because here's what I'd like to paint . . ."

Olive and Ms. Teedlebaum worked until the light that fell through the lace curtains turned from diamond-bright to pearly gray. Rutherford delivered replacement jars of paint. Mrs. Dunwoody wandered in with cups of tea and cocoa, forgot what she was doing, and wandered out again. Olive's arms started to look as though she had a case of rainbow-colored chicken pox. The tips of Ms. Teedlebaum's kinky hair dragged through the wet paint, adding their own delicate brushstrokes to the work.

At last, when the downstairs clock chimed six, Ms. Teedlebaum stopped painting. Olive put down her palette. Together, they looked around the room.

Brushes and jars and palettes and drop cloths were scattered across the floor. The smell of fresh paint hovered in the air, tangling with the older scents of mothballs and stale potpourri. And on the walls around them, just beginning to dry, was a brand-new painted world.

On one wall, sunrise poured over a field of sparkling

snow. The snow dwindled away into rolling farmland and leafy forests, where a huge stone castle thrust up from the greenery. A meadow full of flowers—and a circle of comfortable chairs—spread out into the Parisian skyline, where a café of little wrought iron tables waited beside the River Seine. Around the corner, the painted daylight dimmed above a street that looked very much like Linden Street. Sturdy old houses gazed at each other across the quiet pavement. Candles winked softly in curtained windows. The hill rolled down to a beautiful pavilion, complete with a raised stage, orchestra seats, a grand piano, and a huge dance floor. Beyond the pavilion, where stars thickened in a violet sky, a torch-lit circus arranged its striped tents. Boats shaped like swans and ducks floated on a silvery lake. One big, beautiful bathtub, complete with gold taps, bubbled near the baseboard. Ms. Teedlebaum had even painted a massive heap of dog toys, safely enclosed inside a high fence.

"I love it!" Ms. Teedlebaum cried, clapping her painty hands. "The circus! The castle! The *bathtub!* It's a fantasy world! Who wouldn't want to live in this place?"

Olive smiled up at the row of painted houses. "Nobody," she said.

Ms. Teedlebaum paused, tapping a still blue-tinted brush against her chin. "Are you sure you *don't* want to add an Apatosaurus?"

"I'm sure," said Olive.

Olive walked Ms. Teedlebaum out to her car. The old stone house glowed cheerily behind them. The air was cold, but less bitter than before—or maybe Olive was simply remembering it that way. She waved as the rusty station wagon rolled slowly down the hill.

Then she froze.

Standing across the street, staring straight at her, was the girl with the red coat and the dark eyeliner.

"Hi," said the girl.

"Hello," said Olive, in a not-very-friendly way.

The girl hurried across the street. She stopped, facing Olive, on the icy sidewalk. For a moment, they simply stared at each other.

"Have you been *watching* me?" Olive asked, before she realized that she was going to say anything at all.

"What? No," said the girl, frowning. "Well . . . Kind of. Yes." She lowered her voice and glanced in the direction of the vanished station wagon. "I've been keeping an eye on your house. Because I think someone might be trying to rob you." She lowered her voice even further. "*Ms. Teedlebaum.*"

"Ms. Teedlebaum?" Olive echoed.

"I saw her sneaking around over here, late at night," the girl went on, speaking fast. "She was talking to somebody who came out of that tall gray house, the one everybody said was empty. At the museum, she was talking about how your house belonged to this great, famous artist, and then that security guard asked me to bring that note to your house." The girl leaned closer to Olive. "I think they might be *in cahoots!*"

This sounded so much like something Harvey would say that Olive nearly snorted out loud.

"Wait," she said, catching herself. "*You* brought that note? The one that was on my porch?"

"I saw Ms. Teedlebaum come to your house the other night and never come out again, and today she shows up and spends hours and hours inside, and . . ." A blush began to rise on the girl's cheeks. "She might be *casing the joint.*"

This time Olive couldn't stop the snort.

"No," she said, laughing. "She just came over to help me paint a mural."

"Oh." The girl's face fell. She took a step backward. "That's all?"

"That's all." Olive glanced around the darkening street. "How did you see all this, anyway?"

"I'm staying with my grandparents over winter break. The Butlers." The girl looked down at her boots. "My bedroom window faces your house, so I couldn't really *help* it. I just thought . . . I thought I might be able to help."

Olive put her hands in her pockets. "Do you like mysteries?"

The girl met her eyes. "Kind of. Yes."

"Me too." Olive shuffled awkwardly in place. "It's . . . it was nice of you to try to solve this one. Thanks for trying to help me."

The girl shrugged, looking embarrassed. "It would have been more helpful if it was a *real* mystery."

Olive shrugged too. "Maybe next time."

They looked at each other for another moment. Olive started to smile.

The girl smiled back. "I'd better get back inside," she said, heading toward the street. She stopped halfway across and gave Olive another look. "My name's Vanessa, by the way."

"My name is Olive."

The girl's smile widened. "I know." Then she ran the rest of the way across the street and through the Butlers' sturdy front door.

Back inside the old stone house, the Dunwoodys were making dinner. Neither of them would remember that the other had already added the cheddar to the big dish of macaroni and cheese, which meant that they would both add it again, resulting in a macaroni casserole that was four times as delicious as usual. They had also invited the Deweys and Walter to join them—multiple times, because they had both forgotten that they'd done so—and at that very moment, Mrs. Dewey was down the street in her own cozy kitchen, spreading the last strokes of frosting onto the Dark Chocolate Cherry Cake that they would all share for dessert.

But Olive didn't know that these surprises were ahead of her. She just knew that her parents were safe, and the kitchen was full of warmth and light and good smells, and upstairs, her friends were waiting for her.

Horatio, Harvey, and Leopold stood beside her in the pink bedroom.

"It worked," said Horatio, staring into the drying painting.

"It's almost as good as Elsewhere," Olive whispered.

"Better," said Leopold firmly.

They gazed around at the glinting walls.

"Horatio," Olive began, "I've been wondering: How did Aurelia know what Aldous did to Albert? You told me Annabelle buried her parents in the graveyard, inside the painting of the Scottish hills. So how did Aurelia end up with . . . with what was inside that silver box?"

An uncomfortable expression flicked across Horatio's wide orange face. "That was my doing, I'm afraid," he said. "I thought she deserved to know the truth about her husband, and about what had happened to her son. And I thought Albert deserved to be remembered by someone who had loved him." Horatio cleared his throat. "It was my responsibility to keep this house and its secrets safe. Instead, intentionally, knowingly . . . I failed."

"No you didn't," said Olive, running her fingertips over the fine hair between Horatio's ears. "It was *my* fault too. I didn't listen to you, and Aurelia used us." She looked at the painted walls again. "But we're all still here. We're together."

"Aye, matey," Harvey whispered.

"I believe the paint is dry enough." With a flourish, Leopold offered Olive his tail. "Would you allow me, miss?"

The entire room began to shimmer as Olive's fingers closed around his sleek black fur. She took a step, and then another step, and then her feet were leaving the worn pink carpet and whispering through a field of dewy grass.

Above her, streaks of sunset faded into a darkness that twinkled with tiny painted stars. Far to her left, she could see the fainter light of daytime above rolling fields of flowers. Leaves rustled in the forest, where the towers of a grand stone castle jutted up amid the green. To her right, waves rippled across the silvery pond. Beyond its shores, the torches of the circus flickered as white horses paced gently in their rings.

And, just ahead of her, the cozy, candlelit houses of Linden Street waited for their families to come home.

"Wow," Olive breathed.

"I couldn't have said it better myself, miss," Leopold replied.

The painted people from the attic shuffled, one or two at a time, onto the dewy grass nearby. Horatio and Harvey stepped in and out of the painted surface, bringing the others through, until the orchestra and dancers and neighbors and birds and Parisians and stonemasons and one small spider were all safe inside.

"My carnival!" shouted Roberto the Magnificent, taking off for the circus tents.

"My bathtub!" cried the woman in the towel.

"Paris!" sighed the Parisians, strolling toward their café with flocks of pigeons scuttling after.

"Harold, look," Mary Nivens whispered.

She and Harold and Morton were gathered in a tight knot just over Olive's shoulder. The light of sunset made Morton's pale face glow.

"It's our house." Morton pointed up the hill. "Right there. Waiting for us."

He flashed Olive a quick, wide smile before tearing off up the hill, his nightshirt rippling into the twilight. Mary and Harold hurried after him.

The others wandered off in streams and clusters, the dancing girls to the meadow, the geese to the farm, the porter and the masons to the castle with Baltus bounding happily behind them. The orchestra and dancers had rushed straight to the pavilion. Olive could hear the sound of a waltz already beginning, soft and sweet as summer mist.

"I don't want to leave," said Olive to the three cats, who had gathered around her. Leopold was watching the rest of Morton's neighbors climb the hill to their homes. Horatio was grooming his silky whiskers. Harvey was eyeing the swan boats on the lake through an imaginary spyglass. "*Boom,*" Olive heard him whisper.

"But you can't stay here," said Horatio. "Paint is still paint, and you're still alive—as long as you don't stay too long." His eyes glittered. "Besides, there are plenty of people in the real world who are waiting for you."

Olive watched the reflected stars shimmer on the water. "That's true."

"You can come back for a visit tomorrow," said Horatio, giving his whiskers a final stroke. "You can always come back." He offered her his slightly scorched tail.

Olive turned back to the pink bedroom. The surface of the painting shimmered as she and the three cats stepped through it. She felt the ground turn back to carpet beneath her feet. The air grew warm and still.

Olive paused for a moment, feeling the house gaze back at her. So much about it had changed . . . and yet, so many things had stayed just the same. And Olive wanted it that way.

Down the hall, in her own bedroom, Aldous McMartin's paint-spattered easel waited, holding Olive's assortment of ordinary paints and canvases. In the shadowy library, her first finished painting sat beneath the pine tree, closed in one of the empty frames and wrapped in silvery paper, with a tag that read *To Mom and Dad*. In the attic above, lace dresses and painted china and one small, battered cannon nestled safely in their corners. Next door, Walter was changing his sweater in what was now his very own bedroom. Down the street, Mrs. Dewey and Rutherford were putting on their winter coats, getting ready to step back out into the twinkling snow.

As Olive stood, thinking, a small brown mouse zipped across the carpet and darted through the open attic door.

"The counterspy!" Harvey shouted. He whipped off his eye patch. "He's infiltrating the head of head-quarters! Espionage is imminent. Agent 1-800 out!" With a bound, he shot off for the attic stairs.

Olive stooped down to give Leopold and Horatio a quick scratch between the ears. Then she headed back out into the house, its history and its secrets and its high stone walls standing safely all around her, and followed her parents' voices down the stairs into the warm yellow light.

Acknowledgements

A story begins as a wavery little daydream in one person's mind. By the time it travels out into the world as an actual, on-paper book, it has been helped along by hundreds of other people. And by the time it becomes a five-book series . . .

. . . I'll try to keep this short.

MASSIVE, LOVE-LADEN THANKS GO TO:

Jessica Dandino Garrison, who is simply the most insightful, understanding, and trusting editor a writer could ever hope for.

Chris Richman, who pulled Olive out of the slush pile and opened the door, and Danielle Chiotti, Michael Stearns, and everyone else at Upstart Crow Literary who has kept that door open.

Illustrator Poly Bernatene, who blends light and shadow, humor and fear, beauty and oddity in a way I can only hope to imitate with words. Poly, *muchísimas gracias con todo mi corazón.*

Regina Castillo, the superheroine of copyediting, who catches things that can't be seen by the eyes of mere mortals, saving authors from themselves again and again.

Designers Natalie Sousa and Jennifer Kelly, who create books that readers love to climb inside.

The editorial, marketing, publicity, sales, and production teams at Penguin, both past and present: Lauri Hornik, Claire Evans, Kristen Tozzo, Steve Meltzer, Courtney Wood, Emilie Bandy, Marie Kent, Samantha Dell'Olio, Kristina Aven, Bernadette Cruz, Molly Sardella, Lindsay Boggs, Elyse Marshall, Shanta Newlin, Vicki Olsen, Jackie Engel, Felicia Frazier, and every one of the sales reps.

All of the librarians, teachers, parents, booksellers, students, journalists, bloggers, artists, and young readers who have hosted me, written to me, penned reviews and interviews, shared your writing and artwork with me, and otherwise made me feel like the luckiest person on earth. (I hope you know who you are, because I sure do.)

Phil and Andrea Hansen and Amelia West, for their brilliant naming of cats.

The furry ones—Ceili and Brom Bones, and the real Leopold, Horatio, and Harvey—for their companionship and inspiration, and without whom life would be a lonelier, duller, cleaner thing.

The battalion of family and friends who have supported these books, reading early drafts, mounting events, and spreading the word: Cobians (extra hugs to Mom, Dad, Alex, Dan, and Katy), Wests, Swansons, Betzels, McHargs, Nelsons, Kellers, Jenkinses, Lundgrens, Engbergs, Tomasiks, Hansens, and everyone in the wonderful kids' lit community in Minnesota and beyond.

And, finally, my traveling companion, tech support, and teammate Ryan West. I don't know where or who I would be without you, but I'm so glad to be right here.

About the author

JACQUELINE WEST loves stories where magic collides with real life—from talking cats, to enchanted eyewear, to paintings that are portals to other worlds. An award-winning poet, former teacher, and occasional musician, she lives with her husband in Red Wing, Minnesota, surrounded by large piles of books and small piles of dog hair.

Learn more about what Jacqueline is writing and where she'll be next at www.JacquelineWest.com and www.TheBooksofElsewhere.com